THE CASE OF THE MISSING MORRIS DANCER

THE CASE OF THE MISSING MORRIS DANCER

A WISE Enquiries Agency Mystery

Cathy Ace

This first world edition published 2015
in Great Britain and 2016 in the USA by
SEVERN HOUSE PUBLISHERS LTD of
19 Cedar Road, Sutton, Surrey, England, SM2 5DA.
Trade paperback edition first published
in Great Britain and the USA 2016 by
SEVERN HOUSE PUBLISHERS LTD

British Library Cataloguing in Publication Data

Ace, Cathy, 1960- author.
  The case of the missing Morris dancer. – (The WISE
  Enquiries Agency mysteries)
  1. Women private investigators–Fiction. 2. Wales–
  Fiction. 3. Morris dance–Fiction. 4. Detective and
  mystery stories.
  I. Title II. Series
  813.6-dc23

ISBN-13: 978-0-7278-8554-8 (cased)
ISBN-13: 978-1-84751-663-3 (trade paper)
ISBN-13: 978-1-78010-717-2 (e-book)

All Severn House titles are printed on acid-free paper.

Severn House Publishers support the Forest Stewardship Council™ [FSC™],
the leading international forest certification organisation.
All our titles that are printed on FSC certified paper carry the FSC logo.

MIX
Paper from
responsible sources
FSC
www.fsc.org   FSC® C013056

Typeset by Palimpsest Book Production Ltd.,
Falkirk, Stirlingshire, Scotland.
Printed and bound in Great Britain by
TJ International, Padstow, Cornwall.

For my family in Canada, with love and thanks

ACKNOWLEDGEMENTS

Thanks to my family for their love and encouragement, which keep me going. Thanks to the entire Severn House publishing team for their professionalism and support, and to my agent, Priya Doraswamy, for hers. A host of reviewers, bloggers, librarians and booksellers have helped get this book on to bookshelves, and I thank them for noticing my work. Finally, my thanks to you for choosing to share time with the women of the WISE Enquiries Agency. Happy reading.

ONE

Henry Devereaux Twyst, eighteenth Duke of Chellingworth, was terribly worried about his imminent nuptials. He was utterly convinced that Stephanie Timbers was the right woman for him, and absolutely delighted that in less than a week she'd be his wife. *That* wasn't what he was concerned about. No, the cause of his emotional discomfort could be summed up in one word – 'tradition'.

Henry suspected he might blow a gasket if he heard anyone mention it one more time. Precariously perched on a rickety chair set against a wall in the lower library at Chellingworth Hall, he felt he could reach out and touch the word, so many people were saying it to him about so many different things. The entire staff at the Chellingworth Estate had been in uproar since he and Stephanie had decided when they would marry. He should have known how things would turn out back then; even the announcement of the date came with its own 'tradition'.

They'd been reliably and quite forcefully informed by his mother, the indefatigable Dowager Duchess Althea, that they couldn't simply put a notice in *The Times;* they also had to find themselves a *gwadhoddwr* to make the announcement. Not a real *gwadhoddwr*, of course, because roving young male bards were pretty thin on the ground in twenty-first-century Wales, so Ian Cottesloe, his mother's general factotum, had been 'volunteered' for the job. Henry and his fiancé had sat down together to come up with a series of rhyming couplets that told of their love for each other, their engagement, the date and time of their wedding and the fact that all those who heard the announcement were invited to attend both the wedding itself and the festivities that would follow. Then, pretending to be enthusiastic about it, Ian had read the poem aloud in English and Welsh at both village pubs and on the village green, as well as in the Old Market Hall and St David's Church.

Henry and Stephanie had chosen January 25th, St Dynwen's Day, as the date for the announcement to be made – the Welsh patron saint of lovers enjoying a much higher standing in the area than St Valentine – with the wedding itself to take place on March 1st, St David's Day, the patron saint of Wales. The entire village had been vocal in their delight at the news, despite the fact most of them knew it already because the Reverend Ebenezer Roberts had let the word slip over a glass of sherry in the Lamb and Flag after communion the previous week.

And *that* was when the assault had begun in earnest. It seemed to Henry that everyone and their dog had an idea about some sort of tradition that had to be observed for the wedding and everything surrounding it. It was enough to drive a man to drink. Indeed, Henry had found himself racing through his after-dinner brandies rather more rapidly than usual since then.

'People will want to be involved, Henry,' his mother had told him. 'When I married your father he'd been the duke for some time, and, as you know, we merely had a small ceremony in Chelsea Town Hall, as befitting a second marriage. When he married his first wife, his own father was still alive, and the same was true for his father before him. This is the first time the village of Anwen-by-Wye has been able to celebrate the wedding of a sitting Duke of Chellingworth in almost a hundred years. There will be many traditions you'll be expected to follow. And I suggest you do. This is a pivotal time for our family's relationship with the local community. Listen to what you're told and accommodate people. You'll be glad you did.'

Henry knew his mother was right. He silently admitted she usually was. She'd reached the admirable age of almost eighty with a reputation largely intact for her common-sense approach to life and her characteristically forthright attitudes on most topics. Known as a woman who was never backwards in coming forwards, Althea Twyst belied her small stature by holding her head high in any company, and always ensuring her views were heard.

So Henry had listened. *And listened*. Indeed, he felt he'd been more than accommodating of almost every madcap idea thrown at him. But this last one? It was just one tradition too far. With less than a week to go before Henry's big day, he finally felt the need to speak up.

Relinquishing his inadequate chair – the lower library had already been cleared of anything resembling a comfortable seat to allow for 'decorating' to take place – he marched into the great hall, mentally composing weighty, persuasive arguments as he walked.

His arrival in the imposing space was met by complete indifference; everyone was too busy to notice him. Voices were echoing off the venerable marble columns and floors, Edward his butler was shifting a table about and making a terrible racket doing it, his mother was waving her walking stick around and barking instructions about the exact positioning for the half a dozen harps that were due to be delivered on Friday afternoon – *six* full-sized harps! – while her Jack Russell, McFli, yapped at her heels. On the upper balcony, his fiancé Stephanie was saying something about the Morris dancers being late.

Waving a piece of paper under her nose, Henry Twyst whined like a small boy to his mother when he finally said, 'This is too much, Mother. I really do not care for the idea that Stephanie should be kidnapped by the bridal party, locked inside a house in the village, and I should then have to go yomping about the place pretending to look for her to be able to drag her off to marry me. Don't you think we could give this one tradition a miss, Mother? Rather unbecoming for me, don't you think?'

Althea Twyst, Dowager Duchess of Chellingworth, lowered her sturdy cane – which she insisted she carried about only so people wouldn't keep asking her if she was alright – and drew herself up to her full four feet ten inches. She looked up at her son with shrewd cornflower eyes, then down at her darling McFli with exactly the same expression. McFli stopped yapping, and sat quietly. Henry continued to whine.

'I realize it's an extremely old Welsh wedding custom, Mother, but I feel uneasy about it,' he bleated.

Althea bent down and patted McFli's little head, then stood very upright and stared at her son. 'Henry, I dare say at your age you would, indeed, look rather foolish pretending to chase down your bride, but that's not why I'm going to agree with you.' Her son's spirits lifted at the word 'agree'. 'I believe your wedding will be a richer experience for all concerned because you are observing so many of the traditions held dear by those who live on and near our estate, but the particular activity to which you refer is something I have already discussed with the Reverend Ebenezer Roberts, and we both agree it has no place in the twenty-first century. I dare say it meant something when it originated, though I happen to know that, even when its true meaning had disappeared into the mists of time and it had become a tradition more to do with making merry than the forceful taking of a woman from her birth home to her marriage home, many frowned upon it as anachronistic. Women are not property, Henry, as I am sure we all agree. Stephanie should be saved the ignominy of being treated as such. So I agree with you, but maybe not for the reasons you'd hoped. I believe people will understand women are now viewed, quite properly, as beings unto themselves, not mere chattel.'

Henry waggled the paper again. 'Tudor Evans has written to me on three occasions about the matter. He clearly feels it has a place in our wedding day.'

Althea Twyst looked at her son with a sad expression. It annoyed Henry when she did that; it made him feel inadequate. She sighed heavily. 'Tudor Evans might be the landlord of the Lamb and Flag, the churchwarden *and* the chairman of the parochial church council, but he's not God Almighty, Henry. You must tell him how you feel, and be firm with him. In fact, he should be here any minute, so you can tell him face-to-face.'

Henry felt his tummy clench. He didn't care for confrontation of any sort and began to panic that he might be forced to stand his ground, in person, in front of a man known to have considerable power and influence in the village of Anwen-by-Wye; the village sat upon land owned by the Twysts, and most of its inhabitants were Henry's tenants, but Tudor Evans was, to all intents and purposes, its *de facto* ruler.

Henry struggled to hide his emotions from his mother, though he suspected he was failing. She wasn't a hard woman – indeed, Henry knew she loved him very much – but she could sometimes be a little unfeeling with her words. He grappled with his fears, the turmoil making him bite his lip. His fiancé's hand touching his arm made him jump.

'Ah, Stephanie.' He smiled as he looked down into hazel eyes beneath glossy brunette hair. Henry thought his fiancé looked tired, a little drawn. He supposed that wasn't surprising; he felt much the same himself, and Stephanie was bearing the brunt of the organizing duties. True, she'd been working at Chellingworth Hall as a professional public relations expert and event planner prior to their engagement, so she knew what she was doing, but he had to admit she'd been doing rather a lot of it over the past several weeks. At thirty-two years of age Stephanie Timbers was twenty-five years his junior, and much more fit and lithe than he, but Henry had to assume that not even she was possessed of unlimited reserves of energy.

'Henry, the Morris dancers are late,' said Stephanie simply. Henry liked that she wasn't given to dramatics; he could never have countenanced marrying such a woman. He got quite enough of that sort of thing from his sister Clementine. 'They should have been here twenty minutes ago to discuss the exact plan for next Saturday afternoon. I know we have the general idea – that they'll dance ahead of us as we make our way from St David's Church in the village back here to Chellingworth Hall – but it's a pretty long walk, and I do feel we should be sure that they have something properly organized for the whole trip. I'm just going to pop to the estate office to find Tudor Evans's phone number, then I'll be back.' Stephanie flashed a smile at her fiancé, and made to head off to the west wing where the office was located.

At that precise moment the bell rang at the front doors, so Edward abandoned the massive table with which he was grappling to open them, allowing for the entry of a couple of men who needed to be divested of wet outerwear, waterlogged hats and umbrellas. Henry's heart sank as he recognized Tudor Evans's voice in the outer entryway. *Not long now*, he thought to himself.

'Terribly sorry we've been delayed, Your Grace,' said Tudor as he approached Henry, his wet hand outstretched. 'We've been waiting at the market hall for Aubrey Morris to collect us in his van, but he never arrived, so we've made our way on foot.' He looked toward the young man who'd arrived with him. 'I'm sure you know Aled?'

The younger man was in his twenties, Henry thought, so a good thirty years Tudor Evans's junior, and, whereas Tudor was tall and portly, this poor specimen was both short and decidedly weedy-looking.

Beaming at him, the young man stretched out a hand and said quietly, 'Aled Evans, Your Grace. No relation.'

It took Henry a moment to realize Aled meant that, despite the fact they shared a surname, he and Tudor were not related.

'I didn't see much point in dragging the whole troupe along,' said Tudor as the young man fell back behind his much more imposing namesake, 'but I wanted Aled to be here, as he is our caller – the man who will call out the steps and the dances as we progress. Of course I, as the squire, will have overall control, but I am a bit concerned that Aubrey isn't here. He's one of the few dancing musicians in the world of Morris. No standing about on the sidelines for Aubrey – he's known for his frolicking as he plays. Indeed, you could say Aubrey Morris is instrumental to our success.'

The ruddy-faced man stopped and grinned at his own pun. 'Oh – there you go – instrumental to our success!' He laughed heartily and, Henry thought, a little too loudly. A few inches taller than the duke, and somewhat greater in girth, Tudor Evans was the epitome of the sort of chap Henry would expect to be found behind every bar of every country pub. Henry thought the man could have modeled for a Toby jug – he even wore a yellow-checked waistcoat beneath his tweed jacket as if it were a costume from a performance in which he played a country pub landlord. Henry silently hoped the man's famed bonhomie would hold fast when the contentious topic of chasing one's bride around the village arose, but he feared it would not. Despite Tudor's beaming face and jovially rising and falling Welsh accent, Henry knew only too well that Tudor's reputation as the regulator of 'the right way to do things' in Anwen-by-Wye had been earned and honed over decades.

'I've phoned Aubrey, but I didn't get an answer,' continued Tudor, sounding concerned. 'It's puzzling; he's a reliable young man, you see. He's never let us down like this before. Never. Indeed, I don't know where we'd be without him. I was saying to Aled as we were walking here, he might have had a problem with his van. Maybe we'd better start without him? I'll take notes. How about that, Your Grace?'

Henry nodded and forced a cheery expression. *Oh yes, you're all smiles now, Mr Tudor Evans, but it won't last,* were Henry's thought as he, his fiancé and his mother made their way toward the woefully ill-appointed lower library accompanied by the unrelated Evanses, to discuss exactly what might be involved when a troupe of six Morris men, and a dancing Morris musician, were to lead a newly married couple and most of the inhabitants of the village of Anwen-by-Wye along a mile of winding pathways next Saturday afternoon, when the weather forecast promised 'intermittent wintry showers' and a 'brisk wind'.

Henry's tummy was awash with acid. He squeezed his fiancé's hand for courage.

TWO

Monday, February 24th

'Chrissy? You decent, doll?' Annie Parker called up the wrought-iron spiral staircase that led to Christine Wilson-Smythe's apartment at one end of the converted barn on the Chellingworth Estate now used by the WISE Enquiries Agency as its office.

A muffled reply told Annie her best course of action was to make a pot of tea. She was the first to arrive for the Monday morning meeting. She hadn't exactly run out of her little cottage in the village of Anwen-by-Wye, but she had scarpered the moment she'd heard her mother, Eustelle, head for the bathroom. 'Bye, Eustelle, mustn't be late for me meeting,' she'd called as she slammed the small but sturdy front door behind her. She'd just about got used to having to duck her head before she left, or entered, her home of just two months. A far cry from her ex-council flat in Wandsworth, the chocolate-box thatched cottage looked like her dream home from the outside, but she was having a difficult time coming to terms with the fact that four hundred years ago, when the cottage had been built, people weren't usually five feet ten inches tall, as she was. She was just grateful that a previous tenant had been allowed to dig into the foundations of the cottage to create much taller rooms on the ground floor, and that the upstairs rooms reached up into the rafters.

Its dimensions dwarfing her own little cottage, the converted barn was perfect for the agency's new HQ, not least, Annie ruminated as she filled the kettle in the kitchen beneath her colleague's apartment, because they got to use it for free. She'd been able to sell her flat in London for a good deal more than she'd paid for it, and now she had enough money in her bank account to allow her, for the first time in her life, to know she could feed and clothe herself for the next couple of decades without having to worry too much about how long she'd have to wait for a pension, or how tiny that might be when it eventually materialized. Of course, the fact that Henry Twyst didn't just allow them to use the barn for free, but was also allowing her to rent the cottage in the village for a ridiculously small amount of money every month, helped too.

Returning to the bottom of the stairs Annie shouted, 'Kettle's on. Come on, doll, shake a leg. Car and Mave'll be here in a mo, and you don't want to be running about in your ninnies when they get here, do you?'

The Honorable Christine Wilson-Smythe appeared at the top of the spiral stairs wrapped in a floral silk kimono, looking tousled. Annie sighed as she realized Christine would look beautiful if she was covered in mud and dumped on a rubbish tip in a sack. She also knew that, at twenty-seven years of age and a natural beauty, Christine would shortly reemerge with her brunette locks looking lustrous, her flawless skin not needing any make-up and sporting an outfit that flattered her lovely figure. Annie automatically rubbed the fuzz of hair on her shapely head as she thought of this, and cursed at her knobbly freckles, which she felt marred her otherwise silky, dark skin. She reckoned the freckle-bumps came from her African, rather than Caribe, heritage. The freckles *and* her big bum.

'Ten minutes. Promise,' said Christine as she headed for the bathroom. 'Could I have coffee, not tea?' she asked as she disappeared.

'Gordon Bennett, what did your last servant die of?' said Annie half-heartedly as she returned to the kitchen, realizing as she did so she knew the answer to the question; Christine's old Nanny Mullins had dropped dead in the Waitrose supermarket on the Kings Road in Chelsea a few weeks earlier. Annie shook her head silently as she recalled how she'd had to bite her tongue when Christine had told her that her beloved nanny had collapsed while reaching for a dozen quail's eggs.

How the other half lives, thought Annie dragging the cafetière from the top shelf, then she corrected herself mentally, *or the other one or two percent live, in any case.*

'How was your walk from the village to the office this morning, dear?' asked Mavis MacDonald as she bustled into the barn, letting the cold wind follow her through the door.

'Fine,' said Annie, sounding like a truculent schoolgirl. Of the four women who worked at the agency, Annie was the only one who couldn't drive – a fact that hadn't overly concerned her when she'd been living in her beloved London. She'd already admitted to herself it wasn't an ideal state of affairs if they were going to make a go of it in the wilds of Powys, Wales. What she was struggling to admit to anyone, herself included, was that the idea of driving frightened her; it seemed there were far too many things to concentrate on at one time, and she wasn't known for her ability to prevent her mind wandering.

'Tea'll be ready in a minute,' Annie added, hoping to deflect Mavis's inevitable next comments. 'Just in time for nine o'clock. Have you seen Car?'

Mavis MacDonald peered around Annie's back at the tea tray; at just five feet tall she was so much shorter than her colleague that Annie was very familiar with the top of Mavis's head. Annie smiled as Mavis hooked her neatly bobbed gray hair behind her ears and nodded with satisfaction. 'Aye, a couple of bourbons each will be nice for a Monday morning,' she said, patting Annie on the shoulder – a great compliment.

'I'll put out a couple of extras for Car – she's eating for two, so she deserves it,' said Annie as Mavis made her way toward the open-plan office area.

Calling over her shoulder Mavis replied, 'Ach, no you don't. Carol is pregnant, and my words carry the weight of decades of nursing experience when I say she's no' to be encouraged to overeat because of that. And certainly not bourbon biscuits. Put a couple of those apples out, and a banana. Maybe I can talk her into eating a wee bit more fruit.'

Annie smiled inwardly as she arranged the fruit on the tray. She knew exactly what Carol would say about being encouraged to eat more fruit. 'I'm not a flippin' fruit bat,' was something her heavily pregnant colleague was repeating in her lovely Welsh lilt more frequently as the months passed and her midsection expanded.

Just as Christine descended the stairs, Carol arrived. Annie's expectations of Christine's appearance were more than met, and she was also unreasonably annoyed to note how easily the young woman skipped down the spiral stairs; Annie was pretty sure her feet would probably register as flippers if she ever showed them at a public swimming pool, and she was known to be far from light on them – clumsiness being something with which she was wearily familiar.

Carol struggled with her horribly tight winter coat, then finally flopped onto the sofa they'd brought with them from their previous office in London. 'It's cold out,' said Carol, rubbing her arms as if to prove the point.

'It's February,' said Mavis simply, 'and if you're feelin' the cold, you're no' dead.'

Carol rolled her eyes toward Annie and the friends shared a smile at Mavis's expense.

Placing the tray on the table in front of the now-seated women Annie said, 'How's Bump today, Car?'

Carol sighed. 'Bump is fine. And I'm not a Car, I'm a Car*ol*.' Annie grinned at her – this was their little game. 'Bump is getting a bit more active at night,' added Carol. 'I wonder how much more active it'll get before it makes an appearance? I wish it would come out. I've had enough of this being pregnant lark now. Nine months? It feels like nine flippin' years.'

Mavis picked up her cup and saucer – no office mug for her – and replied, 'I was convinced my first bairn was going to play rugby for Scotland the minute he was born, he made such a fuss in the womb, but he's very placid. It was the other way about for my second; hardly knew he was there, then he never stopped still from the minute he appeared, or so it seemed. They're all different.'

No one disagreed because Mavis was the only one of the four who'd had children.

'Business for the day? Plan for the week?' said Mavis.

In her early-sixties, and therefore the oldest of the four, Mavis MacDonald had become the group's meeting leader quite early on; it was as though she had somehow been silently voted chairwoman.

Carol Hill powered up her electronic tablet. The one-time head of computing for a leading reinsurance company in the City of London, Carol's choice to give up her stressful life in the hope it would help her conceive had paid off. Her prodigious talent with computers was underused by the WISE Enquiries Agency, but she enjoyed the work, and was now blissfully settled in a delightful Georgian house overlooking the common at the center of Anwen-by-Wye, where she and her husband David were looking forward to putting down roots. She, too, was a beneficiary of the generosity of the Twyst family, and paid so little rent for the spacious and well-proportioned home it was almost embarrassing. Whenever she mentioned this fact to either the duke or the dowager duchess she was told she wasn't to worry, that the Twysts owed the women of the WISE Enquiries Agency a debt of gratitude for their having got to the bottom of a rather serious incident on the estate the previous year, and it was the least they could do.

Finally able to access various calendars, Carol spoke up. 'Christine's off to London later today for her late-nanny's memorial gathering.' Looking up she added, 'Have you decided when you're leaving yet?'

Christine looked at her watch. 'If you don't need me here, I might head out around eleven.' Heads nodded.

'Going to the do alone, doll, or will Mister B-rrright be on your arm?' Annie's dark eyes twinkled wickedly as she emphasized the 'right' part of the word.

'Alexander will be accompanying me,' replied Christine. She blushed a little as she spoke.

'Cor! Does that mean he's going to meet your father, *the Viscount*?' said Annie, asking the question all the women wanted answered.

Christine sighed, and placed her coffee mug on the table. 'They're both going to be here for the wedding on Saturday, and I didn't want that to be the first time they'd meet. Tonight's get-together will be for lots of families for whom Nanny Mullins worked over the years – the parents and the children. It'll be a mixed bag. It's a good chance for them to shake hands, at least.'

'You mean tonight's a chance for them to give each other the once-over, eh?' quipped Annie with a wink.

'Annie,' warned Mavis. 'We know the circumstances under which Christine and Alexander met and got to know each other were somewhat unusual, and that he is a man not from the same world as Christine—'

'Oh, come off it, Mave,' said Annie, cavalierly flouting two of Mavis's rules at once – no interrupting, and no shortening of names – 'Alexander Bright has a shady background Chrissy'll say nothing about, 'cept that he comes from the estates in Brixton, and his father was probably black. *Ish*. Well, not quite as black as my dad is. We all know he's good-looking and charming and got pots of money, but none of us knows how he made it. And he's not telling. You go for it, Chrissy. He's a good old Londoner. like me, so he can't be all bad. But you'd better watch it, doll, 'cause who knows what your father's going to make of him. Might even give us a quick phone call to investigate his background between tonight and Saturday.'

'It wouldn't do any good if he did,' said Carol. 'If I can't find out anything about Alexander Bright from the age of six to his mid-thirties, then no one can. But Annie's right, Chris*tine*—' she glared at Annie as she emphasized the last syllable of her colleague's name – 'your father might not be terribly impressed by a man who's known for his philanthropic, if controversial, attitude toward housing for the poor, and his impressive but often questionable social network. What have you told him about Alexander?'

Christine fidgeted as she replied, 'Not much. It's very early days. It took me a while to begin to forgive Alexander for how he acted when we first met. And I know we see each other whenever I go up to London, but . . .' She trailed off looking lost, then rallied: '. . . he's a good man, I believe. He's told me a lot about his early life, but I respect his privacy. He can tell the rest of you what he chooses, when he chooses. Whatever he might have done during those "missing years", he's more than making up for it now. And he's so—'

'Darkly handsome?' said Annie with a mock-swoon.

'Knowledgeable about so many things?' said Carol with a warm smile.

'Dangerous,' said Mavis with an implied 'tut'.

Christine grinned and said, 'All of the above.' Having sipped her coffee she added, 'It'll be fine. I'm sure they'll be polite, if nothing else.'

'Aye, I'm sure they will,' said Mavis in a tone that suggested the topic was at an end. 'So, with Christine in London, what are we three working on – so long as you don't go into labor this week, Carol?'

Carol began, 'I have a lot to do on the accounts today, then I'm on Welsh cake-making rota at the village hall tomorrow – for the wedding. However, by this evening I should be able to tell you all if you're going to get paid this month, and, if so, how much. That said, don't hold your breath, ladies. December was largely swallowed up with of all of us uprooting ourselves from London and moving here, so, as you'll recall, we did hardly any work at all. I know Christine was able to complete the job we had in hand for the fashion designer who was worried her ideas were being stolen before she had a chance to launch them. By the way, Christine, if you would drop in with our invoice while you're in London, that would save a stamp. Could you do that today, or maybe tomorrow? Your calendar tells me you're not coming back until Thursday. Is this time off, or have you some plans you'd like to share with us?'

Christine flushed. 'Yes, a bit of time off. I covered as best I could while you three moved all your worldly goods to Anwen-by-Wye from London, and I need to collect the dress I'll be wearing to the wedding on Saturday. Also, Alexander and I thought we might run down to Brighton tomorrow. You know, poke about in The Lanes for something for the bride and groom. I thought Henry might like something a bit quirky. We'll check out the wares at Alexander's antiques business first, of course, but I have something in mind I don't think he'll have.'

'Gold-plated chamber pot that was once Queen Victoria's?' quipped Annie.

Christine answered calmly, 'No, I rather think Henry already has one of those.' Her smile didn't allow Annie to work out if she was telling the truth or poking fun at her friend. She puzzled about this as Christine added, 'I wondered if you could help me out with that a bit, Carol? I don't feel I've got to know Stephanie as well as I might, and I'm not really concerned about what Henry might want, but I'd rather like to find something that might tickle her fancy. If you're not too busy, maybe you could poke about a bit in her online life and find out if she's got any hobbies, that sort of thing?' Carol nodded, and made a note on her screen. 'By the way,' Christine added, 'what are you all getting them?'

'My cousin in Carmarthen is carving them a love spoon,' said Carol. 'He's going to incorporate the Chellingworth coat of arms, as best he can – and he's very good, so I think it'll turn out alright.'

'Althea thought my idea of a set of monogrammed face towels was sensible,' said Mavis.

Annie perked up as she said, 'I was stumped 'til Eustelle gave me an idea. I found a place that lets you pick your own

subscription to online magazines. I got one for each of them.'
As she finished speaking she noticed that Christine's expression clouded.

'I see, so you're all sorted. I think I need that help, please Carol.' Christine sounded worried.

'So, back to business – this week Carol and Christine are spoken for, what about you and me, Annie?' asked Mavis.

'I'm here all week, and my dad arrives from London on Thursday. I have to finish up my report and expenses for the Case of the Gold-digging Girlfriend that I worked on in Cardiff,' replied Annie, looking proud.

'You did a good job there, Annie,' praised Mavis. 'First of all, it was quite a feather in our cap that we picked up that chance to do some undercover work for another agency in Cardiff – it's important we begin to make our strengths known within Wales, as well as continuing to get work we can handle from here in other parts of the country. And a wee birdie told me you got right into character as a barmaid in that club.'

'I'm guessing that "wee birdie" would be my mother Eustelle?' asked Annie, mimicking her colleague's Scottish accent. 'Reckons I'm being paid to be nosey, she does.'

'Your mother is proud you've found a career that suits you so well,' replied Mavis tartly. 'But she's also told me on several occasions, over tea at the Dower House, that she's been extremely worried about you since you left your job as a receptionist in the City to become an enquiry agent. However, I don't think you help matters by telling her you're a "gumshoe", my dear, and encouraging her to read all those lurid detective novels is no' the brightest idea. She might be proud of you, but she's concerned that you're going to be in constant danger and run the risk of peering down the wrong end of a revolver.'

'Annie has been stabbed during one, and kidnapped during another of our cases,' said Carol quietly, 'so Eustelle might have a point. It's something that worries David. You know, about me and Bump. But he's a bit happier now we're out here in the countryside, and he's able to keep an eye on me because he works from home.'

Mavis straightened her shoulders. 'We must admit to ourselves, if not to our loved ones, that what we do doesn't make us at all popular with the folks we discover are dishonest, or who are taking advantage of others, as Christine will attest. I hope you've got over the shock of having that dye thrown over you by the wee man who was stealing those designs at the fashion house, dear?'

Christine nodded. 'Yes. It was something and nothing, really, though it was strange to have a purple face for a few days. I've kept the clothes he damaged as evidence, and I know Carol was able to find out how much they'd cost to replace, right, Carol?'

Carol nodded. 'It's all in the invoice you'll be delivering to them. Itemized. Though I must say I can't imagine how you can walk into a shop and be happy to pay that much for a sweater.'

'Harvey Nichols has such nice things,' mused Christine. The three other women shared a round-eyed look that spoke volumes.

'I've been volunteered by Althea to help with the flower arranging at the church on Thursday,' said Mavis, 'and I know it'll be all hands on deck up at the hall on Friday, so, until then, I'm proposing I visit Builth Wells again, and Hay-on-Wye, just to make sure we've spoken personally to as many people as we can about what services we offer. There's one particular firm of solicitors I want to make sure I see. If we don't have a case to work on, then I can at least try to find us work for the future. By the way, Carol, did you have any luck getting me an appointment with someone at the local Department of Social Security office? That's always a possible source of casework.'

Carol shook her head, 'I'll try again,' she said, then they all waited while Mavis answered her vibrating mobile phone.

As Mavis listened, she got up and walked around the perimeter of the cavernous barn. Peering out of the windows as she made reassuring noises and asked curt questions, her colleagues assumed a personal call, and they chatted quietly over their coffee. Carol declined fruit, Christine poured more coffee and checked her email, Annie kicked off her shoes, peeled off her socks and allowed her toes to wriggle through the sheepskin rug beneath her feet.

Returning to the sofa Mavis said, 'Ladies, here's something we need to discuss. It appears the man who plays the music for the Morris dancers who are due to lead the procession of the newlyweds and all the guests from the church to Chellingworth Hall on Saturday has disappeared. No one can reach him by telephone, and everyone seems convinced it is most out of character for him to leave without word at such a time. Althea is quite upset. I understand there is some connection between the future fertility of the marriage and the Morris dancers – though I suspect that is symbolic, rather than anything of a practical nature.' She winked. 'Now this is the thing: Althea wonders if we could look into this matter, and I know we could. We certainly have the skills and the time to be able to do so. But this is the first instance of the Twysts almost expecting us to be able to work for them as a first priority, no matter what other work we have on our plates. It is a situation I was not looking forward to facing. We are all benefitting from their generosity – maybe myself more than all of you, because I reside at the Dower House with Althea. I have a great deal of respect and affection for her – she might be almost old enough to be my mother, but she has a youthful spirit, and a wonderfully wicked sense of humor. We have each, as I think you all know, found a great friend in the other. That was she on the telephone. I have told her we will make enquiries, but only on the understanding that we will charge our regular fees.'

The ladies all looked around at each other for their communal agreement. 'I think we all agree,' Christine confirmed. 'Henry and Stephanie are due to be married on Saturday and I know that for both of them, especially Stephanie who's being absolutely pulled from pillar to post making the arrangements for this wedding, the last thing they need is to have to deal with a key person going AWOL. Mavis, you're right to say we'll need to be paid, but maybe we can recognize that you three were all at a bit of a loose end anyway?'

Mavis raised an eyebrow. 'The cost of the enquiry will be what it will be. This is what we know so far, and this is what

I propose we do. Are you all listening, and ready to take notes, ladies?' They all nodded. 'Very well. Last evening two representatives of the Anwen Morris, which is what the troupe of dancers is called, were due to be collected from the market hall by Aubrey Morris, the young man who is the musician for the troupe. He did not fulfil his obligation, so his fellow dancers walked to Chellingworth Hall where they had their planned meeting with Henry, Althea and Stephanie. Subsequent efforts to reach Aubrey Morris by both mobile telephone and the landline in his home have failed. Upon checking this morning it has been discovered that his house is locked up, with no signs of anything untoward, and his van is not in its garage. Some casual enquiries suggest no one knew of Aubrey having any plans to leave, indeed, Tudor Evans, the landlord of the Lamb and Flag pub, and the man who leads the Anwen Morris, had spoken with Aubrey on Sunday after church and they had made arrangements for that evening. Althea has known the boy's family for many years, and believes he is both reliable and fully aware of how critical his role will be to the successful performance of the Morris dancers at the wedding.'

'Has anyone called the cops?' asked Annie with a wicked grin.

Mavis continued with a glare, 'Henry has already spoken with the local police who have told him that, as far as they are concerned, Aubrey Morris has simply "gone away" rather than "gone missing". And that might well be the case. He lives alone at his house on the road that leads from the village to Hay-on-Wye, and does not have, as far as anyone knows, any very close friends. I believe we can do a few things: Althea has much more knowledge of the young man than I can get out of her in a quick phone call – I propose I return to the Dower House and speak to her further there; Annie – I think you should go to the Lamb and Flag and use your ability to winkle gossip out of a mute to find out all you can about Aubrey from Tudor Evans; Carol – I understand Aubrey is a handyman hereabouts, and is known in the village as "Morris the Van". At this stage I propose you put off the accounts for a day and present yourself at the market hall for an early rotation on the Welsh cake-making squad. You can enquire there about what is known of Aubrey by those who use his handyman services. Christine – you should, of course, go to London for your nanny's memorial gathering. What do you think, ladies? Is this how the women of the WISE Enquiries Agency should proceed?'

Silence.

Annie held up her hand. 'So you want me to go to the pub. At ten in the morning?'

'It's a professional visit,' replied Mavis.

Annie grinned. 'Fine by me.'

Carol half-raised her hand. 'Aubrey Morris doesn't have what could be called a large digital footprint. I've had a quick look and I'll forward you all the details of his website. Usefully it has a photograph of the possibly missing man. I can't find an obvious social network profile for him, though I'll dig a little deeper before I leave here for the market hall. If I find anything, I'll send that through to all your mobile devices – even you, Christine, because you should be kept in the loop.'

'You're so quick with that stuff, Car,' observed Annie. Carol glowed with pride.

'You can load the dishwasher before you leave, Christine, and I propose that Carol drives Annie back to the village – it'll be quicker, even if Annie waits for Carol to finish her searches. I, in the meantime, will do my best to stop Althea from getting excited at the thought of hunting for "clues" then making wild guesses about what they might mean. She's a surprisingly good natural enquirer, but she doesn't seem to understand we are professional agents with a code of conduct to uphold, and we don't hunt for clues but seek out information and evidence. And that from more than one source, where possible.'

'You can't ignore instincts,' said Annie defensively. 'I've got a nose for this job, and you know it.'

Carol giggled. 'Nosey Parker it is . . .'

'Oi!' replied Annie.

'Aye, on with the job, Carol,' snapped Mavis, 'and I don't disagree that we all bring our life experience to bear upon cases, as well as the skills and knowledge we've acquired through taking training courses, but I would remind you, Annie, that most of the people you seem to read about in those books of yours wouldn't only, in all likelihood, have lost their licences but they'd also possibly find themselves in prison. So, let's remember we are professionals and work the case in an organized manner, taking things step by step. We all know that works best for our team.'

Annie took her telling off like a trooper and smiled cheerily.

'So come along,' continued Mavis, 'let's check we all have our communication devices, and get going. The sooner we start, the sooner we'll have this sorted. I suspect it's nothing at all, and that the poor man's broken down in his van somewhere and hadn't recharged his telephone's battery. But let's get to it.'

THREE

Alexander Bright stood in the middle of his exclusive Shad Thames penthouse apartment and looked out at Tower Bridge. It was almost 10 a.m. but it was still dusk. Pendulous clouds hung above the viscous river promising that drizzle would soon turn to rain. He mused that the weather reflected his own mood almost exactly; something that might turn out to be quite unpleasant was on the horizon, and unavoidable.

Since the moment he'd met Christine, he'd known this day would come. The day when he'd have to stand before the father of the woman he loved and convince him he was worthy of his daughter. Of course, asking the viscount's permission for his daughter's hand in marriage was a long way off – and he suspected Christine would baulk at such an idea in any case. The Honorable Christine Wilson-Smythe had taken all the advantages a title and a good education could offer, had worked hard to become one of the star underwriters at Lloyd's of London and had then walked away, certain the goals to which her City colleagues aspired were not, for her at least, a worthwhile measure of success. As such, Alexander suspected, she was unlikely to believe that her hand was her father's to give.

Christine's invitation to accompany her to the memorial gathering designed to commemorate the life of her late nanny had come as a surprise to Alexander – and he wasn't a man to be taken aback on many occasions; since his earliest days as no more than a street urchin with an alcoholic mother and absent father in the sinkhole that Brixton had been in the 1980s, he'd been developing his skills as an observer. Little got past him. He'd dragged himself, quite literally, out of the gutter by using those abilities – judging people, discerning their strengths and weaknesses, understanding who knew what, and whom, and what was going on where, and when. It was a skill set that was now completely natural to him. He'd used these talents, and a large stash of cash he'd acquired by being an almost mythical courier to the underworld in South London as a teenager, to build a considerable empire of residential property which he owned, renovated and rented to deserving families. The chance for a home where a family could feel safe was all some people needed to avoid resorting to the sort of life he'd led.

Having established himself in this field, which produced an extremely healthy cash flow, he'd invested in an historic, but ailing, antiques firm, which allowed him to indulge his love of the finer things in life – like art and artefacts.

Alexander had done his best to clear his diary for the day; he wanted to be able to consider the evening that lay before him, and have time to research the people he'd be meeting. Christine had mentioned quite a few names, and all were worth investigating. A couple of names he recognized – the others would, somehow, be connected to people he'd encountered within his wide, and carefully developed, social circles. Whenever possible he avoided entering situations where he might unexpectedly encounter figures from his past – or even his present. Hence the research.

Knowing if there were potential allies in the room would help; he could ensure conversations turned toward topics which would highlight his charitable works, his support of the arts and his interests in various sporting endeavors. But he was well aware that his decision to upend the usual model of renting rundown dumps to low-income families had annoyed those for whom the status quo was a good earner; if any of those types had been invited because their income brackets had allowed for the retention of the late Nanny Mullins, he'd have to be on his guard. He consoled himself with the knowledge that his identity as head of Marion Rental Properties was not generally known, so he could hide behind his carefully guarded anonymity under such circumstances.

Before beginning his investigations, Alexander walked to his bedroom and drew back the sleek doors to his wardrobe. He owned any number of immaculate, handmade suits, but he decided the most expensive he'd ever bought, which had a couple of years of service behind it, was the correct choice for the evening. A simple dark tie and a crisp white shirt, plus his handmade English shoes – not the Italian ones because he didn't want to suggest being flash, or nouveau riche – would be the ideal armor for his encounter that evening. He wanted the viscount to feel comfortable in his company, but not for Christine to feel he was wearing some sort of costume for a Royal Command Performance. Though that was exactly what he was doing, of course.

Christine's call came through around eleven, by which time his research was progressing smoothly. Neither of them spoke of the evening that lay before them, instead they chattered happily about running down to Brighton in his Aston the next day, and agreeing where they'd eat fish and chips when they got there.

After the conversation, Alexander was restless. His life had been so strange – his current being designed to be acceptable within polite society, yet his youthful years bleak and dark – that he wondered if this might be the day when it all came crashing down about him. He'd never been in love before. Indeed, he'd always suspected that love was a weakness. It had been for his mother; he now understood that her alcoholism had most likely been fueled by his father deserting her. What if Christine's father pried them apart? Would he try? Could he possibly succeed, if Christine wanted to be with Alexander?

Sitting at his desk, Alexander squared his broad shoulders,

closed his laptop and stared out at the rainclouds that were now causing tourists to scuttle along the Embankment beneath inadequate umbrellas. Heavy drops hit his windows and rolled like tears in rivulets until they disappeared beneath his sightline.

He only had a few hours to follow up on one more task. It was an unsavory one involving the need to arrange the removal of two families from his properties. They'd been causing concern in a street where he was trying to establish a safe living zone for single-parent households, and he couldn't allow their in-fighting to threaten the hard-earned tranquility the rest of the residents there prized so highly. The troublemakers had been given ample opportunities to change their ways, but it had become clear to Alexander they were not going to toe the line. So action was called for. He hated seeing anyone lose their home, but there came a time when difficult decisions had to be made, and then significant actions put into play. It had taken Alexander some years to get together a good team of people who were capable of extracting troublesome tenants in such a way that they were left in no doubt they were gone for good, and that no acts of retribution against people or property would be accepted. He wondered how much he'd have to invest to bring the properties back up to snuff after the evictions – if the last couple of incidents were anything to go by, these people might well have inflicted some pretty significant damage on the houses they'd been renting. It was an unpleasant trend he was beginning to worry was on the increase. Still, as long as they took out their frustrations on bathroom basins and kitchen fittings, at least the people living in the adjoining properties were safe. But it worried him that he was seeing so much more anger being displayed by people for whom he'd only ever had the best interests in his heart. All he could do was give folks a chance – they had to choose to take it, or else.

FOUR

Carol tried not to giggle when Annie got tangled up in her seatbelt as she wrangled her way out of the car and onto the grassy verge beside the Lamb and Flag pub. She knew Annie couldn't help her natural flair for clumsiness, and they often had a good laugh about it. This time, Carol could sense Annie's frustration, so let it pass.

'I'm going to drop the car back at the house, say hello to my lovely husband, then go to the market hall, Annie. If you want a lift back to the office later, just phone my mobile and let me know, alright?' Carol called just before Annie slammed the door.

'Right-o, doll,' was all she caught from her disappearing friend.

As Carol swung the car around the village green toward the house where she, David and their cat Bunty now lived, she still wondered if she should pinch herself. A few months ago, this would have all been a dream. Now it was her reality. Pulling alongside the house, she used the kitchen entrance – they hardly ever used the front door that faced the green.

'Only me,' she called as she shut the kitchen door behind her. Bunty, Carol's beloved calico cat, gave up her prize spot on a chair next to the Aga and strolled over to Carol, allowing herself to be stroked. Her tail signaled her disdain, then she leaped onto the kitchen table and settled on a newspaper, licking a paw in a most luxurious manner.

David's head popped into the kitchen, followed by his comfortably rounded body.

'You're still in your dressing gown. Are you poorly?' Carol almost panicked.

David smiled slowly and rubbed his unbrushed light-brown hair. 'I'm fine. Just haven't got dressed yet. Got a bit caught up with a problem that needed a quick work-around at the satellite office in Zurich. All sorted now. You OK?'

The couple automatically gravitated toward each other in the middle of the large, pleasantly old-fashioned kitchen, and hugged. David rubbed Bump. 'How's it doing?'

'A bit active today,' replied Carol smiling. 'I'm not stopping. I need to be at the market hall, unexpectedly, so thought I'd park here, see how you were doing and then walk over. I didn't think I'd catch you pre-shower. Just because you're working from home nowadays, it doesn't mean you can stay in your jim-jams all day. Bump will be running around the place before we know it. You'd better get used to having to be up and at 'em in the mornings.'

David grinned. 'Yeah, yeah, I know. I tell you what though, I don't miss the commute. Not one bit. I sat down to look at that mess they had this morning, and the solution just came to me. I'm so much calmer than I used to be. And there aren't the distractions, either. You do feel that too, don't you? We were right to do this, weren't we? Even though I'm not earning as much now. Right?'

Carol reached up and held the face she loved so much in her cupped hands. 'David Hill, I promise you'll look back in six months and find out you've got just as much in your pocket working here as an IT consultant for our old employer as you would have done sitting on the Tube going back and forth across London. Our income is down, but so is our expenditure. I don't think either of us will need to buy clothes ever again, and our eating and travel costs are next to nothing. Of course Bump will cost a bomb once its born, but that would be the same either way, and I still think raising a baby here is going to be a lot less expensive than raising one in London. So, let me get off and back to my duties – and I'll let you get back to saving reinsurance executives who don't know one end of a piece of code from another, wherever in the world they might find themselves working today.'

They kissed, and Carol pulled her rather inadequate duffel coat as far around her belly as it would reach, in an attempt to keep the winter chill off Bump.

By the time she'd reached the center of the green, her wellies squelching on the sodden grass, Carol finally lifted her head and turned to look at the house she now called home.

It stood proudly in the middle of one of the four sides of the square that surrounded the green. To its right was a row of mismatched detached homes, then the Lamb and Flag pub. Turning again she took in the vista of St David's Church, its graveyard and the Chellingworth Arms, then she turned again and gazed along the hotch-potch of cottages and houses that sat either side of the market hall – with its delightful sixteenth century, Tudor brick-and-beam original building and its much less appealing Victorian brick "extension" – and the abandoned Jacobean Coach and Horses pub at the corner. Finally she looked across at the infants' school and the Georgian, Edwardian and Victorian buildings along that edge of the green, punctuated by a couple of cottages built during a more bucolic age. The two tea rooms that stood empty, with brown paper blocking out their windows, at the corner near the bus stop made for a rather morbid corner of the square, but she liked the rest of it very much.

She rubbed her belly. 'This is your home, Bump. You'll live in that house, go to that school, we'll buy sweets in that shop, and, one day, you'll probably have your first drink in one of those pubs. The families in these houses will be your neighbors. Your friends. Maybe your husband or wife will have lived in one of them for their whole life. The people who own the shop might offer you a Saturday job. You'll go to cubs and scouts in the market hall – or maybe in the church hall if they manage to mend the roof before the whole thing falls down. You'll be a donkey or an angel, or maybe even Mary or Joseph, in a nativity play in that church which has stood there for over five hundred years, and where you'll have been christened, and your father and I will love you no matter how many ballet or rugby or singing or cycling or football or sheep-dog training classes we need to drive you to as the years pass. But for now, you're going to be a good Bump and let Mam get on with her enquiring – because otherwise Mam might go a bit do-lally-tap and that wouldn't be good.'

Finally arriving at the hall that had stood to one side of the village green since the fifteenth century, Carol tackled the big double doors which were the 'new' entrance, housed in the Victorian edifice that had been unceremoniously added to the original structure. Carol checked her watch; she knew the ladies making Welsh cakes on the rota for Monday would have been at it for an hour or so. She decided her best approach would be to act confused and offer to help, making out she'd mixed up her time and day for volunteering, and blame her pregnancy hormones. She was pretty sure she'd get away with it because the Young Wives group which had cavalierly offered to make them for the wedding celebrations had only just realized what they'd let themselves in for: making a couple of thousand Welsh cakes – by Friday.

Upon entering the hall Carol was overwhelmed by two things – the wonderful smell of warm Welsh cakes and the military style with which they were being prepared, cooked and cooled. Marjorie Pritchard ran the Young Wives group – which Carol found odd because she was neither young, nor a wife; now in her early fifties, Marjorie had been divorced for a decade, but had never been ousted from a group which valued a leader prepared to organize, arrange and manage the funds for any activity they chose to undertake. Marjorie loved it, and everyone benefitted so, as Carol was learning was often the way in Anwen-by-Wye, no one saw any point in changing anything.

Carol homed in on Marjorie who was telling one of the volunteers that she was putting too many currants in her mixture. Her strong local accent and booming tones made Marjorie's voice unmistakable. 'You've got the weights written down, and the scales are right there. Weigh everything. Every batch has to be the same. Come on now . . . oh, Carol, I didn't see you there. Are you supposed to be here today? I thought you were Tuesday, not Monday.'

Carol adopted a 'confused puppy' face, and rubbed Bump. 'Oh, was it tomorrow? I don't know, I think the baby's sucking all the sense right out of my head.' Since moving to the village Carol had found that allowing her natural Welsh accent to blossom, rather than reining it in as she had done when she lived in London, worked wonders. Coming from a village in Carmarthenshire, she knew outsiders were often treated with some level of suspicion, and she wanted to fit in, and fast. Bump would be born a local, and she wanted Bump's parents to be treated the same way.

Marjorie pulled a notepad out of her apron pocket, consulted it and said, 'Tomorrow. You said you couldn't make it today,' she chastised.

Carol smiled sweetly. 'How about I just pitch in? I can come tomorrow as well. Maybe two short days rather than one long one would help me and the baby.' She wondered if Bump knew it was being used as cover for her enquiring duties.

Marjorie looked along the rows of tables set up along each of the two longest walls of the hall. On one side of the hall the dough for the Welsh cakes, which had been made by the women up on the stage, was being rolled out, cut into rounds and placed on platters; on the other, dozens of wire racks had been set out and were covered with cooked Welsh cakes cooling off, ready for packaging. Carol could see through the hatch into the kitchen that only two burners on the stove top were in use; the large, round, cast-iron 'bakestones' were too large for more than a couple to be used at once. The volunteers tending the cooking dough looked hot and bothered.

'I don't think you'd be good going up and down the steps to and from the stage all the time, so would going up there once and measuring out the ingredients suit you? You could sit down for a bit now and again, if you needed it.' Marjorie looked at Carol's pink cheeks and her rounded middle as she spoke. 'Feeling alright, are you? Due any time now, aren't you? Bit hot over here by the kitchen, isn't it. Yes, you'll be best on the stage, as far from the heat as you can be. Keeping it cold up there we are, to help the butter rub in better. Janet can bring you the butter from the fridge in the kitchen so you can cut it up a couple of pounds at a time, alright?'

Carol glanced up at the stage and realized the three women there were likely to be a good source of information about Aubrey Morris, so agreed to join them – but not before she was given a pinafore by Marjorie, who casually mentioned there was a seat due to become available on the parochial church council, and that she'd be happy to put Carol's name forward for it, immediately followed by precise instructions about following the list of ingredients and weighing things properly. Carol edged away from Marjorie Pritchard feeling she'd been ambushed, and worrying about how she could get out of joining the PCC where, by all accounts, Marjorie and Tudor Evans often went at it hammer and tongs for hours.

Finally escaping, Carol managed to settle herself on the stage, surrounded by bags of flour, pounds of chilled butter, dozens and dozens of eggs and what looked like half the world's supply of currants and sugar, and got to work. She thought it best to do something before she began to 'gossip' so worked as fast as she could – which meant she got ahead of what the women she was supplying needed and she was able to relax a bit and put her plan into action. She wasn't as much of an expert as Annie at this part of the job, being more comfortable with a keyboard than a group of women, so she made up her mind to channel her good friend as she enquired.

'Did you hear about Aubrey Morris?' she asked, placing a collection of ingredients next to one of her co-volunteers named Lynette.

'Morris the Van? Gone off, I heard,' replied Lynette, huffing and puffing as she laboriously worked the butter into the flour and sugar with her tiny hands and bird-like arms.

'Is that like him?' asked Carol as casually as possible.

'Not at all. His mam'll turn in her grave,' replied Lynette. 'Below me in school here, he was. Quiet boy. Reliable though. Big in the church.'

'He phoned me to cancel my gutters next week,' piped up the woman at the end table named Mair who Carol always thought of as 'comfortably plump'.

'What's wrong with them?' asked Lynette.

'What's right with them, more like. Might as well be colanders, the lot of them,' replied Mair. 'But there, that's what happens when you put off getting new ones as long as you can. Can't sleep a wink at night now when it rains. Sounds like there's a waterfall right outside the bedroom window. Came and looked at them two weeks ago, said he'd get the stuff, then phoned up and cancelled he did. Said he'd ask a bloke from Hay to come and see to them. Haven't heard a dicky bird since. Rude, if you asks me.'

Carol listened with interest; why had Aubrey cancelled an appointment for a job?

'He does most of the odd jobs round here, doesn't he?' pressed Carol.

'True,' replied Lynette. 'My John's pretty handy with most stuff, but he's out all week at work, and the weekends just seem to disappear, so, yes, he's done a few bits and pieces for us. John won't touch electrics. Good job too. Got to know what you're doing with electrics.'

'And plumbing. And gas. And gutters,' added Ruth, the tallest and oldest of the three women on the stage with Carol. 'Not everyone's good at everything. Bit of painting's easy enough, but there's so many jobs you need special equipment for. Haven't got most of it ourselves. Morris the Van's got everything, for every job. Been at it years his family has, so they would, wouldn't they?'

'It's a shame he's gone away. I could do with some help getting the house ready for the baby,' said Carol, rubbing Bump as though it was a magic lamp.

All three women stopped their kneading and looked at Carol's glowing face with a smile.

'Aww, first one's always special,' said Mair with a wistful look. 'Had Harry when I was just twenty. Didn't know what I was doing. You'll be fine. How old are you?'

Carol answered quietly, 'Thirty-four.'

All three women rolled their eyes.

'I heard you had a big job in London, but gave it up. That why you're so old having this one?' said Lynette.

Carol didn't think thirty-four was that old to have a first child, but she said, 'I had a big job, yes, but I didn't have a husband which is more the point. David and I have only been married for five years . . .' Carol paused, and decided to be open with the women she was trying to pump for information. 'I'd have happily had a baby right then, but not everything happens when you want it to.'

Returning to their tasks the three women agreed with Carol, and several moments of recollections about first, second and even third pregnancies followed. Carol felt compelled to allow the conversation to run its natural course before she finally took a chance to say, 'So if Morris the Van cancelled his appointment to work on your gutters next week, do you think he was planning on leaving to go somewhere after the wedding, Mair?'

The woman held her floury hands up in the air and pushed aside some stray hairs as she considered her answer. 'Well, it sounds like it, doesn't it? Not normal for him to cancel without a good reason.'

'No, you're right there,' added Lynette, 'never one to turn down a job, and never one to let you down neither. Doesn't charge the earth, and steady as Gibraltar. I wonder where he's gone.'

'And why he'd go now, when he was supposed to be playing the music for the Morris dancers on Saturday,' added Carol.

All three women stopped in their tracks.

'He'll be back by then for sure,' said Ruth, 'he'd never let them down like that.' She sounded shocked at the idea. 'Can't do it without him, they can't. Wouldn't be right with no music. They'd just all look like they was *twp*.'

The four women shared a laugh as they imagined the Morris dancers skipping and swooping with no musical accompaniment.

'Be calling the men with the white jackets they would,' giggled Lynette.

'Any girlfriend on the scene for Aubrey?' asked Carol as innocently as possible.

Returning to their tasks all three women smiled and giggled knowingly.

'What?' asked Carol. 'Not into women, is he?'

Ruth tutted. 'No, nothing like *that*. Just a bit quiet is poor Aubrey. We all call him Morris the Van because his grandfather was the first man in the village to have a van, not a tractor or a Land Rover. His father drove the same van till it finally gave up the ghost and they bought the one that Aubrey drives now. But, although we call him "Morris the Van", we probably all think of him as "poor little Aubrey". Always quiet. Always on the slight side. Glasses. Didn't play football or rugby. Never mixed in with the other kids at school. Right, Lynette?'

Lynette nodded. 'Like I said, we overlapped at infants' school. Just one year. He was in the babies' class when I was in the final year before going off to big school in Builth. Even then he was – well, I don't think kids that young can really be swotty, but if they could be, he was. Maybe it was because he was an only child and he grew up in his grandfather's house surrounded by mechanical bits and pieces, but he never played with building blocks, he tried to build things – you know, like proper things – with them. Always knew something the other kids didn't. Even then. Pretty boy, he was. Red hair back then, though I know he's sandier now. Still got those freckles though, hasn't he?'

Chuckling, Mair added, 'Poor dab, runs away from the slightest bit of sun, he does. Says he'll burn to a crisp, like a vampire. He was doing some stuff in my back garden last summer, and he was wearing a get-up that covered him from head to foot. I asked him why he didn't just cover himself in suntan lotion and be done with it. You'll never guess what he said?'

Carol was all ears. 'What?'

'He said, The thought of the dirt adhering to the cream on my body is very unpleasant, he did. Always talked a bit posh. Mind you, I don't know why. Doesn't come from a fancy family, like I said – he's the third generation of handymen in that Morris family. Now the other Morrises, they'd be the ones with the land and the money.'

'Other Morrises?' asked Carol.

'Up near Hay-on-Wye. Big farm they've got. His grand-father's older brother. When the grandfather's father died, the older son got the farm, the younger one – Aubrey's granddad – got nothing. Though they do say it was his brother, the one who inherited the farm, who bought him his first van and gave him the money to buy his house. Sort of pay-off. Sad mind, when a family breaks up over money, isn't it?'

'Was it much money?' asked Carol.

Lynette looked up toward the ceiling and gave the matter some thought. 'I don't know, really, but the Morris farm is one of the biggest sheep farms in the area, and that's saying something. Now I'm not saying they haven't had it rough with all the disease and so on, but I know they've got a lot of land, and the house is pretty big too. Not like Chellingworth Hall, or anything, but, you know, for a normal house – it would put ours to shame. Married an English woman he did, the Morris who got the farm. But there, you did that too, didn't you? You know, married an Englishman.'

Carol nodded. 'For an Englishman, David's very nice.' She grinned. 'And the baby'll be born in Wales, so pretty soon there'll be a majority of Welsh people in our house.'

As the laughter died away and the women returned their attention to their dough, Carol wondered if a quiet little boy, who'd grown into a reliable man with wealthy relatives but a hard-working lifestyle, would have planned to leave the village at such a time. She wondered if there were any other cancelled appointments that might bolster the theory that he had, in fact, planned to leave Anwen-by-Wye after the wedding.

'Need more butter up there yet?' called Marjorie from the floor of the hall.

'Yes, but I'll come and get it – I need to pop to the loo in any case,' replied Carol, wiping her hands on her apron.

Carol made her way down to the main hall, and ambled toward the loos. Once there, she shut the door behind her and pulled out her mobile phone. Dialing Mavis's number she waited, got the voicemail option and left a message passing on the information she'd gleaned.

Washing her hands, Carol decided she'd try to find out if Aubrey Morris had cancelled any other jobs in the village. To do that, she'd have to invent some reason why she needed to mix with the women working on rolling out the dough and cutting it into rounds. She hoped Marjorie would be amenable to her suggestion.

FIVE

'Mavis? Is that you?' Mavis spotted Althea Twyst walking up the incline that led from the lower copse to the Dower House. Standing atop the ha-ha that prevented the animals that had once grazed the rolling landscape from gaining access to any of the human-only buildings, she waved to her friend below.

Mavis could see Althea instructing McFli to run toward her, which he happily did. She waited with McFli who raced around her in delighted circles, pleased to have captured his quarry. Eventually Althea reached Mavis and the pair continued their walk to the Dower House together. McFli ran ahead of them, then scurried back to herd them along.

'Any news?' asked Althea, seemingly keen to hear from her friend what had been decided at the WISE Enquiries Agency meeting.

'Aye. We'll do it. Though Christine is off to London today for a memorial event she cannot miss, so it'll be mainly just me, Annie and Carol working on this one. Annie and Carol went off to the village in the car. Carol will enquire about Aubrey Morris among the women gathered at the market hall, and Annie's been sent to the Lamb and Flag to talk to Tudor Evans about the missing man. As for me? Well, I'm here to talk to you about him. I'm guessing there's a lot you can tell me, so what about a nice pot of tea and a wee natter?'

'Are you going to "grill me"?' asked Althea looking excited.

Mavis looked down into the elderly woman's face – not something she could do very often, given that Mavis herself was only just five feet in height. She had to admit that being with Althea made her feel quite tall and youthful. Strange but welcome feelings. 'Althea, you know very well I'm not going to "grill you". Have you been talking to Annie? She's wont to speak that way sometimes. If we left it to her we'd all wear belted mackintoshes and fedora hats pulled down over our eyes. She reads entirely the wrong type of books and watches worrying films. If she refers to me as a "dame" one more time, I might not be responsible for my actions. And we won't be hunting for clues, either. We'll approach this case as we do all our cases – professionally. Understand? No sleuthing for you. We're happy that you like to help with cases, but you must realize you are not a legal member of the agency. Agreed?'

Althea sighed and nodded. Mavis hoped the petulant look on her face meant she understood the ground rules, and she was glad to see Althea cheer up as they entered the spacious, portrait-bedecked hallway of the Dower House where McFli's excitement gained the attention of Althea's aide, Lindsey Newbury, who promised a tea tray in the morning room within ten minutes.

Finally settled in front of the roaring fireplace, Althea sipped her tea as Mavis pulled out her notebook, hooked her hair behind her ears and addressed her housemate/landlady quite seriously.

'As I told you, Althea, we'll be charging for our time on this matter, so I want to be professional and economical with our efforts. I hope, my dear, that you'll forgive me if I am blunt.'

'I always do,' answered Althea with a smile and a twinkle that Mavis didn't miss.

'Thank you, you're very gracious, Your Grace,' quipped Mavis. 'So – to work. Could you please begin by telling me everything you know about Aubrey Morris?'

'How far back do you want me to go?' asked Althea.

'How far back can you go?'

'To his grandparents.'

Mavis paused. 'Let's begin with Aubrey as a man – your knowledge of him, your impressions of him. Then we can work back if we need to.'

Althea nodded and patted her leg, encouraging McFli to snuggle at her feet, where he lay quietly, his head on his paws, his amber eyes reflecting the flames in the hearth. 'I believe Aubrey's about twenty-five, by now, and I believe he's reliable and hardworking. I have never heard anyone say otherwise. He was a boy, and is now a man, who keeps his own company and prefers books to people.'

'Books? That might not be a bad thing.'

'Very amusing, dear. You know what I mean. Aubrey read a good deal, and I don't think he favored romance novels. It is merely an aspect of his personality I happen to know about, which is why I mention it. He is a regular at church, a gifted musician – I know he plays for the Morris, but he's also a lovely singer – and he comes from a long line of Morrises in the area, who go back for many generations. Not quite as far as we Twysts, but not far short. A few hundred years, maybe.

But you said to speak of him as he is now, and I'm afraid that's all I really know.'

'Girls?'

'Not that I am aware of. He was never habitually in the company of anyone I can recall. Which doesn't mean he didn't have a girlfriend, or girlfriends. However, I do know that, since the death of his father, he has grown his handyman business far beyond the confines of Anwen-by-Wye. I believe newcomers to the area like the idea of a handyman with a heritage, and, of course, they have the money to pay for more works to be carried out on their properties. They might be newer buildings, but they seem to need even more upkeep than something as old as this place.'

Mavis thought for a moment about challenging Althea's certainty on this point; she was pretty sure the dowager had no real insight into the amount of work done by Ian Cottesloe in and around the Dower House to keep it functioning in all respects, but it seemed churlish to point that out.

'So, he's local, he's quiet, he likes books and is generally thought of as reliable,' observed Mavis, her eyes narrowing as she added, 'so why would he take himself off when he'd made arrangements to help represent the Anwen Morris at Chellingworth Hall last evening?'

Althea shook her head, and reached to rub behind McFli's ear. Mavis had noticed she did this when she herself needed reassuring, rather than the dog having shown any signs of wanting to be acknowledged. Mavis judged Althea to be worried.

'I don't know,' said the dowager quietly. 'It's most peculiar.'

'You said you knew the family right back to his grand-parents?' Mavis wondered if she could find out something useful with a different approach.

Althea pulled her hand away from McFli, who looked quite disappointed. She picked up her cup. 'His grandmother. She bred Border collies, I bred Jack Russells. We moved in similar dog-breeding circles. Must be forty years ago, maybe more. Nice woman. Quiet. Intelligent. You have to be with collies. They know, you know.' She winked at McFli. 'You all know, don't you?' McFli nuzzled his nose with his paws in agreement. 'She started the breeding to make some extra money and turned out to be good at it. Good lines, she had, and she made the most of them. An excellent, natural puppy trainer.'

'Why did she need extra money?'

'Ah yes, the farm. Aubrey's grandfather was one of two brothers. The younger of the two. Of course all the land goes to the eldest around here, so he'd always known, growing up, that his elder brother would get the farm and he'd have to make his own way. But the great grandfather died young. Some sort of accident with farm equipment. I'm not sure about that. But I do know Aubrey's grandfather had to make a living for himself a lot earlier in life than he'd expected. Aubrey's grandparents only had one child, Aubrey's father. I don't think she could have more. Aubrey's father married young and they had Aubrey very quickly. Gossips counted only six months between the wedding and the birth. The child could have been early, of course, but I don't think so. Aubrey's mother was never a strong girl. She went when Aubrey was about three years old. Just him and his father since then, and he shuffled off this mortal coil about five years ago.'

'It sounds like something out of a Thomas Hardy novel,' said Mavis.

Althea smiled. 'I suppose it does. But it's really just Welsh country life in the twentieth century. You don't have to go back to the 1890s to see life on the small scale, just look around the village. And the estate. Traditions hold fast. Time is allowed to pass us by as we choose. We grasp only at those parts of it we want. The 1890s or the 1990s – it's all much the same around here.'

'I cannae agree with that, Althea. The children in the village sit at home and watch the telly the same as children all around the world do. They'll grow up using keyboards, not slates. They'll understand the world in a way that we never will.'

'Louis Armstrong singing in your ear, my dear? It is indeed a wonderful world, and they might very well know much more than we ever will – but here, in Chellingworth and in Anwen, all those external influences will be filtered through Welsh mothers who carry their children on their hip, not in some wildly expensive sling that they hump around in front of themselves. Fathers will toil in the fields, will work the hours the animals and the crops demand in all weathers, and will be there for lambing quicker than they'll be wanting to see their own children born. It's the way around here.'

'Och, come now, Althea, don't be such a Luddite. Social media means the young people hereabouts are in contact with others like themselves all around the world,' said Mavis tartly. 'Just because they live in Anwen-by-Wye, young people, and even people like Aubrey Morris, do not live in a bubble of time set aside from the rest of the world. Ach! Now there's an idea!'

Althea grinned at her friend. 'You've had a thought, haven't you?'

Mavis scribbled excitedly in her pad. 'If only we could get into Aubrey's house we could see if he had any online relationships. If he was quiet and reserved, as you say, that might be more his sort of thing than meeting up with a local girl. He might have found true love half a world away, and simply packed his bags to go to meet his virtual sweetheart. Carol said she couldn't find anything about him online, but he might have some sort of alias he uses for that type of thing. If only there was a family member who could let us see his home we might be able to discover some useful information, or even if there were to be a neighbor with a key and the right to enter it would be fine.'

Althea appeared to give this matter some serious thought. That was one of the things Mavis liked most about the dowager – she was intelligent enough to know that a new idea might be worth considering. She took Mavis aback when she said. 'I have a key to his house.'

'Och, away with you!'

Althea stood up and put her hands on her hips, closing her eyes. McFli also stood, ready to act. 'Now, let me think. Where did I put it? Aubrey's grandmother gave it to me, and I'd have put it somewhere safe.' Mavis watched as the elderly woman pursed and pressed her lips almost as though she were chewing something.

'You mean you've had this key for decades?'

Althea stopped munching and said, 'I suppose so.' She moved to the hearth and pulled the bell rope. 'Maybe Lindsey will know where it is. She's reorganized so much since she got here. I think it used to be in with my smalls.'

Mavis had been excited to think she might be able to gain access to the missing man's home, but now she wasn't so sure. 'Can you even be sure the key would still work?'

Althea shrugged. 'They might have broken the lock at some point, I suppose, but why would you change one that worked perfectly well?'

Lindsey Newbury, Althea's large-limbed, terribly sensible lady's aide entered the morning room. 'Can I help, Your Grace?'

'I had a key. Mortice, not Yale. It was about this big—' Althea indicated a couple of inches in length – 'was made of dull iron and had a plain, solid lump of metal at the top. It was on a piece of bright yellow string long enough to hang about one's neck. Do you know where it might be?'

Mavis's heart sank. Well, that was that than.

'Yes, ma'am. It's in the kitchen with the spare knives. Would you like me to fetch it?'

'Yes please, my dear. Then Mavis and I will be going into the village. Could you tell Young Ian I'd like him to drive us, please? As quickly as you, and he, can. Thank you.'

'I'm impressed,' said Mavis with admiration.

'I'm amazed,' laughed Althea.

Not much more than an hour later, Althea, Dowager Duchess of Chellingworth and Mavis MacDonald, retired army nurse and enthusiastic enquiry agent, sat in the back of Althea's favorite vehicle – a Gilbern Invader estate, which the late duke had given her as a wedding anniversary gift in 1970. Ian drove the vehicle with the respect it was owed as the only car ever manufactured in Wales, and was, as Althea often remarked, a genius at keeping it roadworthy.

As they made their way toward Aubrey Morris's home Althea ventured, 'Ian, I wonder if you could tell us anything of use about Aubrey? I am guessing you must have attended the same school as each other?'

'Yes, Your Grace, I was a couple of years ahead of him.

Quiet boy, and a quiet man. Lovely tenor voice, but no interest in football, or rugby, or anything involving activity of any sort, as I recall. Not a slothful boy, but not active, if you know what I mean.'

'Do you see much of him these days?' pressed Althea.

'Other than at church, not really. Like I say, you always know he's there 'cause he does the harmonies so lovely, and the choir misses him on the Sundays he can't make it. But, otherwise, no. Tudor's your best bet.'

'So you wouldn't know if he had a girlfriend?' Althea gave it one last go.

'I can't imagine him having the gumption to talk to a girl,' said Ian tellingly. 'When I say "quiet" I suppose I mean "shy".'

'Thank you, Ian,' said Althea as she and Mavis shared a knowing glance.

It wasn't long before the pair stood outside the small stone-built house, set back from the road to Builth Wells, that Aubrey Morris had called home for his entire life. In the car from which they had just alighted sat a nervous young man; Ian Cottesloe was fit, well-built and ready for anything – but he had to do as he was told, and the dowager had told him to wait for them in the car.

'Your Grace, you might find – anything,' he'd spluttered, unused to disagreeing with the woman for whom he, his father and his grandfather before him, had worked. As general factotum his duties were wide-ranging, but seemed to not include preventing his mistress from encountering possible danger.

'There is no vehicle here, and no signs of life at the house. We will be perfectly safe,' reassured the dowager.

'Aye, we'll be fine and dandy,' winked Mavis as she shut the car door behind her, then whispered, 'just pop your head around the corner as we go and keep an ear cocked, right, my boy?'

The house was rather rundown. It suggested Aubrey Morris wasn't interested in doing odd jobs when he returned from his handyman work in the environs. The paint on the Victorian wooden sash windows was a hideous green and peeling badly, the front steps had seen better days and the front door itself had taken many a knock and ding in the hundred or more years it had hung on its rusty hinges. Mavis noted that, nevertheless, the overall structure of the house seemed sound, but she wondered what the inside might be like, if this was the advertisement for his skills Aubrey Morris was happy for the world to see.

'The front door's the same as it always was,' observed Althea. 'Let's try the key.'

'Just to reiterate – you were given that key by the homeowner to be used when and how you saw fit, is that correct, Althea?'

Althea tutted. 'Yes, it's correct. And I also happen to own the land upon which the house stands. Or at least Henry does, which is the same thing. It's as good as my house.'

'Now come along, you know the law doesn't see it that way, and I have a license as an enquiry agent to protect. But, since the police don't think he's missing, if anyone ever has any cause to ask, let's agree we're just checking that he meant to go. Let's try it.'

The key turned silently in the lock, though the opening of the heavy old door was anything but. It screamed fit to wake the dead.

'Good heavens, you'd think a handyman would own a can of oil or something,' said Althea as the two small women entered the gloomy, tiled hallway.

Flicking a switch Mavis said, 'There. That's better. I don't know why they never do that on those TV programs. It would prevent so many unfortunate situations if they could only see where they were going. Aubrey? Aubrey Morris? Are you here?'

Althea jumped. 'You might have warned me you were going to shout like that.'

'Sorry, dear. Best to check.'

A vague suggestion of fried onions hung in the damp air, and the house was not at all warm. Indeed, Mavis fancied it was colder inside it than out. 'Thanks for getting us in, Althea. Now could you just stay here while I have a quick scout about? Thank you.'

'I'll wait in the parlor,' replied Althea, opening the door of the room to her left as Mavis headed for the back of the house, where she was pretty sure she'd find the kitchen.

Generally speaking the house was tidy, if somewhat sadly filled with shabby old furnishings. As she moved from room to room Mavis could discern no signs of a struggle, nor any sense of the personality of the man who lived there. Every item, every piece of furniture, seemed to be at least fifty years old, some of it much older. All the photographs were faded and displayed in old-fashioned frames. Many showed a bonny baby, then a gradually ageing boy she could see grow into the adult Aubrey. Dust had been moved about a bit, but had settled again, leaving every surface covered with a film of age.

'I'm off upstairs,' called Mavis when she was outside the front parlor.

'Very well, I'll stay here,' replied Althea.

Mavis approved of the cleanliness of the bathroom as she checked inside the small medicine cabinet on the wall above the sink. *Poor boy must be allergic to something or other*, she thought noting the almost empty bottle of over-the-counter antihistamines. The bathroom contained all the accoutrements one might expect a clean-shaven man to use each day – a telling sign – and there was a toothbrush in a glass beside a tube of toothpaste.

The house had two bedrooms – one at the front, and one at the back beside the bathroom. It was clear to Mavis that the back bedroom was Aubrey's. No more than what would be called in a modern house 'a box room', here, at least, was evidence that someone under the age of one hundred lived in the house; the wallpaper was relatively modern – maybe 1990s? – and the bedspread almost matched the curtains, all of which were a sludgy gunmetal color. Masculine? Maybe a single father's idea of a boy's taste, or maybe Aubrey's own?

A Victorian bedroom set of a matching headboard, chest of drawers and wardrobe allowed for almost no floor space in the room. Mavis noted the wardrobe held working clothes, some casual clothes and a few empty coat hangers. The more she saw, the more she was inclined to believe Aubrey Morris had not packed up and left of his own accord. She found a suitcase stuffed under the bed.

Moving to the front bedroom, the first thing Mavis noticed upon opening the door was the smell of wood polish. Turning on the lights she was intrigued to discover that every surface in the room gleamed. Above the bed hung a cross-stitched homily where all the threads had faded to a uniform gunge, but the glass which covered the ancient fabric glinted in the light and had obviously been recently treated to a good old buffing.

Picking up the old-fashioned dressing table set, Mavis noted with a slight shudder there were a few strands of long gray hair in the bristles of the bone-handled brush. Cranberry glass trinket-saver bowls held cheap rings and necklaces – Aubrey's mother's? – and in each drawer Mavis found lovingly laundered, pressed and folded clothes that must have belonged to his parents. Pulling open the wardrobe doors Mavis was pretty sure what she'd find there – and she did. Clearly Aubrey Morris hadn't been anywhere near the dump or a charity shop since his parents had died – their clothes hung neatly, covered in plastic bags. The strong smell of mothballs caught in Mavis's throat, and she felt rather sick. *Poor wee boy*, she thought, then reminded herself Aubrey was in his mid-twenties.

Descending the stairs, Mavis weighed in her mind whether the respect Aubrey had shown for his late parents' belongings suggested any sort of mental condition. Certainly it spoke of a young man who valued physical reminders of their presence, but she couldn't convince herself what she had seen was unhealthy, as such.

Entering the parlor to join Althea, Mavis was in for one last shock. Fully expecting a plethora of mahogany and antimacassars – and maybe even the odd aspidistra – what she found was Althea sitting on a tall metal stool in front of a blank computer screen, flicking through a book that looked as though it weighed a ton, and dressed in a toga. Mavis paused, unsure if the mothballs had caused her to hallucinate.

'I found his man-cave,' said Althea with delight.

'I don't think this is what people mean when they call something a "man-cave", Althea. That's what they call a room in America where a man puts all his sporting memorabilia and to which he escapes when he wants some time to himself.'

Althea smiled. 'Oh, I see. You mean it's like a garden shed is for a man here?'

Mavis nodded. She didn't want to get sidetracked. 'So what have we here? What a very interesting man our Aubrey Morris is. And where did you get that toga?'

Althea pointed to a hat stand in the corner of the room that held another two items similar to the one she was wearing, but in different colors. 'Maybe he had a different one for every day of the week. But at least we know now what he was interested in.' She nodded at the walls which were covered with maps of Wales from Roman times, and of the entirety of the European continent, showing the extent and nature of the Roman Empire. Photographs of centurions' crests, uniforms, Roman encampments and fortifications covered what space was left.

Peering at the computer tower beneath the table which supported the computer screen Mavis said, 'If we just turn this on we could maybe see what he was up to last time he used it, and maybe even find out if he had an online life. What do you think?'

'It'll be password protected, I suspect,' said Althea, surprising Mavis.

'For someone who wants to rein in technology as though it's a thoroughbred in need of schooling, you sound incredibly tech-savvy all of a sudden, my dear.'

Althea grinned like a naughty schoolgirl. 'TV. Nothing to it really. It's your Carol we could do with here. Any chance of getting her to join us?'

Mavis nodded. 'I'll phone her right away. And I'll let Annie know what we've found.' She paused. 'They might not believe me, of course, but I'll do my best.'

SIX

When Carol's car deposited her outside the Lamb and Flag, Annie knew she'd muffed her exit. She wanted to slip around the back of the pub with no fuss, because she guessed her mother might be looking out of the front window of her cottage just across the green; it would never do for Eustelle to see her daughter entering an establishment that sold intoxicating liquor before noon. Truth be told, she wasn't very keen on the idea of Annie drinking anything stronger than Robinson's Lemon Barley Water, which was one of the reasons Annie was struggling with the tiny little bit of glee she was feeling because she knew her mother was going back to London after the wedding.

It had seemed like such a good idea for Eustelle to help her move into her little cottage. But it was a small space and they'd been tripping over each other for a few weeks. Enough was enough. Annie'd been out on her own since she was sixteen – having her beloved mother just feet away from her every moment of the day and night was beginning to drive her barmy.

'Can I help?' The man's voice was deep, and the accent very Welsh.

Annie jumped. 'Sorry?'

'Can I help?' repeated the voice. 'We're not open yet, you know.' The florid, thick-lipped man looked at his pocket watch. 'Not for another hour.'

'I know,' said Annie abruptly. 'I'm Annie Parker.'

'I know,' replied the man. 'And I'm Tudor Evans. Landlord of this hostelry.'

'I know who you are, I live across the green,' snapped Annie.

'But you frequent the Chellingworth Arms,' added the man with a knowing grin.

Annie sighed. 'Alright, doll. We can go on showing off how clever we both are for another ten minutes if you like, but I'd rather sit down and have a proper natter, if it's all the same to you.'

Annie read the look on Tudor Evans's face to be one of slight amusement. He scratched his nose and replied, 'By all means, Miss Annie Parker. It is Miss, am I right?'

Annie arched an eyebrow. 'You know flamin' well it is. Whole village knows. Black and a spinster. At fifty-four. I see the looks of pity.'

Tudor Evans stepped back and gave Annie a long, appraising

look. 'I tell you what, if you want to feel sorry for yourself I'm not going to stop you. But if I were you, I'd sharpen up a bit and realize you're a fine-looking woman with a lot of life ahead of you. If you want to live it with a look on your face like you just sucked a lemon, go ahead. No skin off my nose. But I suggest you take a leaf out of my book. No oil painting myself. Never have been. But that doesn't mean I sit at home moping all the time. I throw myself into everything. I dare say there's a lot of people round here who think I'm a real tartar, but I'm only doing what I think is right. You know – looking after the right way to do things. I might not have a wife or any kids to leave behind, but at least I can make sure people remember me because I was the one who taught them how to do things right.'

'Tartar? Eustelle calls me dad that.'

'Eustelle?'

'Me mum.'

'Why do you call her Eustelle?'

''Cause that's her name.' Annie looked puzzled.

'But . . . oh, never mind. Back to the original question: what can I do for you?'

'I work for the WISE Enquiries Agency. We recently set up shop in a lovely old barn out on the Chellingworth Estate. The dowager has talked us into making some enquiries about this Aubrey Morris's disappearance. Given that you're the one he'd made arrangements to pick up last night, I thought I'd come straight to the horse's mouth.' Annie wondered how Tudor Evans would react to her forthrightness.

His broad features softened into a smile, and he slapped his corduroy-encased thigh. 'Ah yes, the enquiry agents. Heard a lot about you lot we have. Come into the snug. Ladies are allowed there. I'll get you a coffee.'

Annie bristled as the landlord steered her into a part of the pub separated from the main bar by wood and glass partitions. 'Snug, me eye. Is it some sort of rule a woman can't go into the normal bar? Can't get away with that these days. We women have rights, you know.'

Tudor's expression was difficult for Annie to read when he replied, 'I am fully aware women have rights, and, no, it's not a rule. To be honest we don't get many women in here at all. Tend to go to the Chellingworth Arms, like you do. I'm sure you know Sarah, the landlady there. Makes sure it's all nice for the women, she does.'

Annie sat at the slightly knocked-about table Tudor indicated. He fiddled about behind the bar with an antiquated coffee pot, and she took in her surroundings. 'It's not all lace doilies and pot pourri at the Arms,' she said, 'but Sarah has made the place look cheerful and welcoming. Who picked the carpet for you here? A blind man's dog?'

'Quite the one, aren't you?' quipped Tudor as he placed a mug of coffee in front of Annie. 'I guessed milk and three sugars.'

'Lucky guess. But seriously, couldn't you have found something better than this?' Annie indicated the eyeball-assaulting riot of color that comprised the worn carpet. At least it was a relief from the drab beige walls, the muddy brown wood of the furnishings and the bar itself where not even the brass foot rail was gleaming. The pub looked unloved. Smelled it too. It made Annie feel sad.

'It was cheap,' said Tudor, his already ruddy cheeks coloring even more.

'You don't say,' mugged Annie. 'Tell you what, you help me out with this case, and I'll give you the benefit of my interior designer's eyes. I could spruce this place up in no time. It might be called a snug, but it's anything but.'

'Anyone ever told you you're a bit overwhelming?'

Annie judged that Tudor was almost smiling as he settled in the chair beside her. 'Nah. It's never come up.' She winked. 'But enough banter, what about Aubrey? Reckon he's done a bunk?'

'Never let us down before, and he's not the type,' replied Tudor, his features settling into a thoughtful expression. 'What I don't get is why he'd tell me he was going to pick us up at the village hall, then not do it. If he planned to go off somewhere – though where or why I can't imagine – why would he make those arrangements?'

Annie sipped her surprisingly good coffee. 'That's the question, innit? If he's taken himself off, why like this? Any thoughts?'

Tudor leaned across the small circular table. 'I'm pretty sure it won't be a woman, I can tell you that. Quietest bloke I've ever known. Either working, or at church, or with the Morris, or at home with his books. He was a solid type. Liked a lot round here.' Tudor paused. 'Now why did I say he "*was*" a solid type and he was "liked"? That's a bit weird, isn't it?'

Annie shrugged. 'If we were in a gumshoe novel it would mean that your guilty conscience was telling me you'd done him in. You know, blunt object, shallow grave, the lot. But it's probably just that you're thinking of him in the past tense quite naturally. People do, you know. Without it meaning anything menacing.'

'Well that's comforting at least,' mused Tudor. 'To know you don't think I've conked him one. Very comforting. So, having established that I'm not a cold-blooded killer, what can I tell you that might help you with your enquiries?'

Annie placed her mug on the stained oak table and considered Tudor's large face. It reminded her of the English bulldog named Elsie Tanner owned by one of her neighbors in Wandsworth. Of course, that particular creature had been a bitch, named after the character in *Coronation Street*, and Tudor was very definitely the male of the species, but the likeness was notable, nonetheless. As she was thinking all this Annie took in the capable hands that held his mug, the worry lines that furrowed his brow and the glint in his eye as he watched her watching him.

Snapping back to the case Annie said, 'Reliability and bookishness aside, what do you know about Aubrey? Haunts? Likes? Obsessions? Hates?'

Tudor smiled across his steaming mug. 'Right to it then, no messing about? OK. Let's see. Aubrey wasn't one for gossip or chatter. He was usually well informed about whatever activity was being undertaken and spoke intelligently about it – be that the Morris, or the church activities, or whatever. You know what I mean? Always focused on the matter at hand. Not one given to chatting about something off topic. Good like that, he was. Kept people moving in the right direction. Unlike some I could mention, who prefer to run off at the mouth about anything and everything and not give their concentration to what needs to be done. Worth his weight in gold, that boy.'

'Hardly a boy. Mid-twenties, right?'

Tudor nodded. 'Yes, but you know what I mean. Compared with us, a boy.'

Annie bristled. 'Oi, careful now. Speak for yourself.'

Tudor grinned. 'I won't see sixty again, and you've admitted to fifty-four, so we're both old enough to be his parents, which means I reckon we're allowed to call him a boy. But I know what you mean. Perspective. Boy to us. Man to himself.'

'What about that; was he a man to himself? I understand he lived alone. Family all gone?'

Tudor nodded. 'All his family seemed to die pretty young. I've been in Anwen for over thirty years, so I knew of his gran and grandpa. Everyone called her Gran Morris. And I mean everyone. She was woven through the entire life of the village. Knew everyone. Ran everything. Then she died. Very sudden. Shocked everyone. His mam went the same way. Heart, when Aubrey was just a little kid. Terrible sad. His father was a different matter; strong as an ox he was. Got knocked down by a lorry in Builth Wells on market day and never made it to the hospital. Terrible. Aubrey was about . . . um . . . twenty then, I'd say. Yes, it was about five years ago.'

'And Aubrey made – *makes* – his living as a handyman?' Annie smiled as she corrected herself.

Tudor nodded. 'I don't suppose he needed much income. But he worked hard. His prices were fair. Not cheap, fair. And good work always. Never quibbled if you needed something doing at a funny time. So long as it didn't interfere with him going to church on Sunday, he'd do it when you wanted. Like I said, worth his weight in gold.'

'Speaking of which, any family money? You know, is he secretly wealthy?'

Tudor shook his head. 'Aubrey? No, not him. There is money in the family, don't get me wrong. He's related to the Morisses out toward Hay-on-Wye. Lot of land, they've got. Even for around here it's a lot. No title, like the Twysts, but lots of land. Word is that the grandfather was given the money to buy a house by his older brother when he inherited the land. Not a big house, relatively speaking, but out on its own with an acre or two. No more. Aubrey's mam used to grow veg and his dad would do the odd jobs, though he did quite a bit of building work too. You know, barns and so forth. Pretty good with dry-stone walls he was too, as I recall. More or less a lost art that is now. Funnily enough, Aubrey said he was practicing to do it himself. Thought he could pick up quite a bit of work like that around these parts and up on the Brecon Beacons once he'd mastered it.'

Annie felt Tudor was just about to wander into areas that weren't of any use so interrupted with: 'What about other interests? Might he have gone off somewhere to, I don't know, see someone or do something connected with a hobby?'

Again Tudor shook his head. 'That's it, you see, all I know of him is what he's involved with here. His work. His church life. Playing for the Morris.'

'Is he generally musical? Did he study somewhere? Might he have gone off to play somewhere else or to see a performance?'

'His dad taught him. And even if he did have somewhere to go, why wouldn't he have told me, or someone else? Why tell me he'd pick me up at the hall, then just not do it?'

Silence.

Tudor stood up. Annie could tell he was feeling frustrated. Just as she was about to speak, her telephone rang inside her handbag. She managed to find it before it stopped and answered the call.

'Just a sec, Mave. Tudor, it's Mavis, she and Althea are out at Aubrey's house, just give me a minute to catch up?' she announced.

Tudor paced patiently as Annie listened to all of Mavis's news, and the information Carol had already passed to Mavis, then Tudor started waggling his arms at her. Annie wondered if he was having a fit.

'Hang on a tick, Mave. What?' snapped Annie.

'Ask her if the Morris kit is there,' replied Tudor, 'and could she maybe bring it here when they leave? If it's here, it's safe. Then, if I can find a replacement musician, we'll be alright for Saturday.'

Annie was puzzled. She really had no idea what Tudor was talking about. She sighed. 'Here – you talk to her.' She handed him the phone.

Tudor took it politely and adopted what Annie thought must be his posh telephone voice; it made her want to giggle.

'Ah yes, hullo. Tudor Evens here. Landlord of the Lamb and Flag. I was just asking your lovely colleague if you might be able to bring the Morris kit with you from Aubrey's house. I can take care of it here, at the pub. If that would be convenient.'

Annie watched as Tudor listened then said, 'A large brown leather suitcase, with brass fittings. It's a little heavy, I'm afraid. Plus a tall, thin carrying case for our staff. It's about six feet long, again, brown leather. A small wooden box with silver bells in it. Yes, a box full of bells.' Another pause. 'I'm not sure. In the house somewhere, I would think.' A long pause. 'Well, maybe you wouldn't have noticed them if you weren't looking for them?' Annie sipped her coffee as she watched Tudor's neck grow red. 'If you would, yes. That would be most helpful. No, I don't know where else to suggest. Thank you.'

He handed the device back to Annie, his brow furrowed. 'She wants you back again.'

Annie took the phone. 'Here I am again, what's up?'

Annie thought Mavis sounded a bit shirty as she said, 'I will have another check around the house, but, as I just told your Mister Evans, I haven't seen the items he's referring to. If I do find what he wants, we'll be sure to bring it with us, but find out from him what it is he's after, exactly, and maybe it'll shed some light on what's going on. In the meantime, I'm going to take some photographs of everything here, and I'll wait until Carol can come out and have a go at this computer. I wish there was someone from whom we could gain approval for rooting around in this man's life. Looking around the house I'd say he hasn't gone on a planned trip and it's why I think we can justify Carol's intervention. Agreed?'

'Agreed. Talk later.' Annie ended the call.

'So?' asked Tudor, eager for news.

'Mavis will have a proper look for the items you mentioned,

but I should say she's highly observant, and if she hasn't seen them so far – unless they are hidden away somewhere – they might not be there.'

'Well then we're stuffed,' said Tudor, looking totally deflated.

'Come on then, tell me what's in those cases that's so important,' said Annie, intrigued.

'All our stuff for the Morris. The bells, the sticks, and our staff. It's what makes the Anwen Morris the Anwen Morris. Without it we're just a bunch of overweight, middle-aged blokes skipping about the place waving hankies around. It's our history. Our identity.'

Annie bit her lip. Her personal views about Morris dancing had just been put into words by Tudor, but she knew she had to hide her feelings. She forced her face to look concerned. 'Sorry, doll. Can't you just get new ones for Saturday?' She was trying to be helpful.

Tudor looked at her as though she'd sprouted a second head. 'You're kidding, aren't you? New? *New?* That's the whole point. These artefacts are hundreds of years old. They've been handed down through generations of the Morris family to be where they are today. You know I said about the grandfather getting the house out of his older brother when he inherited the Morris farm? Well, he also got the Morris artefacts. The older brother didn't want anything to do with them, nor the Morris itself. Terrible, when you think about it.'

Annie gathered her thoughts, and realized she might have missed something. 'Tudor, I'm sorry if I'm being a bit dim, but is it significant that Aubrey's name is Morris and he owns a lot of stuff you all use for Morris dancing – or is it just a coincidence?'

Tudor nodded and sat down again. 'Of course. You don't know. Why would you? How about I top up that coffee, then I can give you the whole background on the Anwen Morris, and the role of the Morris family?'

Annie nodded. As Tudor brought the pot of coffee from behind the bar she checked her watch. 'What time do you open?'

'Ten minutes ago,' he replied glumly, 'can't you tell by the hordes beating down the door?' He shook his head sadly. 'Tell you what, come through and sit up at the bar then I can see if anyone comes in, will you?'

Finally perched in her favorite position, Annie placed her phone on the bar between Tudor and herself and pressed record. It would save her having to make notes for the others.

'The history of the Morris is lost in the mists of time,' began Tudor in fulsome tones, 'some say it began in pre-history and is a relic of pagan rites, which is why I wear a hat covered in greenery – I represent the Green man – others that the word "Morris" is a version of the word "Moorish" and refers to the types of dances that Moors brought to Britain during the thirteenth century. That might also explain the black faces.' Tudor paused and visibly blushed. 'Is that offensive to you?' he asked timidly.

Annie was touched. She gave her response some thought. 'I can only speak for myself, and I know other people might feel differently, but, first off – and you might not understand what I mean when I say this – I never think of myself as black. I don't look in the mirror and see a black woman, I see Annie Parker; I'm a person, not a skin color. Growing up in London I was used to seeing people of all colors around me, all the time. I never questioned it. People were different, but the same. The same, but different. No one looked down on anyone. Then, when I worked in the City of London I was surrounded by white men pretty much all the time. They all looked down on me because I was a woman, not so much because I was black; misogynists first, racists second. Shocking, but true. The way of the world. Here? I stick out like a sore thumb. But as much because I'm a cockney as black. I just did a job with our agency in Cardiff, working undercover in a bar, and the main thing I noticed was that people would make comments about my *accent* behind my back, not about my color. But Cardiff's had black people for a long time, I s'pose. Big port cities do. Shirley Bassey's from Tiger Bay in Cardiff, right?' Tudor nodded. 'See, what I think is, whatever there is that's different about you, some people will pick on it. Black, tall, skinny, gangly, fat bum, horrible freckles? Whatever it is that people make fun of reflects on *their* insecurities, not mine. Mind you, I s'pose I just listed all mine. If I could change one thing about myself it wouldn't be my skin color, it would be the size of my backside. What about you?'

Tudor smiled. 'My lips. Mick Jagger can have them back.'

Annie and Tudor shared a thoughtful moment, then Annie said, 'To answer your question – does a white person blacking up their face for a traditional dance offend me? – all I can do is say it doesn't offend *me*, but it might offend someone else. Does every Morris group, or team, or whatever, have a blacked-up person in it? Is it a "thing"?'

Annie judged Tudor was relieved at her response. 'Not every group does, and quite a few are stopping, because they don't want to cause offence. But if the dance really is more ancient than the time of the arrival of the Moors, then I believe that the blacking of the face goes back to the simple idea of disguise – that the dancer is hiding their identity to make mischief. Lots of teams, or sides, as we are called, use multicolored face paint these days. It keeps the spirit without the possible racist implications.'

'So, other than that, what's all the equipment about?' prompted Annie, knowing she should make some effort to get back to the office and meet her colleagues at some point during the day.

'Right. There are different types of Morris dance. It's a fascinating field, but I'll stick to us, here, for now. Basically, some dancers use swords – more often than not they are an amended type of sword so they aren't as potentially lethal – and some use sticks. Others use neither and just have pieces of cloth – the hankies to which I referred. The sticks might be made of anything – wood or metal. The Anwen Morris uses cloth and sticks. We also all wear bells on our legs, and we have the additional piece of a ceremonial staff. Some sides have horse-heads that are paraded about – a hobby horse – and some have a man dressed as a woman – known as the Maid or Mary, or even Marion, which probably derives from the time when Robin Hood's escapades were told of in Morris dancing. We don't have a horse or a maid here, just the staff. The Anwen Morris Staff.'

Annie was pleased she was recording Tudor's voice. It was comforting. She felt as though she was being led up Welsh hills and down into Welsh valleys as his lilt rose and fell.

He continued, 'You asked if the name was a coincidence. The answer is no. There's been a Morris family in Anwen since some time during the 1500s. Always been in sheep—' Tudor grinned wickedly – 'if you know what I mean. Lot of money in wool back then. Mainstay of the wealth around here. The Twysts, too. It's why St David's is so big for a country church – wool money. Started building it in 1490 they did, all on the back of sheep. Come the Reformation, they ran from Rome as quick as they could around here, I gather. Of course, they had to swing back that way when they had no choice under Mary Tudor, but they do say that Elizabeth the First came to Chellingworth specifically to worship at St David's, where her father had also knelt while it was still being built. Anyway, one of the things the Morrises spent their wool money on was silver, and a lot of that silver found its way into the bells we wear. Fifteenth-century silver bells around our knees, and a fifteenth-century silver staff at our head. It's beautiful. A long wand of white Welsh oak covered in chased silver, with a large glass orb at the top caged in gold. Got a few dings and dents in it – but then it would, it's very old. And it's used. Never been precious with it. Always been used by the Anwen Morris. With respect, of course. The cloths we use aren't old. They are still made of wool, though. And the sticks? Well, they're a bit special too. Yes, they're just pieces of wood, but they're believed to be about five hundred years old, and to have been made from an ancient tree, so, when you hold them, it's like you're reaching back through time all the way to, well, maybe even the time of Christ. It's quite something.'

Annie was struck by the man's emotional connection to the artefacts he was describing, his broad features softened, his gaze grew wistful. 'They mean a lot to you,' she noted.

Tudor nodded. 'To me and to all of Anwen. The Morrises own them, but they belong to all of us, in a way. Like I said, without them it's all just jigging about. With them, the dance means so much more.' Annie noted a change in his expression.

He looked uneasy as he added, 'It would all feel a bit like a pantomime without the proper kit. Oh heck, I'd better get on the phone. No. No, I'll wait till I'm certain.' Tudor looked horrified as a thought occurred to him. 'If we don't have the kit, and we don't have a musician, then maybe I should just phone the duke and say we can't dance at all. But that would break with tradition.'

Annie felt the man's genuine anguish. 'Tell you what, doll. You stop panicking, and I'll phone Mave and see if she's found anything over at Aubrey's house, alright? And how about another coffee?'

As Tudor Evans scuttled around behind the bar, Annie wandered back into the snug and pulled out her phone. If the items Tudor had described weren't at Aubrey Morris's house, she wondered where they might be. As she pushed the button to speed-dial Mavis's number she also began to wonder how much such items might be worth.

SEVEN

C hristine Wilson-Smythe's day had flown by. After she'd left the office on the Chellingworth Estate she'd spent a few hours on the M4, then an hour or so at her flat in Battersea before she'd headed off toward her parents' home in Knightsbridge. She'd checked in with Alexander as she'd driven up to London. She knew it was a big night for the both of them; introducing the man she'd allowed into her life during the past few months to her mother and father was something she'd been ruminating on for a few weeks. The sad death of her nanny, and the event organized to remember her, had provided the perfect opportunity for a social interaction that would not allow for an overt examination of Alexander, or of her relationship with him, by either of her parents.

Nonetheless, Christine was more than a little apprehensive; every other escort she'd introduced to her parents over the years had been someone they'd either known personally, or they'd known one of his family members, or at least an acquaintance of his. They'd always had a reference point. Alexander was a complete outsider. Indeed, only he and she understood the distance he had traveled, in the social sense, to arrive at the place he currently occupied in the world. Alexander had insisted upon telling Christine everything about his early life as a courier for the South London underworld, and she'd listened, silently judged, enjoyed a jolly good bellow at him, then had reassessed his early-life situation, and had begun to work toward forgiving him. She hadn't quite reached her destination, but she was still content to be on the journey. She truly believed Alexander's business and philanthropic endeavors were now in synch, and both working toward one end: doing much more good in the world than his early nefarious deeds had done bad.

That admitted, Christine was no innocent about Alexander's difficult position; if he were ever to be recognized for his other, young self, and brought to justice for his deeds – none of which were truly clear to him, except for the fact that he had been aware he was transporting unknown items around South London for some incredibly shady characters – then he could face . . . what? Prison? Possibly.

Christine took advantage of her residents' parking permit to be able to leave her car near her parents' house in Knightsbridge, and she walked the damp and busy streets until she came to the restaurant where Nanny Mullins had enjoyed bringing her for any and every meal possible. As a small child she'd wondered why the woman had chosen this place, of all the possible restaurants in London. She recalled Nanny had said it was because she liked consistency, and now, entering its doors for the first time in twenty years, Christine knew what Nanny had meant. L'horloge hadn't changed a bit. The maître d' was still Michel – a little grayer but the same light-footed, smiling gentleman who had seated her when she was seven; the barman was still Stephane, tall with grizzled hair, now white. A waitress she remembered as young and lithe was now round and flat-footed, but she still smiled and even winked at Christine when she entered.

'Ah, the little miss with a pony,' she said with a nod. 'Still out-riding all the boys in the holidays? Making them pay for betting that a girl couldn't ride faster than them?'

Christine had forgotten how she'd loved to talk about her horse-riding escapades with the boys on her family's estate in Ireland. How she'd enjoyed those devil-may-care school holidays when she could throw off her uniform and run barefoot with the locals. As she grinned at the remembrances, she caught her father's eyes across the room, and she felt her face smooth into a polite, welcoming expression. How her father had chided her for her wild ways. Would he do the same about Alexander?

Raising her hand in greeting, Christine picked up a glass of champagne from the bar as she made her way toward her father and mother. The restaurant was hosting about twenty people who were milling about in an area cleared of tables. Christine didn't recognize anyone as she weaved politely between bodies; she assumed they were all people who had also benefitted from Nanny Mullins' care and protection.

'Mother, how lovely to see you,' said Christine as she tapped her mother on the shoulder. A head shorter than her daughter, the viscountess looked barely old enough to have a twenty-seven-year-old daughter, let alone the thirty-two-year-old son who was too busy to attend the event. Warm kisses with her mother, followed by a hug with her father, allowed Christine to gain some sense of normality. She was on edge; Alexander was late. She glanced as surreptitiously as possible toward the entrance, but couldn't see him anywhere. She knew she wouldn't miss him; he'd be about a head taller than anyone else there, and the only person not completely and blindingly white.

Suddenly, and shockingly, he was beside her, handing a glass to her mother, then one to her father. Christine beamed up at him. He looked delightful in his dark suit, crisp white shirt and that subtly stunning tie they'd picked out together. She decided to dive right in, her heart thumping in her chest as she spoke.

'I see you've already met. Good. Mummy, Daddy, this is Alexander. Alexander, my parents.' She knew she was grinning madly, but she didn't care.

Christine was immediately aware that something was terribly wrong; the expressions on her parents' faces were singularly peculiar. They both looked horrified, and they had frozen on the spot. Her mother was visibly blushing, and she was rolling her eyes at Christine's father like a madwoman; her father was adopting the sheepish look he had when he was about to stammer something unutterably stupid – which, for a very bright man, he did with alarming regularity. Alexander was looking cool, calm and confident, as he always did. Yes, his height meant he was literally looking down on her parents, but that was beyond his control. He was extending his hand toward her father in a welcoming manner. So what on earth was going on? Christine couldn't fathom the dynamic at all.

Unable to stand it any longer she looked at her father and said, 'What?' rather abruptly.

'Mr Bright? A pleasure to meet you,' spluttered her father at last, shaking Alexander's hand. 'Christine told us we'd be meeting you here, but we didn't realize you were . . . you.'

'Well who did you think he was?' butted in Christine with disbelief. 'If he was bringing you a drink . . . oh my gracious me, Daddy. You didn't think he was a waiter, did you?'

'I'm terribly sorry, Alexander,' said her mother weakly. 'Terrible faux pas. Probably best if we don't mention it again.'

One look told Christine that Alexander found the whole situation rather amusing. At least she hoped she was reading his reactions correctly.

'Never again, Lady Ballinclare,' said Alexander quietly, his deep voice reassuring.

'It's Fiona, please, and Aiden, of course.'

Alexander nodded at Christine's mother and father then added, 'I'm just going to get a glass for myself. May I freshen yours?' His eyes twinkled as they caught Christine's.

Christine nodded, threw the entire contents of her glass down her throat and handed it to Alexander. 'If ever I needed another, now would be the time. Thanks.' Alone with her parents she glowered at them. 'What on earth were you thinking?' she whispered angrily.

'Christine, don't be so quick to judge,' snapped her father. 'We're in unusual surroundings, sharing a space with people we don't know, and a stranger asked us if he could bring us a drink. What was one to think?'

'You knew I'd invited Alexander, and I know I told you what he looked like. Tall, dark, latte skin, scar on his forehead, well dressed. What more did you need? That he'd written his name on a big label on his chest?'

'Please don't speak to your father like that, Christine. Your beau could have introduced himself to us,' whispered her mother.

'Mummy, it's not 1922. He's not my "beau" and you could have done the same, you know. Good gracious me.' Christine shook her head in disbelief as Alexander rejoined the little group, glasses in hand and a wicked grin on his face. Christine suspected he was thoroughly enjoying her parents' discomfort.

'So, awkward first introductions aside,' began the viscount, 'may I make a toast – to newly made acquaintances.' Glasses were raised and champagne sipped.

'And to Nanny Mullins,' said Christine quietly. A more somber draught was taken by the foursome.

It was then time for the speeches and their attention was diverted for a good fifteen minutes as various ex-charges of Nanny Mullins gave their eulogies and thanks to her 'inspirational' and 'firm' nannying technique. It was when the fourth and final charge was at the bar that Christine became aware that her telephone was vibrating inside her handbag. She felt she should wait before she answered it, so she was glad when things wound up. A general hubbub following a vote of thanks allowed Christine the chance to check her phone.

'Work?' asked Alexander noticing her preoccupation. Christine nodded. 'Urgent?' he added. She nodded again. 'Why don't you phone them back? I'll stay here with your parents. I'm sure we can amuse ourselves for five minutes.'

Christine looked at Alexander, then her parents. She wondered about the wisdom of leaving them to their own devices, but as soon as her father said to Alexander, 'So Christine tells me you're involved in property development . . .' she decided she'd definitely just check her messages, rather than return calls.

A couple of moments later she felt happy to be able to interrupt what seemed to be a complex explanation of social housing planning in inner cities with a rather curious statement. 'Daddy, I think you can help with a case we have.'

'Really, dear?' replied her father looking suspicious. 'I find that most unlikely, but tell me, in what way do you think I might be of assistance?'

'Morris dancing. You're up on that, aren't you?' Christine was confident he was.

Surprisingly her father looked a bit squirrely. 'In what way "up on it", dear?'

'You know a lot about it. I know you do, Daddy. You dragged me to see umpteen of the wretched displays when I was young. All over the place. Mad for it, you were.'

Her father smiled. 'In my younger days maybe I was keen on it for a while. But not for quite some time now. It's been rather taken over by a different type, these days. Haven't seen a proper Morris for years. Just these tourist type things.'

Christine was genuinely puzzled. She'd always assumed her father had continued with what she'd always felt had been a rabid interest in Morris dancing.

'Oh. Well maybe you can't help then,' she said, rather crestfallen. 'It's just that we have a case involving a missing Morris dancer back in Wales, and now it turns out that, while he might have left Anwen-by-Wye intentionally, he's hopped it with what seems to be an ancient, storied and possibly valuable set of Morris dancing implements. I thought you might know what the chances would be of shifting said implements.'

Her father looked vague. 'Sorry. Not a clue.' He shrugged.

Smiling at Alexander, Christine said, 'I don't suppose *you* know someone who might be able to help?' She knew the answer before she asked.

Alexander winked. 'I know just the chap. Want me to give him a ring?'

Christine smiled warmly. 'If you wouldn't mind.' Turning her attention to her parents Christine added, 'Did I mention that Alexander owns Coggins and Sons, you know, the antiques place down near Chelsea Harbour? It means he has a great number of terribly useful contacts.'

'Contacts who might know about missing Morris dancing kit?' asked her father pointedly.

Tutting loudly, Christine said, 'Daddy, come off it, not all antiques fall off the back of lorries. As a family with two enormous houses stuffed to the gills with ancient objects, we know only too well that many of them sit in dimly lit rooms for generations, unloved and unwanted, but having to be dusted and insured at regular intervals. One of Alexander's business interests allows him to ensure such objects end up in the hands of those who value and love them, rather than seeing them as monstrosities that must be maintained. Isn't that right, Alexander?'

Alexander smiled. 'That's an elegant way of putting it,' he said calmly. 'Now, if you'd like to pursue this matter this evening, might I suggest I make that call?'

Kisses and handshakes followed, and eventually Alexander helped Christine into her coat at the door, before the pair of them stepped into the chilly, damp night air.

'Walk you to your car, ma'am? Then I'll scurry back to my spot at the bar to serve the next lot what comes along?' quipped Alexander in a mock-cockney accent.

'Oh good gracious, my blessed parents! I'm so embarrassed. I'm sorry, Alexander, it was terribly rude of them to assume you were a waiter. I'll never let them forget it.'

Alexander hugged her to his side. 'Don't worry, neither will I.' He grinned. 'Now, about the stuff that's missing. Would that be the Anwen Morris artefacts you're talking about? Because, if it is, I know exactly who we need to talk to, but we won't be able to reach him easily on the phone. We're more likely to catch him at a certain pub near the Globe Theatre. It's his second home. What he doesn't know about folkloric treasures you could write on a postage stamp.' Alexander looked at his watch. 'If we take my car it'll be quicker. And we'll end up not too far from my place, so we could eat there, if you like.'

'Or maybe grab a bite at the pub?' said Christine with a wink.

'Probably not,' said Alexander. 'Not really that sort of pub.

Though you know I can rustle up a mean bowl of pasta at no more than a moment's notice.'

'I do indeed,' said Christine, sliding herself into Alexander's Aston Martin for what she knew would be an enjoyable trip across London; Alexander was an excellent driver, and he managed the power of the vehicle with deftness. Buckled in, she sent a text to the girls back at the office to tell them what she and Alexander were doing – promising to report back to them all later on. Given that she'd abandoned them to run off to London for a couple of days, she was rather pleased she was now going to be able to contribute something to the case.

Half an hour later, Christine was standing outside a seedy pub in a street that hadn't witnessed the passing of a street-cleaning gang in, possibly, a decade. Graffiti covered large, industrial wheelie-bins that stood in a forlorn row against one wall, and Alexander was deep in conversation with a small man who looked, to Christine, like a human version of a bird; his long, beaked nose moved up and down as he and Alexander talked. She wasn't close enough to hear what was being said, which was irritating. She knew very well that the WISE agency would flourish if every staff member used every contact they had in the pursuit of information and evidence to help with their cases, and Alexander had some wonderful contacts. She just wished they didn't all have to be met at the dead of night in dismal lanes.

Finally parting from the informant, Alexander rejoined her, a smile on his face.

'So we definitely won't be eating at the pub then?' said Christine as she slipped her arm into Alexander's and they headed for the car.

'As I said, pasta at mine sounds good.'

'Anything useful from that rather odd-looking little man?'

'Wheels are in motion.'

'Ah, as enigmatic, as ever.'

'One of my fortes,' said Alexander, opening the car door for Christine with a grin.

'Which is both a good, and a bad, thing,' said Christine, sliding in.

EIGHT

'Alright, ladies, it's almost seven o'clock, so I suggest we have a quick summary of the day, then abandon the office and head for our homes. Agreed?' Carol and Annie both nodded in response to Mavis's question. Mavis leaned forward in her armchair, while her colleagues remained splayed on the sofa. The office was dimly lit by a couple of standard lamps; it helped make the vast space seem more intimate. 'Carol, could you record this for Christine, please? You can send it as an audio file. Thank you, dear.'

Carol popped her phone onto the coffee table. 'Shoot,' she said to Mavis, who nodded at Annie.

Annie leaned forward and spoke loudly. 'I have established from my contact with Mr Tudor Evans that Aubrey Morris's no-show last night is out of character, and that while he might own all the kit and caboodle he's taken with him, the village sees it as rightly theirs, so Tudor's more than a bit miffed. I got a good primer on the history of Morris dancing, but Mave tells me you're all over that 'cause your dad's into it, so I won't waste your time. That's me done.'

Carol added, 'It's clear from speaking to various women in the village who had jobs booked with him for *next* week that he meant to not be in attendance to carry out the planned work. He had made arrangements for some jobs to be done by other service providers, or had told certain customers that they should make alternative arrangements. I believe he planned to leave the village after Henry and Stephanie's wedding. Maybe you should speak next, Mavis, then I'll talk about the computing input.'

Mavis moved closer to the recorder. 'I gained access to the subject's home thanks to the fact that Althea – our honorary WISE woman – has a key to his front door. I noted the house was clean and tidy, the refrigerator had not been emptied of perishables, his wardrobe was full of clothes and the presence of an empty suitcase suggests to me Aubrey Morris did not pack up and leave home on a planned trip. His vehicle, a van, is not at his home. To confirm – the police have declined, once again, to get involved. When I spoke to them they pointed out that Aubrey might have clothes and luggage we know nothing about, and might even own more than one toothbrush. They believe Aubrey Morris has left his home and Anwen-by-Wye of his own choice. As to where he might have gone? Back to you, Carol.'

Carol cleared her throat and scooted forward on the sofa. 'Mavis phoned me from the Morris home and asked that I join her there. She and Althea had found a computer which they felt might, if accessed, give us some idea of Aubrey Morris's intentions. Having been unable to trace him online using any obvious names he might use, I thought it worthwhile for me to make the trip to his house. Upon my arrival I noted that Aubrey's computer was a few years old, and not terribly sophisticated. I took a little time to work out how he'd set up his systems before I attempted to access anything at all.

Carol paused for a moment, then continued, 'Now, I know you get impatient with me when I spout computer babble as you call it, so let's just cut to the chase. The most interesting information I found was that the browser history told me Aubrey had been searching online auction sites, as well as sites that gave information on inexpensive hotels in Rome, Italy. The man's house tells us he's well-versed in the history of the Roman occupation of the British Isles, especially the area around Anwen-by-Wye, and he also seems to be besotted with Celtic and Druidic history in the area. He has been quite active in chat rooms and on blogs that deal with all these topics, as well as topics connected with Morris dancing and its history, but there doesn't seem to be anything in what he's written to suggest why he'd have left at *this* time. That, when taken with his searches, lead me to believe he's been hunting around trying to find out more about the exact history of, or to be able to prove the historical significance of, the Morris dancing artefacts his family has owned for many generations. It might be possible he's thinking of selling them. There's no trace of the items on any online auction site I know of, though I will do more digging when I get back home tonight.'

'We have no idea if he's actually gone to Rome,' added Mavis tartly. 'No records of flights purchased on his computer.'

Carol added, 'One more thing – although we thought he might be the type to have hooked up with someone online, I can't find any trail of activity in dating sites or dating chat rooms, or anything like that. I hunted about for an hour or so, but no joy, and no frequently used email addresses either, so no electronic breadcrumbs to lead to a possible romantic interest.'

'Thanks, Carol,' concluded Mavis with a nod. Carol stopped recording.

Annie said, 'It doesn't sound like I did very much, but that's probably because I had to spend all afternoon convincing Eustelle I was in the pub on business and not because I'm a raging alcoholic.'

As Carol made several efforts to extricate herself from the cloying embrace of the sofa she said, 'Annie, you did what was needed. That's what we do – we each do what's needed for the team. But talking about Eustelle, it's time we all got going. Bump will be glad to get home tonight. Give you a lift, girls?'

Mavis got her coat, Annie sent the audio file, then Carol warmed up the car while Mavis turned off all the lights and locked up behind them.

NINE

Tuesday, February 25th

Henry woke with a headache. He put it down to the final conversation he'd had the previous night with Edward about the need for extra staff on the day of the wedding. It had to be that, he told himself as he gazed into his bloodshot eyes in the bathroom mirror. It couldn't be the brandy.

He'd agreed with Mrs Davies his cook he would take breakfast in his room for the rest of the week, which meant she
wouldn't have to set up to serve him in the breakfast room, a
great saving of effort for her, he'd been assured, considering
all her extra duties. He was happy to make the concession,
and was pleasantly surprised to discover that eating creamily
scrambled eggs on toast and sipping coffee at the window of
his large bedroom was actually quite pleasant. It also meant
he could extend the period before he had to face any of the
occupying forces decamped in various parts of his home for
an extra hour or so.

Eventually he had to succumb. Stephanie had telephoned
his room to remind him about a meeting they had planned
with the leader of the chamber orchestra that was due to play
for their festivities. He was keenly aware that his fiancé had
spent some considerable time convincing the students at the
music department at the University of Cardiff it would be
worth their while to perform at the celebrations for next to
nothing, if only to be able to say they had taken part in such
an historic event. He'd promised to be extremely hospitable
to the conductor who was making all the arrangements and
had agreed with Stephanie some alcoholic supplies were to
be set aside for the musicians so they could enjoy themselves
'properly' when their services were no longer required.
Libations aside, the Chellingworth Estate was also paying
for the bus that would ferry them from, and back to, Cardiff
on the day, as well as stumping up for the lorry required to
deliver the harps.

Henry wondered if angels would need to be coaxed down
from on high for the occasion too, but he decided it was best
to keep that thought to himself as he watched Stephanie gush,
cajole, smile, instruct, flatter and make promises to the young
orchestral leader as though he were a juvenile Mozart, rather
than the representative of a couple of dozen music students.

Henry watched with admiration as Stephanie talked about
musical selections, running orders and timings. She was no
beauty, in the classical sense, but he wasn't an Adonis by any
means either. They were a well-suited couple – everyone said
so. And he thought it true. The age difference? He tended to

agree with Stephanie that he was an eternal child, so his age really was just a number, and she'd soon catch him up. One thing he did spot was the fact she'd lost weight. His mother's assurances that this was normal for any woman as she approached her wedding day aside, he wondered why he'd gone the other way – he'd gained a few pounds, if his waistcoat buttons were to be believed. He hoped his wedding suit would fit. He'd been measured back in January. He looked at his watch. He'd know in a few hours; his tailor was due to come to the hall for the final fitting of his morning suit.

Tuning back in to the conversation with the musician, Henry realized it was all over bar the farewells. He was relieved. Another bullet dodged. As the young chap with the greasy hair skedaddled, Stephanie crossed through the item on her list and said, 'Right, I'm off to check on Marjorie Pritchard and the Young Wives' Welsh cakes. Then I'll make sure the daffodils will be delivered to the church first thing on Thursday, and that we're on for the choral rehearsal on Friday evening. When will my ring be delivered, dear? What time did you arrange?'

'Pardon?' Henry was confused.

'The ring. The jeweler. You said you'd speak to him and make sure he came today, so we can check it fits me. What time is he coming?'

Henry panicked. 'I'll have to consult my notebook.' He patted his pockets. 'Left it upstairs. I'll just pop and get it. Don't need me for a little while, do you, dear?'

His fiancé smiled warmly, 'No, my darling Henry, I can get along here. But maybe you could just check about the ring. It's rather important, isn't it?'

Henry kissed Stephanie's cheek and took off at a canter. He cursed himself as he tried to get up the main staircase as surreptitiously as possible, which was difficult to do because the bannisters were being bedecked with trailing ivy at every turn.

Leaning his back against his closed bedroom door, Henry looked around in sheer terror. What had he done with the jeweler's telephone number? What had made him forget the ring? It was critical. It had been specially ordered of course, and made from Welsh gold. A simple flat, wide band, the woman who was making it had assured them its reddish gleam would suit the design perfectly and look flawless. Forget traditions – a wedding ring for his wife was at the very heart of the whole matter. 'With this ring, I thee wed,' for heavens' sake! Henry suspected the entire thing would be illegal if he didn't have the ring.

Flinging open his wardrobe Henry stared helplessly at his jackets, wishing the jewelers' card would float out of one of the pockets.

'This is no good,' he said aloud. 'I need Edward.'

A few moments later his butler was at his side handing him a glass of water. Edward's soothing tones calmed Henry with: 'I took the liberty of telephoning the jeweler and he'll be here at three o'clock, Your Grace. I thought it best. I hope it wasn't too presumptuous of me?'

Henry smiled. 'Not at all, though maybe three thirty would have been better. But we'll work around three. Could you let Miss Stephanie know, please, and tell her she can reach me here? I'll just stay out of the way for now.'

'Certainly, Your Grace,' said Edward, closing the door as he left.

Henry was just settling his frazzled head on his pillow when his mobile phone began to vibrate in his waistcoat pocket.

Holding it to his ear he heard, 'Henry, is that you? It's me. I'm in a spot of bother and I could do with my big brother's help. Have you got a mo?'

Henry glared at the instrument in his hand, then put it back to his ear. 'No, Clementine, I don't have a mo. Have you forgotten I am to be married in a few days? And can you begin to imagine the state of chaos and uproar that's reigning here? No you cannot, because we haven't seen hide nor hair of you for weeks. Mother's been leaving messages for you all over London. It's terribly unfair to the staff at the Belgravia house to keep ignoring her requests to telephone – she keeps asking them, and they keep asking you, no doubt. So what's the matter? Run out of money?' Henry was usually cross with his sister, and today was no exception.

Instead of anything approaching a cogent response, all Henry heard was sobbing. He waited, less than patiently. It was probably all a ruse, he told himself. Typical of Clemmie. For once this was supposed to be a time when Henry was the center of attention, but there she was trying to throw herself into the limelight. As per usual.

'I'm sorry, Henry. I didn't mean to spoil your wedding . . .'

'You won't,' snapped Henry, 'come or don't, I couldn't give a fig. Mother would be mortified if you didn't attend, of course, so come for her sake. But you won't ruin my wedding. *You* couldn't.'

'Henry, oh Henry – I'm in hospital, and I think I might have killed someone. I'm sorry it's at such an inconvenient time,' sobbed his sister.

Henry paused. 'I beg your pardon?' he said slowly.

'I smashed the car. My leg's broken. Three places, they say. And they found a bicycle, but no bicyclist. I'd completely squished it. It's a tragedy.'

Henry could feel his temples throb. 'When you say "they", I presume you mean the police?' he felt he'd spoken quite calmly, given the circumstances.

'Yes,' said Clementine simply.

'I see. And you're at which hospital?'

'St Stephen's, Kings Road.'

'Completely immobile?'

'Utterly.'

'Will they release you?'

'I'm not under arrest, Henry. There's no *actual* dead body.'

'I meant the hospital.'

'Oh, I see. Yes. I've been here for a few days already. They say I can go home. But I don't want to go to the house in Belgravia, I want to come back to Chellingworth Hall. *Home* home.'

'You've been in the hospital for days?' Henry could hear his voice moving up the scale. 'Why did no one from the London house inform us of this?'

'No one there knew.'

'Because?'

'Because I thought I could sort it all out myself.'

Quite how his sister had imagined she could 'sort out' a

broken leg and a possibly fatal road traffic accident all by herself Henry had no idea, but, knowing Clementine, she'd come up with some bizarre notions and had blithely stuck to her guns. Until now.

'I suggest you telephone Gordon at the Belgravia house post haste and get him to drive you here. Even if your leg is fully extended it should fit in the back of the Bentley.'

'Could I have a nurse when I get there?'

'I beg your pardon?'

'I can't do anything for myself, Henry,' wailed Clementine. 'I'll have to have someone to help me with all the necessaries. Someone who's used to managing the human body and all its requirements.'

Henry's tummy churned. 'I'll speak to someone about it. Now I suggest you telephone Gordon and make arrangements. Are you up to doing that for yourself?' Henry knew he sounded snippy.

'Thanks, Henry. You're very kind, and a good egg.' Clemmie hung up.

Henry counted to ten, then he counted to twenty, then he telephoned his mother. He made a conscious effort to not whine when he spoke to her, but he couldn't help believing that was what she'd hear as he told her about his sister's plight, and plan.

Buoyed by his mother's response – that he'd handled everything perfectly and he'd done just the right thing – Henry finally left his room an hour after he'd entered it feeling that, for once in his life, he'd accomplished something all on his own.

Making his way to the estate office where he knew he'd find Stephanie, he drew her to one side, filled her in on what was happening regarding his sister, and asked her advice about a nurse. Two minutes later, he was being whisked off by Edward to the comparative privacy of the lower library so he could have an emergency meeting with Tudor Evans. Luckily for Henry he was in such a state of shock that the imminent arrival of the intimidating Mr Evans left him undaunted, which meant when Tudor and he sat alone in the library on two rickety chairs, he was ready for anything. Or so he thought.

'So you see, with the inaccessibility of the Anwen Morris artefacts, and with us not having our musician, I think it best if we pull out of the wedding altogether,' Tudor Evans was concluding regretfully, just as Stephanie joined the two men, which she had promised to do.

Henry thought she sounded a bit on edge when she said, 'We can't have that, Tudor. We must have the Anwen Morris to lead the journey from the altar to the bed. That is, from the church to the hall. It's a well-established tradition designed to ensure the fertility of the marriage. At my age, I'm not taking any chances. Surely you can perform without the artefacts, and I'm sure you could find another Morris musician. Don't you chaps all know each other? Don't you all use basically the same tunes?'

With both men hovering beside their chairs, having risen from them upon Stephanie's arrival, Tudor Evans looked uncomfortable as he replied, 'To be honest, yes, we do all know each other pretty well, but no, we don't all use the same tunes, and no, it's not going to be possible for us to find another musician. There is one man, up in Radnorshire, who might have been able to help, but he's visiting relatives in Australia at the moment, so he's out of the picture. And he was the only one anybody could think of.'

'What about pre-recorded music?' asked Stephanie, summoning an encouraging smile from Henry.

'Well, if we'd thought about that beforehand and actually recorded the music, then, yes, that could have worked,' replied Tudor, 'but we haven't got our music in pre-recorded form. And it's not the sort of thing you can buy on a record, or even over the internet. All our music is – well, it's an acquired taste.'

'You know this is just a tradition, Stephanie, don't you, my dear?' said Henry gently. 'The fact that we won't have the Anwen Morris to lead us here on Saturday will not impact our likelihood of having children, I promise.' He smiled at the woman for whom he had the utmost respect, and with whom he knew he would be in love forever. As he gazed into her lovely brown eyes he saw them fill with tears.

Henry feared Stephanie was finally cracking. Within about

thirty seconds she'd dissolved into hysterical sobbing, and Henry was left flailing, steering her toward an utterly inadequate seat, and barking at Tudor Evans that his fiancé needed a glass of water.

A few moments later, Stephanie had regained some composure – as had Henry – and she was sipping cool water which Henry also dabbed at her wrists with a damp pocket handkerchief. She reassured him he could leave her alone, which Henry did, dragging Tudor Evans toward the door.

Once there Henry held the man's lapel in his fist and whispered angrily, 'I do not care what you have to do, you will find either Aubrey Morris or a replacement musician, and you will find the Anwen Morris artefacts, or other items with which you are able to perform at my wedding on Saturday. You have the women of the WISE Enquiries Agency to call upon, and I am asking you to get in touch with them immediately you leave this room to make my wishes known to them in no uncertain terms. I fear I am in no mood to speak to a woman at this time. Do you understand me, man?'

Henry felt that, for once in his life, Tudor Evans was in no doubt he was not the most important man in the room. 'I understand perfectly, Your Grace,' was all he needed to say.

Henry heard the man speaking into his mobile phone as he left, 'Annie, that you? Boy oh boy, have we got trouble . . .' was all Henry caught, then he made his way back to his exhausted and crushed fiancé. He determined to be of more help to her over the next few days. This was *their* wedding, and it was time he pulled up his socks and got on with making sure it all went as well as could be expected.

'Right-o, my dear. Let's have a look at that list of yours, and start to make it ours, shall we?' he began. He meant well, and Stephanie knew it.

TEN

C arol Hill half-rolled over in bed to look at her husband – not the easiest thing to do given Bump's size. Despite the overnight rain she'd left the windows ajar and now she could hear the birds singing in the trees around the village green, and she knew the early bus for Hay-on-Wye was late because it hadn't roared around the corner yet. In the peace of the village, that sort of thing was audible. At their old flat in Paddington? All this would have gone unnoticed. As it was, she'd listened to the village throughout the night, unable to sleep well, because her mind was whirring with what she'd found out the evening before.

Carol had done as Christine had asked and had trawled through as much of Stephanie Timber's online life as she was able, trying to find out if the young woman had any hobbies or interests that might make the selection of a wedding gift easier. When she'd found nothing she'd carried on digging – into Stephanie's parents. And she'd been surprised at what she'd found. It seemed Stephanie's father had an interesting background, and some of the information Carol had gleaned suggested it might not be the sort of personal history a duchess would shout about, if Stephanie was even aware of it. What was more to the point was the fact she'd discovered some possible intersections between John Timbers and Alexander Bright during a period about a decade earlier. She'd been grappling with her conscience about how much she should say about her findings to Christine, because the upshot was it looked as though Alexander might not be very happy to become reacquainted with Mr Timbers.

Deciding to talk to Mavis about her dilemma, Carol was delighted when David groaned, and reached for her, connecting with Bump long before the rest of his wife.

Snuggles and breakfast behind them, Carol briefed her husband on her plan for the day – a quick trip to the shop for some supplies, then off to do her planned stint at the village hall making Welsh cakes. Feeling pretty relaxed about the case, because there wasn't really much they could do about a man simply choosing to take his own property and go off on some sort of jaunt, with or without his toothbrush, she gave Bunty one last loving stroke as she pulled the hood of her duffel coat over her head and made off through the kitchen door.

Pleased the rain had died down, but disappointed the keen wind was even chillier than the day before, Carol pushed into the beating drizzle and made her way diagonally across the village green. Her red wellies made her feel fearless as she splashed through the sodden, muddy grass, and she was quite lighthearted when she pushed open the door to the general store and made the little bell tinkle, announcing her arrival. She was sure of a cheerful greeting; Sharon Jones was a lovely girl, and the village benefitted from her presence in the shop. Her parents had run the place for decades, then they'd retired and sold up to a young couple who'd imagined that running a general store and post office in a little Welsh village would offer them an idyllic lifestyle with a healthy income. They'd been proved wrong in pretty short order, had decided that village life wasn't going to suit them after all and had just about given the business away in their urgency to escape. Sharon Jones had returned to her beloved Anwen-by-Wye, having found that life in Cardiff wasn't all it was cracked up to be, and was now judged to be the perfect person to restore the original *status quo* in the village.

'Hello Mrs Hill,' said Sharon as Carol entered, shaking rain off her dripping arms. 'How are you and Bump today? Alright? Is today the day, do you think?'

'Oh, who knows? I don't. But yes, I'm tidy, ta, and it's Carol, I keep telling you,' replied Carol allowing her full Carmarthenshire accent to bloom. 'Mind you, I could do with it being a bit warmer. Oh my giddy aunt, it's nippy. Let's hope it's not like this for the wedding, eh?'

'Oo, I know. Terrible bad that would be, wouldn't it. I hope it picks up for them. I mean, what will anyone wear if it's like this? Got to walk all the way from the church to the hall

up there, haven't we? Bit *twp*, if you asks me, expecting us all
to do that. I expect they'll be alright, mind. Going in a pony
and trap, aren't they? Just the likes of us have to walk it.'

Carol tried to look chipper as she wondered about the
possible sources of a rumor about a pony and trap. 'I believe
they are walking too. The Morris dancers are leading them.'

'Not with Aubrey gone, they won't be. I said that to him
last week, I did, when he got all his money out. I said, "What
will they do without you?"'

Carol was on full alert. 'What do you mean, when he got
all his money out?' She realized as she said it she shouldn't
have sounded quite so interested, because Sharon retreated
into her shell.

'Oh, nothing really. I suppose I shouldn't say. You know,
post office business.' She looked a bit sheepish and Carol
noticed she'd reddened around her hairline. Carol needed to
get Sharon back to a place where she was prepared to talk.

'Oh well, never mind. Now, I've come in for some supplies
for the Welsh cakes. I'm on today. What have you got?'

Luckily Sharon took the bait and smiled. 'Thank goodness
Marjorie phoned me a few weeks ago and warned me about
all this, or I'd have run out of everything by now. I tell you
what, someone should have phoned the *Guinness Book of
Records* or something, all the stuff you lot are going through.
I've got it all, what do you need?'

'Everything,' said Carol grinning. 'We all agreed we'd buy
four pounds of flour each, and all that goes with it, so could
you put that together for me, Sharon? Ta. I dare say you know
the recipe off by heart by now.'

Sharon busied herself behind the counter of the general
store part of the shop. As she did so, Carol wandered around
the post office area looking a bit lost, and poking through the
stationery supplies and sundries that surrounded the counter
where Sharon took in and passed out post and parcels, stamps
and greeting cards. Carol's brain was humming along, nineteen
to the dozen.

'How are you going to carry all this?' asked Sharon, looking
at the heavy bags that ranged along the counter.

Carol pulled a face. 'Drat, I hadn't thought of that. I can't, not in one load.' She looked out of the glass door and made another face. '*Uch a fi!* The weather's not fit for a dog. I know, I'll phone David. He can help.' She winked at Sharon as she patted Bump, 'It's his fault I'm like this anyway.'

Carol phoned her husband, who promised to arrive with the car as soon as he could. Passing time until his arrival Carol said quite nonchalantly, 'It's such a shame they won't have the Morris dancers on Saturday. All to do with fertility, isn't it?'

'Yes,' said Sharon. 'Getting on a bit, Stephanie, isn't she? You know, to be starting a family. Could do with all the help she can get, I dare say.'

Carol decided to risk it. 'Not like Aubrey to let everyone down,' she ventured.

'No,' agreed Sharon then, peering around at the empty shop as though someone might be listening from behind the canned peas, she added, 'everyone's due a holiday when they need one. And he does work very hard. Mind you, I didn't think he was going till *after* the wedding. In fact, that's what he told me. Having a bit of time off here this week to pack and get ready, then off next Monday. That's when the insurance was for.'

Carol tried to not sound over enthusiastic when she replied, 'See, now that sounds more like him. Take a bit of time to get sorted, do what he'd said he'd do, then off to go. I bet he was looking forward to it.'

Sharon nodded eagerly. 'Oh he was that, poor dab. Never does nothing he doesn't. Why shouldn't he go off to Europe and have the time of his life?'

'He wouldn't miss this weather would he? You know, *there*,' punted Carol.

Sharon looked a little confused. 'Well, I don't know where he was going exactly. Just that his insurance was for Europe. Though why he bothered I don't know. I told him about how to do it without. But yes, I suppose it's nice in some parts over there now, though I'd have thought most of it would be like this.'

'True,' agreed Carol. *What next?* 'Did he say he was nervous about going?' *Worth a try.*

Sharon shook her head. 'No, just excited. Said they'd waited their whole lives for it.'

'*They* had?' Carol was tingling with excitement.

Sharon smiled and winked knowingly. 'I'm pretty sure that's what he let slip, but I couldn't draw him out about it. Clammed up like a cockle past its best, he did.'

'Shame,' said Carol, her meaning being somewhat different from Sharon's when she agreed.

'I got the impression he'd known whoever he was talking about from school, though,' added Sharon, almost as though speaking to herself.

'Really?' Carol tried not to sound too interested.

'Well, not exactly. But he said something about them plotting at their desks. I don't know where else he'd be at a desk, do you? I mean it's not like he worked in an office.'

Carol nodded thoughtfully.

'He'll enjoy spending those thousands then,' said Carol, trying to fish for information about how much money Aubrey might have withdrawn.

'He certainly will,' agreed Sharon, just as the little bell rang out and David plopped into the shop, dripping, smiling and ready to go.

'Thanks, Sharon,' said Carol as she picked up the one bag she was allowed to carry and followed David out into the rain.

'You're welcome,' replied Sharon with a smile, oblivious to how happy she'd just made Carol.

Once she'd slithered into the seat beside her husband and buckled up, Carol said, 'Right, drive away from here, quick as you can, then park up behind the market hall, will you, love? I have to phone Mavis and report in. It's important, and it might mean that I have to duck out of the Welsh cake thing today. So, if you don't mind hanging on for a little bit, maybe I'll drop you back home and take the car.'

ELEVEN

A nnie and Mavis had met at the office at eight thirty and were well into their second pot of tea when Carol rang. As Annie had noted, it wasn't as though they'd been skiving; Mavis and she had read the report Christine had sent through at some ungodly hour the night before, and they'd been discussing what it might mean for their enquiries. All of which meant that when Carol phoned they were easily able to come up with a plan of action, and they agreed she should join them.

Fifteen minutes later all three women were hunched over their desks undertaking their allotted tasks, and, within an hour, they were all in a position to reconvene around a fresh pot and nibble bourbon biscuits as they shared information.

'I'll speak first,' said Mavis, thereby calling the meeting to order. Annie and Carol settled back on the sofa ready to listen and learn. Mavis hooked her hair back, straightened her shoulders and began: 'Following up on a lead I obtained from Althea, I have now established there is someone we can speak to about Aubrey Morris's early years in school. A Mrs Lewis was the head teacher at the infants' school in the village when he attended, and she still lives in Anwen-by-Wye. Carol, she's your next-door neighbor, in Rose Cottage. I understand she's now quite elderly, somewhat hard of hearing and, if Althea is to be believed – and I suspect she is – then the poor woman might be having a few challenges when it comes to differentiating between yesterday afternoon and ten years ago. As we all know, this would usually be my area of specialism – the old and infirm having been my main responsibility as a nurse, especially in the latter part of my career at the Battersea Barracks. But I am more than happy to take a back seat if you'd like to step up and build some connections with your neighbor, Carol. She'd need to be seen without delay.'

Carol paused as both Annie and Mavis raised their eyebrows

in her direction. Carol disliked the smell of old age, and was immediately apprehensive about how she might deal with a woman who wasn't quite with it. She knew it wasn't her strong suit. 'To be honest, Mavis, we all know you're really good at that sort of thing, and I think you should do it. Let's stick to our strengths for this one.'

Mavis nodded. 'Very well, I shall make my way to the village as soon as we finish up here. I have also established that Christine and Alexander are indeed heading off to Brighton today, that she will deliver the invoice to the design house tomorrow and she's sorry there's nothing specific to report after she and Alexander met up with that chappie last night. I must say the fact she was able to tell us, through this contact, that there is no news of the Anwen Morris equipment being available for sale within the parts of the underground antiques business with which he's familiar is good news, rather than no news.' Mavis looked at Carol and Annie as she added, 'Alexander seems to know some quite extraordinary people. We're fortunate to have his knowledge at our disposal.'

Annie grinned. 'Yeah, and that's the only reason Chrissy keeps seeing him, innit?'

Mavis shot her a warning glance, and Annie bit into a bourbon biscuit with such determination that it disintegrated.

'Since Annie's making a mess over there, what about you, Carol? What have you discovered?'

'First of all, just let me tell you that all the photographs I am about to show you on my laptop have been sent to you both, and to Christine, as attachments to an email, so you can each access them on your mobile devices. I have found a photograph of Aubrey's van, so we all know what we're talking about when we refer to it.' She motioned to her laptop screen. 'This is it. I've seen it in the village often, though I know you swear you've never noticed it, Annie. As you can see, it's hard to miss. The letters spelling out his name are two feet tall and bright red. I also have these additional photographs of Aubrey himself – thanks for taking snaps of the photos he had at his house, Mavis, and I can now also show you what the Anwen Morris artefacts look like. Thanks to the information Christine gleaned from the bloke she met in the pub near the Globe

Theatre last night, I've been able to find these approximations to what's missing. I still find it hard to believe that no one in Anwen-by-Wye has a photograph of the actual items in question, but, failing that, these will have to do for now. According to Christine's source, the Morris staff would look rather like this—' she pointed at her screen – 'but with a glass knob at the top, covered in a gold cage. The missing sticks look like this, and the bells like this.'

'They just look like ordinary sticks, and a collection of cat bells,' said Annie, unimpressed. 'Your Bunty's got one just like that on her collar, Car.'

Carol sighed. 'I know that, but I am doing this for clarity. If items have gone missing we should all know what they look like, just in case we happen upon them.'

'Well them sticks look just like sticks,' said Annie with finality.

'Come now, dear. They've been carved so they have rounded ends, and they are of a particular, standard dimension. We can see that at least,' said Mavis tartly.

'And they ain't missing, neither,' added Annie. 'They are his, and he's taken them. That's not missing, that's gone. Like him. This is all a flamin' wild goose chase – when the goose in't missing, but gorn!'

Carol sighed wearily, then half-smiled at her friend. 'The Twyst family has asked us to look into it. We're being paid to do so. We must be professional, Annie, and we must be able to show what we have done with the time for which they will be billed.'

Mavis smiled at Carol with pride. 'You're learning, girl.'

'Backhanded compliments – her specialty,' sneered Annie with a wink.

'And how have you spent your time, Annie?' challenged Mavis.

Annie cleared her throat and used her most professional tones: 'I've spoken with my contacts in Cardiff.' She smiled proudly – Mavis and Carol knew she was talking about the people she'd worked with when she was doing an undercover job a little while ago, but they allowed her her pride. 'And they tell me that, around these parts, the best way to shift such items as we see here—' she waved at Carol's laptop – 'would be for scrap. They also tell me that if Aubrey hasn't got any paperwork to prove he owns the stuff, which we all reckon might be the case because they're so old, then he wouldn't be likely to be able to shift it at all, except to one bloke, and he's somehow connected with Cardiff Castle and a billiard hall in Cathays.'

'Explain your use of the word "connected", please,' said Mavis.

'They say he works at Cardiff Castle as a sort of guide, and when he's not there he can be found at a billiards hall called the Cathays Billiards Hall, in Cathays. Not all that inventive when it came to the name of the place, it seems.'

'And do we have a name for this man?' asked Carol.

'Jones the Watch,' said Annie, rolling her eyes. 'And before you ask, no, no one knew why he's called that. He just is.'

'Any chance you could meet up with one of your "contacts" and track down Jones the Watch at either his place of work or this billiards hall, Annie? Today maybe? He might be able to tell us if Aubrey Morris has made an attempt to sell the artefacts on the local market,' said Mavis. 'After all, although Alexander Bright might be well connected, we have to assume he doesn't have a path to every dodgy dealer in the entire United Kingdom. Our role as enquiry agents is to make use of every single route toward every single lead and it's wonderful that we have the connections of a man like Alexander to call upon, but we must not allow that to prevent us from discovering, developing and using our other connections. That's what this business is all about – knowing where to look for the information we need to lead us to the evidence we require.'

Annie shrugged. 'Eustelle won't be best pleased if I leave her to clean up the cottage ready for Dad's arrival all alone, but work's work, so she'll have to lump it, I s'pose.' Her colleagues could tell Annie wasn't enamored of the idea. 'I'm just not sure what it will achieve, though,' she added pensively. 'See, if Tudor can find another musician, and some bits of stuff for them to all use, I don't see why Henry or Althea would really care if Aubrey's not there on Saturday, nor his stuff. And it is *his*, after all. I mean, it's not like they asked us to track him down as a person, just as someone whose absence could mess up the wedding plans. I think I should see how Tudor's coming on with his plans to find a back-up before anyone goes off and does anything.'

It was clear that Annie had given the group some food for thought.

Mavis nodded. 'I think you have a point, Annie. Shall I telephone Tudor Evans to establish the state of play?'

'No, I'll do it,' said Annie quickly. *Almost* biting back her enthusiasm she added, 'We've talked for hours about this already so we have a sort of, you know, rapport. I'll give him a quick bell.' She uncurled herself from the sofa and picked up the mobile phone on her desk to make the call.

Mavis and Carol shared a secretive wink and listened intently, while pretending to discuss the comparative merits of bourbons and custard creams.

Returning to stand beside the sofa, Annie was beaming. 'Tudor's found himself a bloke who can play the accordion on Saturday, and he reckons he knows enough of the right sort of songs and tempos for them to be able to manage, and the bloke with the accordion – who's coming up from somewhere near Somerset – is going to drop into some village in Gloucester and pick up all the bits and bobs they need. It won't be the Anwen Morris kit, but they'll have bells and sticks and they'll make do. He's done ever so well, ain't he?'

Mavis stifled a smile as she replied, 'That he has, my dear. Your Mr Evans seems to be a very resourceful man.'

Annie's expression wouldn't have been out of place on Scarlett O'Hara's face as she replied coyly, 'He's not my Mr Evans, Mave, and well you know it.'

'We should check in with Althea and Henry,' said Carol. Mavis nodded her agreement. 'They might say that's an end to it. Has Tudor Evans told the Twysts about his new arrangements yet?'

Annie shook her head. 'He was just about to phone Henry and tell him the good news. Let's not steal his thunder? Give it five minutes, then how about Mave phones Althea? Henry'll probably do whatever she says anyway and I can't imagine Stephanie gives two hoots.'

The three women returned to their desks and began to square away all the notes they'd made on the case. By the time Mavis spoke to Althea, Carol had three little bundles ready for billing. They listened as Mavis explained the situation, then held the handset silently, nodding.

Eventually, Mavis hung up the phone and looked at her colleagues. 'Well, that's a turn up for the books, and no mistake.'

'What?' chorused Annie and Carol, frustrated.

'They've found Aubrey's van. It was parked just off a lay-by on the Builth Wells road. It's not damaged and there's no sign of life inside it, or around it. No blood, no signs of injuries at all. The police have had it towed away, but they are still not prepared to act as though Aubrey is a *missing* person, merely noting he has left a motor vehicle at a lay-by where no overnight parking or unattended vehicles are allowed and they will issue a ticket. There's no way of telling how long it had been where it was found. Althea is, of course, delighted that Tudor Evans has been able to make arrangements for the Anwen Morris to participate in the wedding, but she now feels she owes it to her friendship with Aubrey's late grandmother to ask us to continue to try to find out where he's gone, and now, of course, what's happened to him if he's no longer with his van.'

'We need to find out everything we can about that van,' said Annie.

'Agreed,' said Carol . 'It's more of a priority than the billiards hall lead. But, I tell you what, I could do that – I can find out what the police know about the car, and I can even go to see it at the impound if they'll let me. I'm the only one of us three with their own transport after all, and, once I manage to get the seatbelt around my middle, I'm quite comfy in the car. If you make the most of your time with Eustelle, Annie, and Mavis goes to see Aubrey's old teacher – just in case we can get somewhere with identifying who it might be from his old schooldays that he was planning to travel with – then we might understand why the van ended up where it was.

No sign of the Anwen Morris artefacts in the van, I suppose Mavis?'

'Not a sausage,' she replied, shaking her head.

'I wish you hadn't said that,' groaned Annie, 'now I'm going to want a sausage sandwich for lunch. With lots of HP, and a dash or two of Eustelle's special hot sauce for good measure.' Annie beamed as she spoke, which made her colleagues chuckle, though the thought of pouring what she thought of as the equivalent of battery acid into her tummy made Carol's insides quake.

'Perhaps they serve sausage sandwiches at the Lamb and Flag,' quipped Mavis. 'Maybe you could drop in to congratulate Tudor Evans on his achievements.'

Annie looked thoughtful, oblivious to the tone of Mavis's remarks. 'That's a good idea, Mave. I might just do that.'

'Go on, away with you,' said Mavis smiling, 'I'll phone Christine and tell her what we're all up to.'

TWELVE

'People will start to talk you know,' mugged Carol as, for the second time in as many days, Annie Parker once again emerged in a tangle of arms and legs from Carol's little car in front of the Lamb and Flag before it was open to the public.

Annie grinned. 'Think I in't used to that, Car? Every time I walk anywhere round here there's a stiff breeze whipped up by all the net curtains that get twitched. But don't worry, I'll get used to it, or they'll get used to me. Anyway, I'm not going straight in there, I'm going to get Eustelle first, then me and her can have a bite in the pub together. Not in the snug, mind you, but sitting in the proper bar.'

Carol shrugged, not understanding the distinction. 'So why did you let me drop you off here? I could have taken you to your own front door.'

'Exercise,' said Annie blithely, and began to stride the

hundred paces or so she'd need to cover with her long legs before pulling out her front door key.

Carol drove away, bemused. She loved her friend dearly, but had no misconceptions about how unpredictable Annie could be. As she headed away from Anwen-by-Wye along the B roads that wound through the lush countryside of Powys she felt she should hug herself, she was so happy. It was wonderful to be living in Wales again, having left it behind in the belief that her only hope of finding herself and growing into a complete person was to leave it and her family and head out into the world, specifically London. Of course, if she hadn't taken the job as the head of programming at the Swiss conglomerate she'd grown to hate, she'd never have met David.

When he'd been recruited to the team that reported to her, she'd immediately spotted him as being the brightest spark in the group, and it hadn't taken long before she'd noticed a good few other things about him too – like how funny he was, and how he was always ready to help out when someone needed an extra hand or a chance to get away early. They'd ended up working on some big projects together, and the late nights in the office had led to respect, friendship, the odd drink and then proper dates.

If only for the reason that she'd met David, Carol knew that moving from her family's farm in the Carmarthenshire countryside to the chaos that was London had been worth it. But she knew she was back where she belonged; the verdant countryside wrapped itself around her like a comfy old Welsh tapestry blanket, and she was happy to *cwtch* in for all she was worth.

The first set of traffic lights she encountered made her pause in her journey. As she hummed 'Cwm Rhondda' she allowed her gaze to wander up the hill which mounded beside the road. Sheep dotted the dappled green, almost-vertical pastures, and she could see the tracks carved into the hillside over countless generations of both sheep, and farmers. A thought popped into her head and she reached up to hit the button on her earpiece; she put a call into the office.

'Mavis, is that you?' she snapped when the ringing stopped.

'Aye, I've not set out yet. Everything alright?'

'Yes, but a quick question – have we got an address for the

Morris sheep farm? You know, Aubrey Morris's grandfather's farm. Do we even know if it's still owned by a Morris family member?'

'Now that I can tell you. Hold on.' Silence. 'Here you go. Morris Farm, *Ty Gwyn Fawr*, Builth Road, Powys. Not the most informative of addresses. Althea says that Aubrey's grandfather's brother still lives there. Does that help?'

As Carol resumed her progress along the narrow road she smiled. 'Yes Mavis, it does, ta. Listen, I'll give the van and the police my attention first, but I might well stop by the Morris farm on my way back to the village. Given that the address is "Big White House" in Welsh, I think I might have just spotted it up on top of the hill here. Looks like it might be the place, anyway. I'll let you know. I think it might be worth checking face-to-face if they've had any contact with Aubrey.'

'Aye. A nice piece of journey planning that'll make the petrol money worth spending,' replied Mavis. 'I'll be off now. I have my mobile if you need me. Bye for now, dear.'

'Tarra,' said Carol cheerfully, and she resumed her humming – much more loudly; this time it was 'Calon Lan' delivered with real *hwyl*.

When she arrived at the police station on the outskirts of the market town of Builth Wells, she managed to find a place to park that meant she didn't have to walk too far. By the time she presented herself at the front desk she could feel her cheeks glowing, and even though her duffel coat didn't quite cover her entire body any more, she was warm.

The young policeman behind the counter looked up from his computer and caught her standing in front of him wiping the dew of sweat from her brow.

'Are you feeling alright? You look like you're having a bit of a turn,' he said, sounding concerned.

Carol felt just fine, but she made a split-second decision. 'Well, I don't know, the baby's being a bit active at the moment, and I suppose I could do with a bit of a sit down. I don't suppose you could rustle up a glass of water for me, could you?' She adopted her 'pathetic' face, and smiled, reaching behind her for a chair as though it was a great effort.

'Just a tick, let me give you a hand,' said the young constable opening the secure door to the waiting area. 'My sister's pregnant. Always going red in the face she is, too. You sit down.'

A few moments later Carol was sipping water and the solicitous young officer was finally asking why Carol had come to the police station.

Taking her cue, and laying on the Welsh accent as heavily as she dared, she told a pretty tale about how the four women were trying to make a go of it in the countryside as enquiry agents, showed him her credentials, then spoke emotionally about how she, pregnant and the only Welsh member of the group, was having to struggle to make sure she kept her end up. The sympathetic young man seemed impressed by how much effort she was prepared to put in to find out about Aubrey Morris's van, and he allowed her to access a great deal of information, even though he didn't really need to.

Half an hour later she sat in her car, pulled out her laptop and typed up a memo for the rest of the team.

TO: MM, CW-S, AP
FROM: CH
RE: Aubrey Morris Van – police information

1. Information gleaned from PC Stephens at Builth Police Station. I have seen the files, but wasn't allowed to bring any hardcopies away. I gained an opportunity to leaf through the file alone when the kind officer left me to bring a second glass of water. That means we don't officially have some of this information.

2. Aubrey Morris's van was discovered around 2pm yesterday afternoon by a Mrs Russell of Hay-on-Wye who stopped her car in a lay-by for her dog to relieve itself. The dog ran off, then attracted her attention to the unattended van. She phoned the police when she returned home, saying she waited until then to do so because there was no mobile signal where she found the van.

3. The police ascertained the van had no occupants. The doors of the van were closed, but not locked.

The contents in the rear of the van were the sort of tools the police assumed would be carried about by a handyman, and were undisturbed. A note, and some photographs, convince me the van was parked so it could not be seen from the road.

4. Other than tools and work bags, the police noted there were no obvious personal items in the van (e.g.: no luggage etc.) no mobile phone, no paperwork etc. There was nothing to indicate to the police why the van had been abandoned in the manner it had been, and they state there is no way to tell how long the van had been there.

5. Comments: PC Stephens seemed to be of the opinion that the fact Aubrey Morris has chosen to leave Anwen-by-Wye at this time is mildly interesting, as opposed to being ominous, or criminal. That appears to be the general consensus. I spun the young man a story about Aubrey having taken a critical piece of domestic equipment from my kitchen to fix it, and it being in the back of his van. He confirmed the location of the van for me, and told me I could mention his name if I wanted to have a quick look at the van at the impound. I will do that next.

Carol was satisfied with her little update, then buckled up and drove off along Builth Wells' narrow high street toward the animal market and show grounds, then around the swinging curve that led to the water meadow and the ancient bridge over the river Wye. Taking the road to the left, heading away from the town center, Carol kept her eyes peeled, looking out for the turning that would deliver her to the police impound. The roads were quiet, and the journey didn't take long. Finally she pulled up outside a sadly tatty Portakabin with metal grilles on its windows and a rather inadequate couple of steps leading to its metal door.

Teetering on the steps, Carol hammered at the door which was eventually opened by a small man engulfed by a large, luminously-yellow jacket.

'*Ydw?*' said the man in a surprisingly high-pitched voice.

'*Bore da*,' replied Carol, hoping to get on the man's good side. 'PC Stephens sent me. I've come to take a look at the white panel van that was brought in from the Builth Road earlier this morning. The Aubrey Morris van.' She decided it was best to keep things simple.

Suspicious, slightly beady eyes regarded Carol with uncertainty. 'Not police, are you?'

Carol reached into her pocket. 'No. Private enquiry agent.' She showed her picture ID and smiled.

Regarding her photograph, then Carol in person, the small man's face betrayed a modicum of respect. 'Can't be too many of you, can there? Pregnant Welsh women private investigators. Hardly two a penny.'

Carol nodded sagely. He wasn't wrong. The question was, would he let her peer inside Aubrey's van as she wanted.

'Send you over from the station, did they?'

Carol nodded. And waited. The small man's eyes flickered as he considered the matter. He looked at Carol's bump, then reached for a set of keys. 'It's over by here. Follow me.'

Carol waited while he locked the door of the Portakabin, and followed him toward the van.

'Here you go,' he said, handing her a pair of surgical gloves. 'It's not locked. You can open it. You can look. You can't take nothing. Right?'

Carol nodded, and did what she was allowed to do with the aid of a torch she pulled from her handbag. She also took a lot of photographs with her phone's camera. Peering over her shoulder toward the man she said, 'Can I open the glove compartment?'

The small man looked around furtively. 'Go on then, but quick mind, and don't go disturbing nothing.'

Again, Carol did only what he'd suggested she was allowed to do. 'Thanks,' she said as they walked back toward her car.

'S'oright,' said the little man, 'gets a bit boring round here usually. When's it due?'

Carol was taken aback. 'Any day now.'

'Thought so. Our third's due around now. Wants to call him Fred, she does. 'Orrible name for a kid, innit? Still, it'll keep 'er happy see. Tarra for now.' The man clambered back up the rickety steps, let himself into the cabin and clanged the door shut behind him.

Takes all sorts, Carol thought to herself as she reinserted herself into her car, glad the odd little man had at least been so accommodating. She checked her watch. The pubs were open, and she knew a loo and a warming cup of coffee were in her not-too-distant future, as well as a Wi-Fi signal which would allow her a chance to send a couple of emails and some photos to the girls.

She swung the car onto the main road and headed back toward Builth's High Street; there was a pub with a comfy lounge where she knew she could get everything she wanted, and a sandwich for lunch too. Now all she had to do was find somewhere to park, not easy on the narrow high street, but she crossed her fingers and headed off.

THIRTEEN

Annie was feeling pretty chuffed with herself; she'd managed to talk her mum into accompanying her to the Lamb and Flag for lunch, which was quite an achievement. All in all it hadn't taken her long, though now she was counting her fingers while she waited for Eustelle to find a jacket that would complement her red skirt, which Annie knew wouldn't be easy.

Appearing at the doorway to the little sitting room, Eustelle Parker had obviously plumped for her orange mackintosh, the one Annie had talked her into buying in the sales at John Lewis in Kingston with the words, 'Yes, of course orange can be a neutral, Eustelle.' That had sealed the deal, because her mother had been on some sort of kick to eradicate all patterns from her wardrobe – something Annie was totally convinced would never happen.

'Do you t'ink the green scarf, Annie?'

'We're only going to the pub for a sandwich, Eustelle.'

'But do you t'ink the green scarf?' Eustelle swathed her

head in a vivid emerald satin scarf and posed for her daughter, pulling a face.

'Watch the wind don't change,' said Annie with a grin.

'It already did, many years ago, child.' Her mother winked at her and pulled open the front door. 'I got me stuff wit' me,' she added, patting her large handbag.

'I don't think we'll need it there,' said Annie, wondering how Tudor Evans would react if her mother produced a bottle of hot sauce to add to whatever it was she might order for lunch.

'Just in case,' said Eustelle ducking as she left the cottage. 'Mind your head, child,' she cautioned as Annie followed her out. 'Tiny little people those old Welshies.'

Annie didn't comment, knowing full well that with her mother being five nine, and Annie herself being five ten, or even five eleven on a tall day, ancient Welsh cottages weren't the only places where doorways had to be treated with respectful caution.

Although it was almost March, Annie felt the keen wind sting her face as she and her mother walked, arm in arm, around the outer edge of the village green. They stuck to the pavement, knowing that neither of them were shod well enough to contend with the soggy grass of the common itself. Even so, it didn't take them long to reach the welcoming warmth of the Lamb and Flag.

Pushing open the double doors Annie said to her mother, 'Now it ain't as primped as the Chellingworth Arms, but the man who runs the place is very pleasant.'

Giving her a sideways glance Eustelle replied, 'Not a word you use lightly, child. "Pleasant"? You said that about Denzel Washington – I wonder if this one's as good-looking as him.'

'Lovely to meet you, Mrs Parker,' said Tudor as the women entered. He rushed forward and ushered Annie and Eustelle to two bar stools.

Annie's mother grinned toothily at Tudor and said, 'If you're a friend of my child, you're a friend of mine. I'm Eustelle. Everyone calls me that, even me own daughter, so you should do the same t'ing. And I'll be callin' you Tudor. Never knew a Tudor until now. Strong name. And you looks like a strong man.' Eustelle laughed throatily, her deep voice echoing in the empty pub.

Tudor nodded a little uncomfortably. 'Righty-ho, Eustelle it is then. Here are a couple of menus for you ladies to look at while I get you a drink each. On the house, of course. Your usual, Annie, I'm guessing, and what about you, Eustelle?'

Annie felt the sharpness of her mother's glance. 'You got a "usual" drink here already, child?' asked Eustelle slyly.

Annie felt herself get warm. 'Not really, Eustelle. Only been here once before and that was for work.'

Tudor was already pouring a gin and tonic for Annie, but paused, blushing. 'Have I got it wrong?' he asked.

Annie smiled. 'That'll be lovely, Tudor. Ta. And Eustelle will have a tomato juice, right?'

Her mother nodded. 'No'ting fancy in it, just the juice in a glass. I got me own sauce wit' me.' She patted her handbag lovingly.

Tudor busied himself with the drinks, and poured himself a glass of tomato juice. 'Now you've mentioned it, I fancy one myself,' he said with a smile. 'Tomato juice is like that, isn't it? Once you want it, it's that or nothing. Like Marmite.'

Annie watched Tudor eyeing the way Eustelle poured hot sauce into her drink with amusement. 'Fancy some of Eustelle's sauce yourself?' she asked innocently.

'Alright then,' said Tudor a little uncertainly. 'Try most things once, me. Maybe not too much though. Just a bit.'

Eustelle poured, they both swooshed, then drank.

'Put hair on your chest, that,' proclaimed Eustelle, smiling.

Tudor looked at the drink with an expression of pleasant surprise. 'Nice that. Tidy. Not too hot.' He took another swig. Two seconds later Annie could see that the heat of the capsicum had kicked in, because Tudor blanched, then turned quite red and began to sweat.

'I'll give you two a minute to look at the menu,' he croaked, and Annie stifled a giggle as he found a good reason to leave them and disappear into the bar of the snug.

Eustelle laid her hand gently on her daughter's arm. 'You're a wicked child,' she said with a wink.

Reappearing a few moments later, Annie noticed Tudor's

pink, watery eyes and reddened cheeks. 'See anything you fancy on the menu?' he said as casually as he was able.

Eustelle turned her attention to the card in her hand. 'Do you make your own faggots?' She peered over her spectacles, and Annie could tell her mother's 'look of death' was having the same effect upon Tudor Evans it had been known to have on any wayward youth who'd dared to mess with her mother's launderette over the years – not that she owned the launderette in question, but she had managed it for all the years Annie had been living at home in Plaistow, so, as far as Eustelle was concerned, it was as good as her own.

'I don't make them myself,' confessed Tudor, 'but a good friend of mine who runs an excellent butcher shop in Llandrindod Wells does, and he knows his faggots. Won prizes with them at the National Welsh Show he has. And not just once. His grandmother's recipe, with a bit of a twist on the spices, he says. Not that he'll tell anyone the recipe, of course. I haven't had any complaints about them. Always consistent, and delivered fresh every couple of days, they are. The gravy comes with – he makes that too, from stock he makes himself. So it's all home-made, just not made in *this* home. Peas and mash we do here ourselves. Up to that, we are. Will that suit?'

Eustelle handed him the menu. 'I, too, will give most things a go, once,' she said, smiling – quite coquettishly, thought Annie.

'I'll have the same as Eustelle, thanks Tudor,' said Annie, knowing if she ordered something else she'd end up preferring the look of what was on her mother's plate in any case.

Smiling, Tudor said, 'Righty-ho, back in two ticks,' and scuttled off toward what Annie assumed was the kitchen.

As soon as he was out of sight her mother asked, 'Got any children?'

'Tudor?'

'Yes.'

'No.'

'Lucky. They might be as ugly as him.'

'Eustelle!' Annie was shocked. 'He's not ugly. He's just . . . you know, not good looking. In the usual sense.'

'He could turn milk,' was all Eustelle had a chance to say before the beaming Tudor was back in his spot behind the bar.

'Quiet today,' observed Annie with a smile that was possibly a little too bright.

Tudor nodded. 'Not unusual, I'm sorry to say. I sometimes think I might as well not bother opening up on these winter afternoons. Especially a day like today when it never really gets light, and everyone's busy rushing about their business. But a pub's a pub, and people expect you to be open, even if they don't usually come in. Still, it's a bit better in the summer, when the hall is open to the public and the day trippers come through.'

'Will you be shut on Saturday, because of the wedding?' asked Annie.

'Yes,' replied Tudor. 'There's more to life than profit in the purse, isn't there? It'll be a rare treat to dance at a duke's wedding. For all that I go on about him, he's not a bad sort, and I think that Stephanie could be the making of him. Knows what's what she does. I bet she'll throw herself into everything quick as you like. Not that I'm saying the dowager did a bad job, but she's bit past it now.'

Eustelle's deep tones sounded menacing as she replied, 'Althea Twyst is a fine woman, Tudor. I've been lucky enough to spend a bit of time wit' her and Annie's friend and colleague Mavis.' Annie was relieved when she broke the tension she'd caused by then laughing aloud and slapping her thigh as she added, 'Like two schoolgirls them two. One's younger than me, one's older, but I t'ink they both six years old in here.' She smacked her chest hard. 'I kept up wit' de walking, though. Sometimes it helps to have long legs, 'specially when you're walking about with short folks.'

Annie had noticed heads turn in the village as Mavis, Althea and Eustelle had gone for lengthy walks over the past couple of weeks.

'You're right to say the dowager is a fine woman,' replied Tudor quickly, 'and she was an excellent duchess. But it's like a job, isn't it? I mean, when her duke died, she sort of retired. It's just that this duke didn't have a wife, so there's been a sort of void. The daughter doesn't seem to know the village exists, and we've come to expect that Elizabeth Fernley, you know, the Chellingworth estate manager's wife, will do most of the things the duchess would. Well, some of them, anyway.'

Tudor paused and Annie jumped in with, 'Do you think her nose'll be put out of joint with the new duchess coming on board?'

Tudor's expression suggested he didn't think so. 'Be glad to be rid of most of the duties, I expect,' he replied. 'It'll be up to the new duchess to step up and try to do something about the church hall, for example. Always the duchesses domain, that. And it's in a terrible state. Can't use it at all now. We'll have to have the next PCC at the market hall.'

'PCC?' enquired Annie.

'Parochial Church Council,' explained Tudor. 'I'm the chair. Vicar's not up to it. Good at all the religious stuff, but when it comes to getting things done? Not his forte. Let's leave it at that. And now we've got to meet at the market hall. Not right. PCC should be at the church hall – or even at the vicarage. Unmarried vicars are all well and good in theory, but in actuality you need a vicar's wife to do quite a lot of the heavy lifting. And the Reverend Ebenezer Roberts never did marry, which is a shame for all of us in his parish.'

'And why hasn't a fine man like yourself married, Mr Tudor Evans?' asked Eustelle with a cheeky grin and a wink in her daughter's direction.

Tudor studied his shoes as he replied, 'Never found a woman prepared to look past this horror of a face of mine and see the man inside, I suppose.'

Eustelle sucked her teeth. Loudly. 'Got to want to be seen, ain't you,' she said sagely, then added, 'and where's the toilet in this place?'

Tudor's head shot up and he gave Eustelle directions. 'Top up?' he asked, turning his attention to Annie. She nodded. 'Nice woman your mam,' he observed, pouring steadily. 'Speaks her mind. Always best.'

'Really?' replied Annie. 'I find it gets me into all sorts of trouble. Usually with Mavis.'

Tudor smiled to himself, seemingly preoccupied for a moment as he picked up a gleaming glass and began to polish it. A little buzzer broke his reverie. 'Ah, tidy. Grub's up. I'll just go and get it. Now would you and your mam like to sit up here at the bar to eat, or go to a proper table.' He waved his arm at the empty pub. 'You'll be pressed to find a spot, but maybe I can squeeze you in somewhere.'

With a plate of aromatic faggots, fluffy potatoes and suitably mushy peas, all topped with glistening gravy in front of them atop a little table near the fireplace, Annie and her mother oh-ed and ah-eh their way through a delicious meal.

'See,' said Annie, licking her lips as her mother finished her last two mouthfuls, 'didn't need the hot sauce, did it?'

'Honest, child, you'd swear I force-fed you hot sauce against your will.'

'You do, Eustelle. You put it on everything you ever serve me.'

'And what do you do with the bottles I give you to use at home then? Pour it down the drain? No, you put it on your food like a good girl.'

Annie nodded. 'Yes, I do, Eustelle. I'm a good girl. Like you said, it's what keeps me as thin as a rake, and able to eat what I want.'

'Keeps the metabolism ticking over, child,' said Eustelle, patting her daughter's hand as though she were five years old.

'You lovely ladies alright over by here, are you?' Annie thought Tudor looked apprehensive as he approached the women, and wondered why.

'Perfect, ta very much, Tudor,' replied Annie brightly. 'Eustelle and me both loved the faggots. You've got an earner there, I'd say. Better than everything we've eaten over at the Chellingworth Arms, in't that right, Eustelle?' She couldn't work out her mother's expression at all, which annoyed her because she'd just taken a course in reading body language, and facial expressions had been the test where she'd got the highest score. But her mother might as well have had a sack over her head for all that Annie could work out what she was thinking as she stroked her daughter's hand and smiled.

'You alright?' she felt compelled to ask.

Eustelle nodded her head slowly as she replied, 'A mother

never knows when it'll happen, she can only be sure it will. And here we are.'

'What's up? Come on, Eustelle, you're beginning to give me a turn.' Annie's voice conveyed the anxiety she felt.

'Never better, child, but I am lookin' forward to seein' your father soon. Three weeks is a long time to be away.'

That must be it, thought Annie.

'You'll all be at the wedding?' asked Tudor sharply.

'Oh yes,' said Annie with a grin. 'Eustelle's got a particular hat she wants to wear on Saturday, and Dad's bringing it with him when he comes on the train. Then they'll stay with me until Monday and get the train back to London together.'

Annie thought Tudor looked pleased at her answer for some reason. He then noticed some people had come through the door and said, 'If you'll excuse me, I appear to have some other customers to serve. Why don't you look at the menu to see if there's anything sweet you fancy. The spotted dick with custard is very good, and, yes, it's made right here.'

Tudor left the Parker women to tend to his new customers and Eustelle leaned in to her daughter's ear. 'He's lovely, Annie. Grab him with both hands, child, and don't let go. This is it, child. This is it.'

'Gordon Bennett! Pull yourself together, Eustelle,' was all Annie could manage before she dragged her phone out of her handbag and answered the call she could see was coming in from Christine. 'Chrissy's on the phone. Why don't you order me some afters and I'll talk to her?'

She turned on her seat to be able to concentrate on the call, which also allowed her to see Tudor in full 'landlord' mode. She had to admit, he was good at it.

Putting the phone to her ear Annie said, 'Hi Chrissy.'

'Annie, don't speak, just listen,' said Christine breathlessly. 'Alexander and I are in Brighton. As I said we've come to try to find something a bit special for the happy couple. Anyway, we've been poking about in the antique shops in The Lanes and I think I've found them!'

'What?' asked Annie.

'The stuff. The Anwen Morris artefacts. I'm sure I've found them. I've taken some photos and I'm sending them to you.

Can you find someone there to take a look at them and tell us if this is really the stuff that's gone missing?'

'Yes, I'm with Tudor. And Eustelle. At the pub. I can show Tudor. He'll know.'

'Are you alright, Annie? You sound a bit . . . off.'

Annie held the phone in front of her face and cursed at it silently. Returning it to its rightful position she spoke as evenly as she could, 'I'm fine, thank you. We've just enjoyed a lovely lunch of local faggots and we're about to have spotted dick. With custard. But I'll show Tudor the photos and phone you right back. Where are you exactly?'

'Outside the shop with the swag, so hurry up 'cause it's cold down here and I need something inside me to warm me up.'

Annie grinned. 'You mean like a nice cup of tea, I s'pose?'

'Hardy-har-har, Annie. Yes, a nice cup of tea, and some fish and chips,' replied Christine acerbically. 'I'll hang up so you can do your thing there.'

Christine did as she'd said, and a moment later, when Tudor had served the two customers at the bar, Annie beckoned him over and showed him the photographs.

Tudor took forever. At least, that's how it felt to Annie. She fidgeted on her seat as he gave the photographs a good deal of attention.

Eventually he said, 'No. Not ours. Very similar, but they're from North Wales. I know these pieces. They come from a team up there that originated in the flint mines. They packed it in – oh, it must be twenty years ago now. That would be how these are out there on the market. Mind you, I tell you what, if your friend could find out what they want for them, we might be in the market for some kit with a bit of history if our stuff's gone forever. Could you ask her?'

'You're sure they aren't the Anwen pieces?' Annie knew her disappointment showed in her voice.

'Positive.' Tudor's face told her he was, and she trusted his judgment.

'I'll give her a ring and tell her, and ask about the price too. Won't be a tick.' As Tudor wandered off to tend to his bar, Annie passed the disappointing news to Christine.

'Two grand,' she mouthed and gestured to Tudor.

He mugged a belly laugh, then shook his head mouthing, 'No way.'

'That's a lot of money for a few old sticks and some bells,' observed Eustelle as Annie hung up and tucked her phone back into her handbag.

'Maybe that's why this lot have gone missing, along with the elusive Aubrey Morris,' said Annie, grinning as she noticed a bowl mounded with spotted dick and glistening with sunshine-yellow custard. Her tummy rumbled.

FOURTEEN

Mavis's morning visit to Aubrey Morris's old teacher had been fascinating. And a little worrying. Mrs Iris Lewis was now a widow, well into her eighties and had a penchant for budgerigars. Her small cottage was filled with cages of all shapes and sizes, inside which lived, and chirped, her feathered companions. Mavis could see quite clearly that the creatures were delightfully colored, beautifully marked and certainly well cared for. The cages were clean, and the house had no overwhelming odor because of their presence, but the incessant noise they made grated on Mavis's ears from the moment she set foot in the claustrophobic sitting room until she left. The birds irked her, and she found herself becoming cross with their owner, which annoyed her even more. Her unflappable demeanor was lost to her, and that in itself was cause for concern.

All in all she only had to share the small space with Mrs Lewis and her pets for about half an hour, but it felt a good deal longer to Mavis, who was aware of every moment as it dragged by – accompanied by theoretically cheerful chirping.

Finally escaping to the peace and quiet of the village green, Mavis regrouped. She felt the best way to tackle her temper was to walk it off, so she marched as fast as her short but sturdy legs would carry her. When she let herself in through the front door of the Dower House she was slightly breathless, pink in the face and quite returned to her normal self, which was a relief. Mavis prided herself on her ability to deal with any amount of pressure in a cool and professional manner. Her matron, when she'd been training, had drilled into her that the most critical ability any nurse could possess was to be able to act calmly in any and all circumstances, especially those which, to others, constituted an emergency. Mavis had taken that to heart, and was well able to because, by the time she decided to become a nurse, she was a woman of almost thirty with two small boys at home – not some flibbertigibbet of a young girl wanting a job where she might be able to snare a doctor for herself. No, Mavis had taken up nursing because she'd realized she had a calling for it and, since her earliest days, she'd put her natural self-possession to good use.

'You look utterly discombobulated. What's wrong, dear?' said Althea as Mavis entered the comfortable sitting room.

'Mrs Iris Lewis has birds. Very noisy, annoying birds,' said Mavis simply, as she plopped herself onto a comfy old sofa that beckoned to envelop her with great posies of country garden flowers in faded pinks, blues and greens.

Althea nodded. 'I'd forgotten about that. Yes. Always was a keen birder, when she could get about. Does she still have dozens of them in every nook and cranny?'

'Aye.' Mavis knew she sounded cross. 'I must say I didn't care for it. The noise they made was quite . . . unsettling.'

Althea held her silence for a moment then said, 'The woman who ran the nursing home where your poor, dear mother passed away kept birds, didn't she? I seem to recall you mentioned something about them being in her office? Sometimes our poor brains make some peculiar connections.'

Mavis sighed and nodded. 'Now isn't that queer? I'd quite forgotten about those birds in that woman's office. You're right, dear. She did have some.' She paused for a moment, then added, 'I wonder if it's the mind that plays tricks on us, or the other way about.'

Breaking into her friend's reverie Althea asked, 'Anything helpful regarding Aubrey?'

Straightening her small shoulders Mavis replied, 'I think,

though I cannot be sure, that Mrs Lewis's memory for times long gone is better than for a fortnight ago, so I'll give her the benefit of the doubt. She told me that Aubrey, albeit a quiet boy, was always seen about the place with a girl. A quiet girl. Not from the village itself. "A farmer's girl" was what she called her. No name. Couldn't manage that. But a description. Short for her age, long brownish hair, always in two plaits, poorly maintained clothing. Otherwise, nothing. It made me think – if we were to go back to Aubrey's house, do you think we might now be able to look at his possessions and find something that might lead us to a girl with whom he had a close friendship at infant's school which, according to Mrs Iris Lewis at least, continued when they went off to the senior school?'

Althea gave the matter some thought. 'I think we could. Now Carol has unlocked the computers we can have a look there, though if it was a school-aged thing, we might look for more prosaic methods of keeping in touch, or mementos. We're talking about fifteen, twenty years ago, aren't we, dear? Bit of a long shot, I'd say.'

Mavis nodded. 'It is. But we've nothing more to go on. It's up to you, Althea. You're the client now.'

Althea's cornflower eyes twinkled. 'Indeed I am. And the client says we should have lunch then head off to Aubrey's house again. I'll let Ian know he'll be driving us. What's the time?'

Mavis regarded her watch, which was pinned to her chest – a habit retained from her nursing days. 'Lunchtime,' she said smiling.

'Just as well, because I am rather peckish,' noted Althea. 'Lunch, McFli,' she added rising from her seat. McFli launched himself off the sofa and twirled three times yapping with excitement. Smiling down at her furry companion Althea said, 'And I bet you're peckish too, aren't you, boy?'

McFli wagged his tiny tail in agreement, and the three friends made their way to the dining room where Mavis knew Cook would serve them soup and cold cuts, as usual. She wondered what the pickle of the day would be – the only variant on the lunchtime menu at the Dower House.

FIFTEEN

S
ettling herself into her car after a delicious lunch of thickly cut home-baked ham, crusty bread and some ill-advised piccalilli, Carol Hill pulled out of the tight parking space with caution and took the main road back toward Anwen-by-Wye. Once she reached what she thought was the general area she kept a beady eye open for any hint there was a turning of some sort for what she hoped was the Morris farm.

She knew she was making the man in the Land Rover behind her angry, but she also knew she had to drive at a snail's pace. Eventually she spotted a weathered wooden stump that said 'Morris', just in time for her to indicate twice and swing off the main road. The Land Rover's horn hooted as the driver revved the engine and roared off. She imagined a fist being shaken and some choice words being uttered. Probably in Welsh.

Driving up the hillside Carol wished she was in a Land Rover herself; she took her time and finally crested the hill, spotting a large whitewashed house with black trim ahead of her. The slate roof was dark with rain, there wasn't a window without a curtain drawn across it and, to all intents and purposes, the place looked as though no one had lived there for donkey's years. Carol's tummy tightened. *Was this wise?*

Crunching to a halt outside the house she sat for a moment before unlocking her seatbelt. Pulling her phone out of her handbag she checked for a signal. One bar flickered, then disappeared. *Drat!*

The thought of grinding back down the rutted lane without having even tried to achieve anything forced Carol to extricate herself from the car, pull up her hood to protect herself from the sleety rain and march to the front door with an air of more determination than she truly felt. There wasn't a bell, just an old-fashioned painted, iron knocker, so she hammered it as loudly as she could. Glancing around as she waited for a response she took in her immediate surroundings: a little way down the other side of the hill was a higgledy piggledy collection of what appeared to be animal barns, as well as one clearly identifiable hay barn. Dry-stone walls made a patchwork of the receding hillside and the road below was lost in the wintry shower. To her right, a little way off behind the house, were a few more stone buildings with good roofs – probably places where humans worked, Carol surmised. An upbringing in the countryside meant she could imagine the purposes for everything she saw except one building, which she could hardly see because it was so far off. She couldn't imagine why anyone would want to build anything so far from the farmhouse.

Carol knocked again and jumped when the door was opened almost immediately. The creaking it made told her it wasn't the usual means of access used for the house. As the door opened Carol noticed two things: the inside of the house was gloomily dark, and someone had recently boiled a cauliflower . . . or maybe a dozen.

The almost-bald head of an elderly man peering around the door was all she could see. She reckoned he must be in his mid-eighties, so probably Aubrey's grandfather's brother. Guessing it was the right thing to do she greeted him in Welsh.

'*Helo. Sut ydych chi? Ai* Mr Morris *ydych chi?*' Be polite and check he's the right man, Carol told herself.

'*Ie. Pam? Saesnes ydych chi?*' The old man's voice was as thin as his hair and cracked as he spoke, suggesting he didn't talk much.

'*Nac ydw, Cymraes ydw i.*'

'Might say you're Welsh, but talk Welsh like the English, you do,' the old man all but squeaked.

'Sorry,' said Carol. It seemed appropriate to apologize. 'I was looking for Mr Morris.' She smiled as widely as she could.

'Like I said, why?'

'I am trying to find a member of his family who has gone missing.' *Best to be forthright.*

The man's shoulder and arm appeared. He was wearing what Carol would have thought of as a jumper fit only for the dustbin – it was more darned and un-darned holes than knitted garment, and it sagged over an open-necked shirt that must, at one time, have been white. She felt grubby just looking at him.

'No one's missing,' he snapped, and began to close the door. Carol was too quick for him and inserted her foot so he'd have to be thoroughly ungentlemanly to shut it all the way. It turned out he was, and pushed the heavy door hard against her.

'Ow! That hurt,' said Carol, keeping her foot where it was.

'Your own fault,' said the man, a glint in his rheumy eyes.

'Aubrey Morris has disappeared from Anwen-by-Wye,' said Carol quickly. 'I know he's related to you and I thought you might know where he's got to.'

The man allowed the door to open a little, taking the pressure off Carol's foot and allowing him to peer at her once again.

'And what's it to you?' asked the man, jutting his stubbly chin toward her.

Carol decided it was best to be truthful. Pulling her ID card from her pocket she showed it to the man. 'My name is Carol Hill and I am an enquiry agent. Our company has been retained to locate Aubrey Morris.'

The elderly man squinted at the wallet. 'Could be anything, that. Come in while I gets me glasses.'

He pulled open the door and Carol was almost overcome by the smell of grease, cauliflower and something burned. She swallowed hard a few times, resisting the desire to gag. 'Thanks,' she said, quite feebly as it turned out.

Venturing inside the farmhouse made Carol feel uneasy. One dim lightbulb tried hard to illuminate the hallway, but it was set in a fitting meant for four bulbs, so it didn't achieve much at all. As the door closed behind her the weak light of the wintry afternoon disappeared altogether and she was enclosed in a stinky, gloomy world.

'Glasses are in the kitchen. Follow me,' said the man as he shuffled along the Victorian tiles which, had they been clean, might have been very attractive. As it was they were so grimy they were treacherously slippery. Carol walked with great caution, allowing her eyes to adjust to the dimness of her surroundings.

The kitchen wasn't much brighter despite the fact it had a large window without a curtain. A film of grime coated the glass, filtering the daylight, and a bare strip of fluorescent tubing hummed above a large kitchen table completely covered with the detritus that remained from making what appeared to be vegetable soup – which went some way to explaining the smell.

'Show it me again,' snapped the man holding out his hand for Carol's photograph and credentials. Peering through greasy spectacles the man took his time, mouthing words silently as he read them. Eventually it seemed he was satisfied and he handed the wallet back to Carol.

'I'm Morris,' he said. 'Herbert, me. Aubrey's father's uncle. Haven't seen Aubrey in, let me think . . .' He took his time doing so. 'Twenty years?'

'You're telling me you haven't seen Aubrey Morris in the last twenty years?' Carol wanted to be clear.

'About that.'

'So you didn't go to his father's funeral?'

Herbert Morris looked grumpy. 'Well, yes, I suppose I did. But I haven't seen him since then.'

'So you wouldn't have any idea where he might be?'

'How would I? Never welcome here, he wasn't.'

Carol pounced. 'Why's that?'

Herbert pulled off his glasses as he said slyly, 'No reason, really. Just, you know, family stuff.'

'Anything to do with the question of inheritance?' asked Carol with a leap of faith. Herbert's reaction told her she'd hit a raw nerve.

'I don't see why you'd say that,' he almost squealed. 'Village gossip, that's what that is. This farm's gone down the line of eldest sons like it's supposed to – to me, and it'll go to my eldest when I'm gone. It's not unfair, it's what's right. Lot of fuss people make about things that have nothing to do with them. My younger brother, Aubrey's granddad, didn't expect to get the farm – no more than my sister did. We do things the right way here.'

'Did you set up your sister when you inherited, like you set up your brother near Anwen-by-Wye?' Carol was curious.

'Didn't need to,' replied Herbert grumpily, 'stayed on here, she did. Her and her family live in the house down there. All of them.' He stubbed a thumb toward the kitchen window.

'You mean the house a little way down the hillside?'

Herbert nodded. 'Nice set up for them.' Carol noted he didn't speak with any malice and his smile seemed to signify kind thoughts.

'Would your sister be likely to know anything about Aubrey's whereabouts?' Carol thought it a question worth asking.

Herbert Morris hunched his bony shoulders and stuck out his chin, then he spat out, 'Absolutely not. She and her . . . family have had no contact with that boy for many a year, not since he left school, and they won't have again. So there. I don't know nothing, so be off with you, woman.'

There were few worse things Herbert Morris could have done than fling Carol's gender in her face as though it were an accusation. Resisting the temptation to let rip at the man, Carol took a deep breath, nodded abruptly, turned on her heel and made for the front door. She knew she didn't dare say a word, or she'd overstep the bounds of professionalism before she'd finished a sentence.

Striding out in anger, Carol forgot to be as careful as she should have been on the greasy tiles. About halfway along the hallway she felt her right foot slide from under her just as she put her full weight onto it. She couldn't do anything but flail her arms and let out a little shout as she skidded forward and toppled backward at the same time. As she fell onto her rear end she put out her hands to save herself, and heard something give way. It was the last thing she heard for a moment or two. She realized she must have closed her eyes, because, when she opened them, Herbert Morris was standing over her waving his arms about and shouting.

'Please phone for an ambulance,' said Carol calmly, 'and tell them I'm pregnant – in my final month.'

'I'll phone my niece too,' said Herbert.

'999 first, please,' said Carol firmly.

'Right-o,' replied Herbert and Carol caught parts of conversations, then decided to rest her eyes for a moment.

'Feeling a bit better now, are you?'

Carol heard a woman's voice far, far away. She tried to focus on what it was saying. She peeled her eyes open and said, 'I'm here.'

'Yes, love, I know you're here. Now just lie still. Ambulance is on its way. I'm Netta Roberts. Herbert's my uncle. He phoned me and asked me to come over. Just in case. Ambulance shouldn't be long.'

Carol tried to sit up, but Netta pushed her down, gently. 'Now, now, stay down,' she said firmly, 'you don't want to move until the professionals are here. Nowhere to go, anyway.'

'Thank you,' said Carol quietly. 'I think I heard something break when I fell but I can't feel any terrible pain anywhere.'

Netta and her uncle looked at each other. Carol couldn't see any family resemblance – indeed, Netta was about twice the size of her uncle, in all directions. 'That might be good, or not,' she said, 'I don't know. I'm not a nurse.'

It occurred to Carol she should let David and her colleagues know what had happened. If the ambulance was going to take her to hospital her car would be stuck at the Morris farm until David could get a lift to come to collect it, and he'd need it if he had to visit her in hospital, or collect her from there. She knew Althea would probably loan out Ian Cottesloe for the job, but she hated to ask. However, with Christine away in London with her car, the only other option for David would be a taxi, and that would cost a small fortune. Then there was the enquiry – what should she do about that?

'What are you worrying about?' asked Netta. 'I can see the hamster running round the wheel from here. Can I phone someone for you, is that it?'

Carol reeled off telephone numbers to Netta, who wrote them on her hand, promising to make the calls. 'Terrible mobile signals up here,' she noted, confirming Carol's own observation upon her arrival, 'and the phone in the kitchen won't reach you here in the hallway, so I'll phone your husband first and explain to him what's happening, then I'll phone him again once the ambulance people tell me what they're doing with you, alright? Maybe your work can wait though? Not so urgent, is it really?'

'It's your relative, Aubrey Morris, who's missing. That's what I came here to enquire about,' said Carol sharply. She noticed Netta Roberts stiffen when she heard the young man's name.

'You don't have to remind me about that, Uncle's just told me.'

Carol was surprised by how tense the woman had become. Herbert Morris had been evasive, but his niece was . . . *what?* . . . frightened. That was it. The news that Aubrey was missing had frightened her. Just as Carol was thinking this was an odd reaction, she caught the sound of sirens in the distance and a flood of relief washed over her.

Netta said, 'There they are. I'll phone your husband now. Back in a tick.'

She disappeared in the direction of the kitchen, leaving Carol alone with Herbert standing over her. He'd been silently watching the two women but finally spoke. 'I never touched you. Fell all on your own, you did, rushing off without even a "thank you". You make sure you tell them that, right?' Then he followed his niece out of Carol's sight.

On the edge of her hearing Carol caught, 'If Aubrey's gone too, I bet I can guess where she is. With him. I bet they never stopped. I just hope her father hasn't found out . . . he's been acting funny the past couple of days, and you know how he can get with that temper of his. I thought he was acting strange because she hasn't been in touch at all but if . . .'

The sirens drowned out anything else, and Carol lay completely still, waiting for a paramedic to tell her if she and Bump were going to be alright. She clutched her belly and tried to get her heart to stop thumping with worry. *Please let our baby be alright, please let our baby be alright . . .*

SIXTEEN

Althea's tapping foot signaled to Mavis the dowager was beginning to lose her patience with waiting quietly while Mavis herself sat in front of Aubrey Morris's computer and scrolled through what seemed to be endless emails about almost nothing at all. Mavis felt she'd made good headway, and was glad she could read as fast as she could. She was also pleased that Aubrey Morris seemed to have an effective method of using clear titles for emails, so she could quickly discount most as being related to jobs he was doing, or she could take the time to read those about his hobbies – ancient Welsh and Roman ruins.

Aware that Althea was being quiet, though fidgety, Mavis looked over at her companion and said, 'There's nothing says you can't go and have a little look around the place if you want, you know. I'm sure it's best if you don't go digging too much, but you're the one who's commissioned this investigation, so practice your skills. Being one quarter each Welsh, Irish, Scottish and English might mean we're happy to have you as an honorary WISE woman, but we are also enquiry agents, so please feel free to enquire . . . within.'

The two women smiled at Mavis's little joke. Althea launched herself off the high stool where she'd been perching for no more than fifteen minutes – though it clearly felt like a lot longer to the woman – and headed off up the stairs to Aubrey's bedroom. 'I'll be up here,' she called to Mavis. 'Long time since I've been in a strange man's bedroom,' she added. Mavis was heartened by the chuckle in her friend's almost-octogenarian voice.

Half an hour later, Mavis was still lost in her task and was startled when Althea rattled a tin near her ear.

'Och you dreadful woman – you gave me a fright,' chided Mavis playfully. 'What's that?'

Althea held up the large, battered old biscuit tin triumphantly. 'What do you think it is?'

'Button tin, I'd say. Every house used to have one.' Looking
at her surroundings Mavis added, 'This is exactly the sort of
house where I'd expect there to be a button tin.'

'I wonder if people have them anymore,' said Althea quietly,
'or if they just throw out clothes without removing the buttons
first. Terrible waste if they do. My mother had one, and I have
it now. I'm not sure I've added many buttons to it myself –
not since the children were small. Odd that, isn't it? One of
those things that might die out, d'you think?'

'Aye. Like us,' replied Mavis. 'Have you opened it?'

'I can't' said Althea looking disappointed. 'That's why I
brought it down. It seemed odd to me that a young man would
have a button tin in his own bedroom, and when you shake
it, it sounds as though the buttons are being muffled by something else. But the lid's so tight I can't get it off. Fingers aren't
quite what they used to be,' she added with a disappointed
glance.

Mavis took the tin and tackled the lid. 'It's certainly snug,'
she observed. Refusing to be beaten, she worked her way
patiently around all four sides of the cube-shaped tin, trying
to ease up the lid which showed a painted representation of
The Mutiny on the Bounty. 'Odd picture for a tin of Peak
Freans,' she observed, straining at her task.

Finally the lid flew off, and Mavis caught it before it hit
Althea in the face. A couple of dozen buttons also bounced
up, a few landing on the floor. 'Ach!' said Mavis, bending to
collect up the stray buttons.

'So? What's in it? Anything interesting?' Althea sounded
like an excited schoolgirl.

'I think you've got a nose for this enquiring, Althea dear,'
replied Mavis smiling. 'There are letters in here. Proper hand-
written letters in envelopes, with stamps on them. Well, some
have.'

Mavis smiled at the sight of Althea almost quivering with
excitement. 'Who are they to? Who are they from? What do
they say?' Questions tumbled out of the woman in much the
same way as they'd do from someone seventy years her junior.

'First things first,' said Mavis. Instead of pulling the letters out of the tin, she placed the tin carefully beside the computer on the desk in front of her and reached into her handbag. 'We don't know what we're dealing with yet, so please put these on.' She handed the dowager a pair of surgical gloves.

'You haven't raised the necessity for me to wear these as I've been making my way about Aubrey's home. Why would you do so now?' Althea took the gloves from her friend with the tips of her fingers. She looked at them as though they were made from something corrosive.

'The house? Likely to be lots of prints about the place and it would be easy for anyone to eliminate ours, should it ever come to that. These letters? They might be critical and more telling in terms of those who have had contact with them – especially the pages of the contents rather than the envelopes. I do not want to run the risk of contaminating them. Those gloves won't kill you, Althea, please put them on.'

Althea wrestled with the uncooperative latex for a couple of moments, and was finally triumphant. While she struggled, Mavis, already gloved, pulled out several of the letters and lay them on the desk, examining the envelopes before she made any move to reveal their contents. She took photographs with her phone.

'These are all written by the same hand,' she commented. 'I'd say it's a woman's writing – neat, rounded. Penmanship mattered to this person and they took time writing these addresses. All are addressed to Aubrey Morris, here. The post-marks, where I can discern them, show me the letters were sent over a long period of time, beginning back in the late 1990s.' Mavis spread all the letters across the table and peered at them. 'Look – this second, smaller bundle just has the letter "C" on the envelopes, and they're all grubby and dog-eared.' Mavis paused. 'That's all the envelopes can tell me. Now let's see who they are from, and what they say.'

Mavis selected three letters – an early one, a later one, both properly addressed to Aubrey, and the topmost of the seemingly un-posted envelopes. She carefully pulled out the letters and lay them beside their envelopes.

'Who are they *from*?' urged Althea.

Mavis turned over pages until she reached all three signatures. 'Boudica. That's all it says.' She turned the sheets over again. 'The letters are written to Cariad Caradoc, that being Aubrey, according to the addressed envelopes.'

'Interesting,' said Althea, 'Boudica and Caradoc were two famous warrior leaders who each fought the Roman invaders of Britain. The warrior queen Boudica in the Midlands and eastern counties of what is now England, and Caradoc led his men against the Romans here, in Wales. Whoever this Boudica might be, she and Aubrey saw themselves as facing a common foe. What does she say?'

'I cannot say, dear,' was Mavis's disappointing reply. 'Look.'

She allowed Althea to peer at the letters. 'Oh dear. And I can't help at all.'

'They're all written in a mixture of Welsh and Latin,' said Mavis sounding glum. She sat back in her chair and hooked her hair behind her ears.

'You do that when you're thinking hard about something,' observed Althea.

'I do not,' replied Mavis tartly.

'Indeed you do. And when you're getting ready to say something significant. So, come on, which is it?' The dowager smiled kindly at her friend.

'Maybe a little of each,' said Mavis with a playful smile. 'How's your Welsh?'

Althea faltered. 'When I married Henry's father and moved to Chellingworth Hall I took lessons. But it didn't stick. It's a terribly difficult language and, of course, I had trouble just making the right sounds back then. With more than fifty years of living in Wales under my belt the sound of the language is more familiar, and my own ability to make the shapes needed to pronounce it has improved, so it's now much easier for me to comprehend and even reproduce. When we have the Lord's Prayer in Welsh in church I'm quite good at it. But I've always found reading it to be beyond me. Not a linguist, you see.'

'Henry?'

'Hopeless.'

Mavis could feel Althea waiting for her to come up with something. She sighed. 'Right, first things first – Christine went to all the best schools and I'm sure she'd have been taught Latin. I only know whatever I've picked up in terms of medical knowledge, and you?'

'I might have married a duke, but my schools weren't what you'd call "posh",' replied Althea. 'We had Latin at grammar school, but it's long gone from my poor old brain. The bits I use for crosswords are about it. I think Christine's our best bet for the Latin. She's much younger, she won't have forgotten as much.'

'Aye. Best thing I can do is to take photographs of a few letters and email them off to her. See what she says. As for the Welsh? You have a lot of staff whose first language is Welsh – there's Ian, sitting just outside here in the car, for a start. But I'd rather not get any of them mixed up in this. These letters might contain some personal and private information about a man they know. Carol's mentioned that, since she's returned to Wales, she's regaining her Welsh vocabulary. She might be able to help, and she's one of us. That would be best, even if she can only give us the gist of the Welsh parts. Let's get the photographs taken, then I can send them off. I'll just open a few more in case any of them are in English, though, given Aubrey's proclivity for Roman history, and the fact he clearly shared that passion with this female, I doubt we'll find any. The idea that he made a pact with a girl at school, as mentioned by his old teacher, makes a good deal of sense. And it seems to have been an enduring relationship. Hopefully, by the end of the day, we'll have an insight into the nature of that relationship, even if we don't know who this Boudica is.'

Althea nodded and helped Mavis with her photographic task. Half an hour later Mavis had spoken to Christine, who explained she did, indeed, feel she might be able to tackle the translation of the Latin, but it would have to wait until she'd driven home from Brighton. Mavis couldn't get an answer on Carol's mobile, so she left a voicemail message and sent the photos. 'I hope she checks her messages soon,' said Mavis as she and Althea made their way back to Ian and the car.

'She's a good girl,' noted Althea, 'and diligent too. I'm sure she'll get back to you as soon as possible. Meanwhile, why don't we go back to the Dower House and clean up a bit before dinner? I feel rather grubby having poked about Aubrey's house for ages.'

'You're right,' replied Mavis. 'Poking about in people's lives can make a person feel that way.'

SEVENTEEN

Unable to take tea in the lower library – as was usual – Henry Twyst looked across the morning room at his fiancé and thanked everything holy he'd chosen to marry this woman. They'd been discussing the problems in the kitchen, and Stephanie had already managed to talk him down from one of the highest levels of anxiety he'd ever felt.

'Cook Davies will come round, Henry, you know she will. She's got a bark, but no bite. She indulges you, you know that, so you're the one who has to talk to her. You know she's still struggling to accept the fact I've been here for a couple of years as "one of them" and now I'm going to be "Your Grace" along with you and the dowager. Mrs Davies has been here quite a while longer than me and sees the kitchen as her domain. It's only natural. I know she initially agreed to the idea of having the caterers come in and use some of her facilities, but it's beginning to irk her. You need to talk to her, dear.'

Henry watched as Stephanie replaced her cup and saucer on the tea tray. The firelight reflected off her dark hair, and he smiled inwardly as she pushed up the sleeves on her serviceable brown polo-necked sweater. Having grown up at Chellingworth Hall he knew how difficult it was to dress in the winter – most of the time your teeth were chattering because cold air seeped into the place somewhere in every room, but when you did manage to get close to a source of heat you'd end up pink-faced and glowing within moments. He'd learned how useful cardigans could be, and was confident Stephanie would too, with time. He liked the idea they'd both end up getting old together, wearing cardigans.

'You're not thinking about what you're going to say to Mrs Davies at all, are you?' observed Stephanie with a smile.

'Pardon? Oh, yes, of course I was,' spluttered Henry.

Stephanie shook her head. 'I'm delighted to say you're a terrible liar, Henry dear. Now come along, focus. Mrs Davies. What will you say to calm her down?'

Henry stood, replaced his own cup and saucer on the tea tray and moved to stand in front of the fireplace. Despite the fact the fireplace in the morning room wasn't as grand as the one in the drawing room, it was a position he liked to adopt. It made him feel at peace with the world because, as he stood there, he could imagine his forbears having done exactly the same thing for the past few hundred years. He enjoyed the sense of continuity and depth of connection to his home it gave him. 'I shall remind her she said she understood she couldn't cope with feeding a few hundred people who'll all be looking for as much free food as possible after our wedding, and that she even had a hand in selecting the catering company we're using. I'll further remind her she's the one who insisted she'd find the arrangements to be perfectly acceptable.'

'Maybe you could be a little more generous than that, Henry? Maybe begin by thanking her for all she's done, and for all she's going to do. I think you should also suggest she finds time at the end of the reception to be able to be brought into the gathering to be thanked in public.'

Henry beamed at his bride-to-be, 'She'd like that,' he said warmly.

'I know,' replied Stephanie.

A knock at the door of the morning room was immediately followed by the sight of Edward's head peering in. 'Might I interrupt, Your Grace?'

Henry's tone was puzzled. 'Come in, Edward. What's the matter?'

Edward's usually neutral expression had been replaced by a pink face and a frown. He entered the room carrying an awkward load.

'Good heavens, you look as though you're off on your holidays, Edward. What on earth is all that? Is that a suitcase?'

'Yes, Your Grace, I believe it is a suitcase. An extremely

old one,' said Edward evenly, placing the items close to his employer's feet. 'These items were discovered outside the door of the New Buttery. A note said "For the duke's wedding". Since the items weren't wrapped as gifts, nor delivered by the usual methods, I thought Your Grace might want to see them now.'

Stephanie stood next to her betrothed as she and Henry stared at the strange collection; a battered, hard-sided leather suitcase, a long columnar brown leather case and a small wooden box, bashed at the corners. 'Henry – you know what it is, don't you?' squealed Stephanie.

Henry regarded his future wife with what he suspected was a quizzical look. 'Haven't the faintest.' He gave the matter some thought. 'Some sort of painting kit?'

Henry noted Edward staring at the ceiling when Stephanie said, 'Painting? How do you get "painting" from that lot?'

Henry knew his voice sounded defensive when he replied, 'I used to paint, you know. I thoroughly enjoyed it, and I don't think I was too bad at it. I can quite imagine an easel being in the big long case, paints and brushes in the suitcase and a pot for water and so forth in the little box.'

Stephanie's gaze lingered on Henry's face for a few seconds, then his heart warmed as she smiled and said, 'How clever. Yes, it might well be. I tell you what, why don't we open everything and find out?'

Henry agreed, and he moved toward the suitcase.

'Would Your Grace like me to do that?' asked Edward.

Henry replied coolly, 'I think I can manage to open a suitcase myself, thank you, Edward. But, please, stay while we see what's here. I'm sure the entire household is desperate to know what this is all about.'

Henry suspected Edward's completely unchanged demeanor resulted from decades of service rather than a lack of interest, so he leaned down and lay the suitcase on the rug. Feeling the rolls around his middle as he bent, Henry struggled with the brass latches that seemed determined to frustrate him.

Finally managing to open the case, Henry lifted the lid to reveal . . . a collection of battered wooden batons. 'Oh.' Henry was terribly disappointed.

'Wonderful,' said Stephanie with what Henry could only assume was mock-enthusiasm.

'It's a suitcase full of sticks,' said Henry, unafraid of stating the glaringly obvious.

'They're the Anwen Morris sticks,' said Stephanie.

Henry was truly puzzled. 'The what?'

He thought Stephanie sounded a little annoyed when she replied, 'The sticks that Aubrey Morris had as part of the kit the Anwen Morris dancers use. You know very well what I mean, Henry. When Aubrey disappeared the kit went too. Tudor told us about it.' Henry could see the light of hope in her eyes as she said to Edward, 'Did anyone see who left these items?'

Edward shook his head. 'I'm sorry, Miss Stephanie, nobody did. I already asked. You know how it's been here – all sorts of people coming and going all over the place. And you can't see the entrance to the New Buttery from anywhere.' He cleared his throat politely, 'It has been suggested that that's why the items were placed there – out of sight, and where no one could see who left them.'

Stephanie nodded, and Henry thought it best to follow suit. 'Let's open the rest, just to be sure,' he said, determined to retain control of the situation.

When everything had been opened it was clear that all the missing items were present, and in good order. 'Well, this is quite a turn-up for the books,' observed Henry. 'I dare say someone should be informed.'

'Your mother told me she has taken on the responsibility of retaining the women of the WISE Enquiries Agency to track down Aubrey,' said Stephanie thoughtfully. 'I suggest you give her a quick ring.'

Henry checked the time on his pocket watch. 'I'd expect her to be at home taking tea at this time of day. I'll ring the Dower House. Edward, why not take these items out into the . . .' Henry paused. He'd been about to instruct his butler to deposit the Anwen Morris artefacts in the great hall, where they could stay until someone was able to collect them, but he was painfully aware of the frantic level of activity out there, what with all the decorating and placement of what seemed like an extraordinary amount of furnishings for a simple toast or two and some nibbles upon the return of the happy couple from the church to the hall. 'I tell you what,' said Henry with uncharacteristic certainly, 'leave it all here, but tuck it away in a corner somewhere so one doesn't run the risk of tripping over it all. I'll get in touch with the dowager duchess and we'll take it from there. I dare say someone will be along at some point to do something or other with it. Thank you, Edward.'

Edward nodded and followed his instructions. Henry, meanwhile, strode to the corner of the morning room where a telephone sat upon a hexagonal table inlaid with the most exquisite marquetry. A few moments later Henry rejoined his fiancé beside the fireplace. 'Mother is in Hereford. At the hospital.'

Stephanie's reaction was more passionate than Henry could have imagined. 'Oh no, Henry. What's wrong with her?' She grabbed his hand and squeezed it with a ferocity that quite took him aback.

Surprised that his statement had elicited such a response, Henry realized, too late, that he sounded dismissive when he said, 'Nothing at all. Carol Hill has taken a fall and Mother has seen fit to drive Carol's husband David to the hospital. It would appear he had no means of conveyance available other than Mother's car, driven by Ian. It's quite extraordinary that she puts herself out so much for those people.'

Just one look at Stephanie's face told Henry he'd done something reprehensible, but he wasn't at all sure what it was. His bride-to-be didn't leave him in any doubt for long.

'Henry Twyst,' said Stephanie forcefully, 'sometimes you are quite unbelievable. First of all Carol is pregnant, so of course her husband would be worried sick about her and the baby, so why wouldn't your mother want to help out the poor man? And secondly, "those people", as you casually put it, are your mother's friends. Haven't you noticed a change in her since Mavis MacDonald took up residence with her at the Dower House? Your mother seems as though she's ten years younger. There's a spring in her step, she has some real interests in life now that she's "enquiring" with the other women and she's not just hanging about talking to McFli all the time.

She converses with a woman close to her own age about things that, presumably, interest them both. Mavis MacDonald and the other WISE women have done your mother the world of good. She knows it, and she's admitted them all into her life as friends – especially Mavis. The least you can do is recognize that, Henry.'

Henry felt the warmth of the firelight suffuse him with more heat than he thought natural, and he suspected he was blushing. He nodded and replied quietly, 'You're right, Mother has changed.' He sighed. 'I'm not always sure it's for the better, because she sounds as though she's enjoying snooping into other people's lives on occasion, but I agree, she does seem to have more vim and vigor these days. She never ever used to back down in an argument, but, recently, I've noticed she doesn't seem to have them so often. Maybe she's too busy meddling in other folks' business to be too bothered with mine, I don't know. But it's certainly a noticeable difference. I shouldn't have spoken that way about the women, you're right.'

'You're the one who introduced her to them, Henry, after all,' noted Stephanie.

Henry sighed. 'Right again.'

'And you were quick enough to ask her to ask them to help us when Aubrey went missing.'

'Yes.'

'They are a part of the fabric of our lives now, especially since you've given them the use of the barn and the cottages in the village.'

'That was all Mother,' said Henry quietly, 'though she wanted them to think it was me.'

Henry noted that Stephanie twirled her hair as she gave the matter some thought. She sounded quite cheery when she replied, 'I think your mother was right about that. You are the duke, she is merely the dowager duchess. You really are the one who makes the decisions about the estate, or at least you should be – but I see why she wanted to do what she did, and you were right to agree with her.'

Henry felt as though he'd been patted on the head – which he realized wasn't a bad feeling. Indeed, it reminded him of how he and his mother had interacted when he was a boy. He smiled at Stephanie. Life with her would be good.

'So, if we don't know the situation regarding the location of Aubrey Morris, should you telephone Tudor Evans to tell him that the Anwen Morris now have their original artefacts to use on Saturday?'

'Good idea,' said Henry brightening.

'And then we can go to talk to Mrs Davies in the kitchen,' added Stephanie.

Henry immediately felt his mood darken. 'That could wait until after we get rid of this stuff, and maybe even until Clemmie arrives. She should get here from the hospital in London soon. What time did the agency say the nurse would arrive?'

Stephanie checked her watch. 'I requested the person they are sending to be here by five o'clock, so not too long now. Oh Henry – I think I just had an idea that could help out a lot of people all at once.'

Henry felt apprehensive – sometimes Stephanie's bright ideas involved quite a lot of participation on his part. 'Yes?' He tried to sound encouraging.

Stephanie gave the matter some thought. Henry realized her eyes twinkled a good deal when she was thinking something through, and he enjoyed watching her formulate a plan.

Lifting her head Stephanie said, 'We've been talking about how we can assuage Mrs Davies's anxiety in the kitchen, and we both know Edward could do with some help. What about inviting your mother and Mavis to decamp into the hall here from the Dower House until Monday? If they shut up the Dower House that would release your mother's cook Mrs Wilson, as well as Ian Cottesloe, who could back up Edward's work, and your mother's aide, Lindsey Newbury who is an extremely capable woman. They could all be accommodated here quite easily. Also, we are retaining a nurse to attend your sister, who has a broken leg. That nurse could also oversee any post-hospitalization attention that Carol Hill might need. If Carol and David Hill stayed here through the wedding weekend as well, that might help everyone concerned. What do you think?'

Henry gave the idea some thought. His initial reaction was to not like it one little bit, but he'd learned that Stephanie didn't care for it when he gave an immediate negative reaction to something she'd said, so he tried to make his face look as though he was thinking hard. He furrowed his brow, and pushed his lips together. Eventually he dared, 'I think the idea of everyone moving to the hall is very good. As for the Hills moving in? I'm not so sure about that. For one thing I know they have a cat which would need to be catered for – and I dislike cats enormously. And then, of course, there'd be the question of Clementine "sharing" her nurse.' He paused and felt a wash of turmoil in his tummy. 'She wouldn't like that, and she can become quite dramatic when she doesn't like something,' he concluded nervously.

Rising from her seat and straightening her brown corduroy slacks Stephanie said, 'You're right. She does.' Henry wondered if he'd caught a glimmer of a wicked twinkle in her eye as she spoke, or if it was merely a trick of the firelight. 'And maybe that would be an imposition on the Hills in any case who would probably prefer to be in their own home at a time like this. You're right, Henry. Good thinking. Why don't you speak to your mother about everyone from the Dower House moving here as soon as possible? But, for now, why not phone Tudor Evans and make arrangements for someone to collect all that—' she waved toward the pile of bags in the corner – 'then we'll have a nice chat with Mrs Davies downstairs in the kitchen and by then, I dare say, we'll have a nurse and an ailing relative to deal with.'

Henry nodded and made his way back to the telephone. He realized how wonderful at all this Stephanie was. Thank heavens!

EIGHTEEN

When David Hill was allowed into the curtained cubicle where his wife had been stripped, swaddled in a backless paper garment and hooked up to various machines, it was clear to Carol that the sight of her laying there horrified him.

'I'm fine,' were the first words out of her mouth.

'You can't know that,' replied her distraught husband. Turning to the tall, lank young woman who was reading something off a monitor David said sharply, 'What's wrong with her? Is she alright? Is the baby alright?'

The young woman smiled indulgently and said, 'The doctor will be here in a minute,' then she pulled aside the curtain and left.

Carol held out a hand, as best she could, toward her husband. 'Come over here – I don't have as many attachments this side,' she said gently.

A few moments of silence ensued, and Carol thought she could sense David's anxiety growing again. Sure enough, 'Where the devil is that doctor?' was out of his mouth before five minutes had passed.

'She's probably with someone who really needs her,' said Carol.

'*You* need her.' David launched himself from his seat. 'I'm going to track her down and find out what's going on. What's her name? Who am I looking for?'

Carol sighed. 'Sorry, love, the name didn't stick. I'm sure the nurses will know. But listen, before you go stomping off, could you get permission for Mavis and Althea to pop in for a mo?'

'Why?' snapped David.

'Because they are my friends and I'd like them to see that I'm OK,' said Carol pointedly.

David climbed off his high horse and sounded contrite when he said, 'Oh, alright then, I don't suppose it can do any harm. But I don't want them tiring you out.'

'We're not all going to have a game of rounders, David. I just want a few minutes with good friends, thank you.'

'Promise?'

'Cross my heart – no running about the ward in my beautiful backless gown, I promise,' said Carol with what she hoped was a whimsical smile.

'Right then,' said David as he swooshed the curtain aside then marched out of Carol's sight.

A couple of minutes later Carol was relieved to hear Mavis saying, 'Knock, knock. Can we come in?'

'Please do,' said Carol, beaming as her friends entered her tiny 'private' space.

'Good color, that's a relief,' were Mavis's first words as she made her way straight to the monitors beside Carol. 'What have they said?'

'Thanks to you both for bringing David here, and for getting him so well organized,' replied Carol. 'They've said I'm fine, the baby's fine, but they might keep me in overnight for observation. How are you?'

'We're fine too, dear,' said Althea. 'It's you we were worried about. You and the baby. It's wonderful to know they think you're going to be alright. And one night's not the end of the world. It's such a relief to see you looking so healthy. What do the machines tell you, Mavis? Anything?'

Mavis didn't turn to look at the women. 'Everything seems to be good,' she said with authority. 'All your vital signs are within normal parameters, as are those for the bairn.' She finally gave her attention to her bedridden colleague. 'So, tell us exactly what happened.'

'I checked out the police report on the van, and discovered . . .'

'Ach no,' snapped Mavis. 'Not work. You. What happened to you?'

Carol said quietly, 'I just slipped on a tiled floor and fell on my bum. That's all.'

'Did you lose consciousness at all?' snapped Mavis.

Carol knew she didn't dare hold anything back. 'I think I might have done, but only for a moment or so.'

'And you've told the paramedics this, and the doctor too?' Mavis was on a roll.

'Yes, Mavis, I did. My health, and the well-being of this baby are my first priority, you know. I'm not going to tell fibs just so they'll let me go home. There is no way I'm taking any chances with this baby.' Carol sounded more angry than she'd meant to, but she was getting a bit fed up with people seeming to assume she didn't understand how serious all this could have been.

Mavis stood down from full-on bossy-nurse mode and smiled at her friend. 'What will we do with you?'

'Sorry,' said Carol, and she meant it. She didn't want to be in a hospital bed, and she knew the whole situation had really arisen because of her temper, but she decided to not mention that. 'I did overhear something I think is important – I must tell you before David gets back.'

'Very well then, spit it out,' said Mavis tartly.

'All my notes and photos about the van are already in emails to you all. But at the Morris farm I met Herbert Morris – Aubrey's grandfather's brother, and his niece, Netta Roberts. They mentioned that a female at the Morris farm was also missing and they suspected she'd be with Aubrey. I don't know who they were referring to, but they said something along the lines of "they never stopped" which suggests to me that Aubrey and this girl had a relationship.'

Mavis looked thoughtful, and Althea said, 'The letters! They must be referring to Boudica.'

'Boudica?' asked Carol.

'Briefly, we found some letters written in a combination of Welsh and Latin at Aubrey's house. They were written to him as Caradoc from a Boudica. Christine's working on the Latin translation and we were hoping you'd take a look at the Welsh.'

'Happy to,' said Carol. 'I'm not doing anything else. Have you got them here?'

Mavis shook her head. 'I sent you photos. Have you got your phone?'

'I made sure they brought my handbag, and my phone's in there. I think they stuffed it behind my bed. If you could reach it for me I could do the translation while I'm sitting here . . .'

'And what translation would that be? Something to do with a flamin' case?' snapped David as he reentered the suddenly-crowded curtained area. 'You are supposed to be resting! Mavis, what are you thinking, asking her to work when our child's life hangs in the balance.'

Carol could tell that Mavis was struggling with her natural inclination to respond to David sharply. She was relieved when her colleague said simply, 'No, I am not asking her to work. I simply wanted to check that certain information had got through to her on email.'

You're a pretty good liar, Mavis, thought Carol, relaxing a little as her husband's face softened.

'Hmm, well, alright then. But no work. No way. Agreed?'

Both Mavis and Carol nodded their agreement, leading David to raise his eyebrows toward the dowager duchess who said, 'Oh absolutely. Nothing to do with me, David. As you know, I was merely the one with the car. But I wonder, I've been quite some time without a drink of anything, do you think that maybe you, or Mavis might be able to rustle up a cup of tea for me? Am I being a terrible old bother asking that?'

David looked at Mavis suspiciously. Carol judged he wasn't about to leave her alone with his wife again.

'Why don't David and I do that together?' said Mavis brightly. 'You can have the chair for a few minutes, Althea. I'm sure you'll feel better after a cuppa and a wee sit down, won't you? I'll put an extra sugar in it, if we can find any at all. Come away with you now, David. You know very well that if I'm with you I cannot encourage Carol to do anything she shouldnae be doing.'

'Will you be alright?' asked David solicitously of his wife.

'To be honest, I wouldn't mind a cuppa myself, if they say it's OK,' replied Carol. She knew it was the encouragement her husband needed.

'Right, we'll get teas all round,' said David holding open the curtain for Mavis. 'Back as quick as we can.'

Once alone, Althea leapt into action, and, with Carol's complicity, they achieved a great deal in the ten minutes that followed. When David and Mavis returned with four cardboard cups containing what purported to be tea, Althea fluttered her eyes, as though on the edge of sleep, and then made an effort to rouse herself to drink the reviving beverage. Carol inwardly applauded the dowager's acting skills.

When the doctor arrived about half an hour later, Mavis and Althea hugged Carol then left the couple to listen to what the medic had to say. Several moments later David emerged to confirm he'd be staying with Carol overnight. Ian had brought the bag from the car which David had hurriedly prepared according to Mavis's instructions, and it was agreed that Mavis and Althea would return home, while David would telephone

Althea when plans were cemented for Carol's discharge in the morning – if that was when it was to be. Althea promised she'd make arrangements for someone to collect the Hills from the hospital and have them taken to their home, as well as getting somebody from the estate to collect Carol's car from the Morris farm. Car keys were found and secured by Mavis, and Carol began to suspect that Althea was, truly, flagging.

Finally, Carol asked a nurse to hold open the curtain so she could wave goodbye to Mavis and Althea. With David's back to her, Carol also gave a double thumbs-up to Althea whose eyes, she noted, glinted with schoolgirlish wickedness.

NINETEEN

In the car once again, heading to the Dower House, Mavis and Althea sat in the back seat and kept their voices low.

'Were you able to get her to do some of it?' hissed Mavis. Althea nodded.

'And did you get anything useful?'

Again, Althea nodded. Mavis saw her shoulders jiggle as she suppressed a giggle. 'This is fun,' she said, eyes wide with excitement.

'We'll talk properly at home,' said Mavis with a wink. 'But can you give me any hints?'

'Boudica and Caradoc are not just firm friends, but good, old-fashioned sweethearts too,' replied Althea meaningfully. 'It appears she addressed him as *Cariad* for good reason; he's her Dearest, and she's been soppy about him for years. Carol said the word *gwraig* was used – which means "wife". She really only scanned the last letter, but she thought it said something about being excited to be his wife.'

Mavis said thoughtfully, 'So, a possible elopement.'

Althea squeezed her friend's hand and whispered gleefully, 'How romantic – to be young and so much in love.'

The two women settled to watching the lights of the houses of Hereford through the sleet. As they left all signs of human habitation behind them and entered the blackness of the true countryside, all Mavis could do was reflect on the follies of young love, and then that she'd been pleased to see a small-scale and apparently well-run hospital taking excellent care of Carol.

The motion of the car through the darkness was soporific, and Mavis realized she wasn't concentrating on anything except the glutinous white sleet on the glass, so she was startled when her mobile phone rang.

Answering it swiftly she listened to Annie babbling on about something she couldn't understand.

'Slow down, dear,' Mavis began. 'Now start again, more slowly. You say Tudor Evans just telephoned you?'

'Yes,' replied Annie, sounding very far away. 'Can you hear me?'

'Yes, dear, but you're fading in and out a little. What did Tudor say?'

'The Anwen Morris stuff has been . . . at Chellingworth Hall.'

'It's been what?'

'Delivered to the hall.'

'All of it?'

'Yes.'

'Any sign of Aubrey?'

'What?'

'Any sign of Aubrey?'

'No . . . tomorrow morning . . . best thing.'

'I'll phone you from the Dower House. Bad reception.'

'OK.'

'What?' said Althea, tugging at Mavis's arm. 'What's happened?'

'I think the gist of it is that the Anwen Morris artefacts have been delivered to Chellingworth Hall, and that they are intact, but there's still no sign of Aubrey,' replied Mavis, tucking her telephone into her capacious handbag.

Mavis watched as Althea gave the matter some thought. Leaning forward the dowager said, 'Ian, please take us directly to the hall. I'd like to find out what's going on, and by far the best thing to do is go there ourselves.' Mavis watched as the woman tried to get some light on her wristwatch. 'When we get there it'll be time for dinner. I'm sure Cook Davies will be able to rustle up something for us, so why don't we plan on dining with Henry and Stephanie, and maybe they could get you something in the kitchen, Ian?'

'I could drop you off at the hall and run on down to the Dower House to let them know what's happening if you like, Your Grace,' replied Ian. Mavis liked the way he was always so sensible – he reminded her of one of her own sons, Duncan.

'Good idea, thank you, Ian,' replied Althea.

'I'd much rather grill Henry about it all face-to-face than on the telephone,' said Althea with relish.

'Ach, all this talk of "grilling"? You're spending far too much time with our Annie.'

'Nattily-angled fedoras were all the rage when I was young, you know,' said Althea impishly, 'and I was told they quite suited me. Sometimes I miss the days when men wore hats. Proper ones, not the things they wear nowadays. And a belted mackintosh? I remember thinking Bogie was very handsome in his. So dashing.'

'Dashing can bring a world of trouble,' said Mavis sagely. 'My late husband was dashing, so I should know.'

'Ah yes, the draw of a man in uniform,' said Althea quietly, 'though my late husband wore velvet and ermine, not khaki and brass.'

'I dare say either would do at a pinch,' said Mavis with a smile.

Both women sighed deeply, each looking out of the window nearest them, lost in their own worlds.

'Just about twenty minutes now, Your Grace,' announced Ian eventually.

'Thank you,' replied Althea automatically. Turning toward Mavis she clutched the woman's arm and said softly, 'I'm so glad to have you as a friend. There's no one who understands a widow like another widow. It's wonderful to see Carol and David at the beginning of their journey toward building a family, and of course Christine is so full of youthful vigor with that terribly handsome Alexander falling all over himself to get on her good side.'

'I'm not sure it's her good side he's interested in,' observed Mavis wickedly.

Giggling, Althea added, 'Poor old Annie's a worry though. Even Eustelle is lucky because her husband's still alive. But us? Like I say, no one understands a widow like another widow. None of them understand how it feels. Well, how could they?'

'True,' replied Mavis. The headlights from an approaching car flashed across their faces, shining on Althea's face for long enough for Mavis to see tears in her friend's eyes. Patting Althea's arm she whispered, 'I bet a lot of people don't think that a duke and a duchess can possibly have a truly loving marriage, like we normal folks do. But I know how you felt about him. And when the man you love dies, it rips a hole inside you that you cannot explain, you can only feel. Words don't do it justice. The tears that come unbeckoned, the reminders that tap you on the shoulder when you least expect them, thinking you see the back of his head in a crowd. It's all called grief, but just because it has a name doesn't mean it's understandable by those who've not felt it. I'm grateful to be able to sit quietly with you of an evening, firm friends in understanding, Althea. It's a great gift you've given me.'

'My husband would have loved all this enquiring. But my son? Too bothered with appearances. My fault, I suppose. He's not keen on me being involved with you lot. Thinks it's not seemly for a dowager. A bit too serious for his own good is my son,' said Althea sadly.

'Aye, my husband was too. Dour chap some said, but I knew he was loving and reliable. Not an ounce of inquisitiveness in him, though,' replied Mavis. 'That's no' something they care for much in the armed forces,' she added.

They sat in silence for the rest of the trip.

TWENTY

'Her Grace has just alighted from her motor car at the front entrance, Your Grace. She has said she will be joining you for dinner.' Despite the fact that Edward managed to make the announcement sound totally neutral the duke began to feel his neck throbbing.

'For goodness' sake, who else will be here before the night's over?' said Henry to Stephanie in exasperation. 'Very well, Edward, you'd better tell Cook we'll be an extra two for dinner and she can serve it as soon as possible because that Evans man will be here to collect the Morris dancing gear before too long.'

Edward retreated and Henry thanked his stars it wasn't he himself who had to tell Cook to cater for even more at dinner than she'd imagined.

'How did the nurse seem to you, Stephanie?' he asked his betrothed. 'I don't have much experience in that sort of thing myself, though I know you told me it was a good agency.'

Stephanie pondered her answer as Henry watched. They'd both changed for dinner, of course, and he liked it when she wore a dress. Shapely calves, a neat waist and what he knew people referred to as 'childbearing hips' – he almost blushed at the thought – meant she looked very presentable as she hovered beside a hurriedly set-up arrangement of drinks on top of a sideboard in the drawing room. Henry wondered if any rooms at all would be useable by Friday – it was as though Chellingworth Hall was shrinking about him, and this in a place that had 268 rooms. Of course most of them were never used at all, but the ones he enjoyed all seemed to be out of bounds to him. Henry sighed and waited for Stephanie to answer, then wondered why she hadn't. He realized her attention was being given to something behind him, so he turned to see his sister, Lady Clementine, being pushed into the room in a wheelchair. Her right leg was fully extended, encased in plaster and swathed in magenta chiffon, which proved to be more of a draw to the eye as opposed to being effective as any sort of camouflage.

'Henry, it's so wonderful to see you again,' called his sister, stretching out her arms as if she expected him to run to her.

Henry didn't move. He thought it best to remain in front of the fireplace and stand his ground. 'There you are, Clemmie. Edward told me you arrived about an hour ago. Where have you been?'

His sister's tone had already informed Henry she was going to play the tragedy card. He sighed, waiting to be bludgeoned to within an inch of his life by what he knew would be her unyielding self-pity. It didn't take long for her to land the first blow.

'It's taken so long to get everything sorted out and arranged. I suppose it was your idea that someone should make up a bed for me in the east wing, on the ground floor. The place hasn't been used for so long, Henry, it smells of old . . . everything. Can't I use my own apartment?' Clementine Twyst sounded like a truculent twelve-year-old, belying her more than fifty years of age. Henry seethed internally that she'd always been allowed to get away with all sorts of unreasonable demands, while he'd always had to toe the line. The fact she'd left the artists' village near Arles, where they'd both been living and painting when news of their father's death had come through, for no more than two weeks – whereas he'd never been able to return there again – rankled with Henry.

'Clemmie, you know that's not possible. We don't have any lifts here, and I won't have people carrying you up and down stairs all the time. It's not something we can expect of the staff. Besides, the bathroom Grandfather installed off the old music room when he broke *his* leg, and where Edward has arranged for a bed to be placed for you, is more than adequate. You'll be fine.'

'It's not a nice bathroom, Henry. I suppose it's got most of the right bits and pieces, but it's so ugly. It's horrid.' Clementine grabbed the magenta chiffon from her leg and flung it about her shoulders in a very dramatic manner.

Henry glowered at the way it clashed with the acid-lemon dress she'd chosen to wear. At least the pink matched her current hair color, he thought. 'The only alternative is that you use your apartment and never come downstairs,' snapped Henry. 'I know very well you'd agree to that in an instant, then create as much of a stink as Stilton because you changed your mind and wanted to come down. This is the only viable option. Besides, your nurse can be close to you down here; they've made up a room beside yours for her.'

Finally turning his attention to the navy-clad woman behind his sister – who he thought would have made Hattie Jacques look like a waif – he said, 'I hope your accommodations suit, Nurse . . . um?'

Abandoning her charge about a third of the way across the drawing room, the nurse strode toward Henry in what he thought was a most alarming manner. *Were the silver candlesticks on the stone mantle shaking?*

'I'm Thomas, Nurse Betty Thomas, Your Grace,' said the woman in a voice so deep Henry imagined she could have sung as at least a baritone, if not a bass, in a male voice choir. She thrust a huge hand toward him and he allowed her to almost shake off his arm. 'Accommodations are excellent, thank you,' boomed the nurse with a grin that frightened Henry not only because it was wide and full of teeth, but because it disappeared immediately. She marched back toward Clementine, who was wafting her chiffon about her as though she might swoon. 'Where shall I park you, Lady Clementine?'

'Near the fire, but not so close that I'll get too hot,' replied Clementine in the voice of a woman close to death.

Henry stopped himself from tutting by saying, 'Mother is joining us for dinner. Have you told her you're here?'

'Why would I?' asked Clemmie, wriggling about in her seat as best she could. 'I thought you'd do that.'

'Henry's been terribly busy with the wedding arrangements, Lady Clementine,' said Stephanie, moving to join her fiancé and taking hold of his hand. Henry thanked her with a smile.

'You'll be my sister-in-law in a few days, Steph, so drop the "lady", won't you?' sneered Clementine.

His sister's tone wasn't lost on Henry who leaped to

Stephanie's defense. 'Clemmie, let Stephanie be. Save your venom for those who are more used to it.'

He was relieved when his mother and Mavis MacDonald entered the drawing room. He felt reinforcements were in order.

'Clemmie's here, Mother,' he announced, completely unnecessarily.

'I can see that,' replied Althea Twyst with what Henry judged to be a startled look. 'What have you done to yourself this time, dear?' she asked as she walked toward her daughter, bent down to kiss her, then moved to sit in a chair set back from the fire. 'I'll take a large sherry, please Henry,' she added, almost without drawing breath. 'I assume we're helping ourselves tonight? There's no one here to serve.'

'Yes, Mother,' said Henry moving toward the sideboard, 'and no, there isn't anyone tonight. It seems there's been something of a crisis in the Orangery that demanded the attention of most of the able-bodied people in the house this evening.'

'The Orangery? I didn't know you were using the Orangery on Saturday.' Althea settled herself on her straight-backed chair, and motioned that Mavis should do likewise.

Henry began to pour as he replied, 'We weren't planning on it, but it seems it's been necessary to call it into service to act as some sort of preparation area for the chamber orchestra. Edward said they went to air out the place this afternoon and found wasps' nests in there.'

'Wasps' nests?' Althea sounded surprised. 'Won't the wasps all be asleep at this time of year?'

'Maybe, but we had to get in a man to remove them, and he commandeered ladders and all sorts of help. I must say, I hadn't expected wasps.'

'They are the Spanish Inquisition of the insect world, Henry. No one ever expects them,' replied Althea tartly

'Pardon? The Spanish Inquisition? They never came here to Chellingworth. Are you feeling quite well, Mother?' Henry panicked – what was his mother babbling about? As he saw a sly smile curl his mother's lips, he knew she was playing with him. 'Is that one of your Monty Python things again?' he asked sharply. Whenever his mother said something bizarre out of the blue, it usually had something to do with that lot.

'Very good, Henry,' replied his mother with a wink, 'you're learning.'

'Really, Mother,' was all he could manage. He felt flustered, and what made it worse was that he spied Stephanie trying to stifle a grin. 'You too?' he couldn't stop himself from wailing at his fiancé.

'Now Henry, you know what I always say about your sense of humor,' said Althea seriously. 'And I might add that, if ever you needed to overcome the bypass it received when you were an infant, now might be the time. Where's my sherry, dear? And one for Mavis too, I think. We've just come from the hospital, and it's been a long day.'

'We heard you were there,' said Stephanie helping Henry at the makeshift bar. 'What's happened? Is Carol alright? And the baby?'

'Who's Carol? What baby? What are you all talking about?' Clementine Twyst was clearly not impressed that she wasn't the center of attention. 'Nurse Thomas, I'm too near the fire here and I can't see anyone properly. Hoick me around a bit.'

'I beg your pardon, Lady Clementine?' growled the nurse.

Henry was amazed when his sister said meekly, 'Could you move my chair a smidge, so I can be a little less close to the flames, and have a better view of Mother, please, Nurse Thomas?'

Henry looked at the large woman standing beside his sister with immediate admiration.

'Certainly, Lady Clementine,' replied the nurse, and did as she'd been asked.

'Been with the agency long?' asked Mavis MacDonald of the nurse.

Moving Clementine's chair, the woman replied, 'About five years. It suits. I can see from your watch that you have some service yourself.'

Henry saw Mavis pat the watch she had pinned to her chest. 'Aye, thirty years. Army. Mavis MacDonald. Last ten years as matron at the Battersea Barracks.' Henry wondered if some sort of nursing-based power struggle was about to break out in his drawing room.

'Thirty years is a good long time, isn't it,' rumbled Nurse Thomas. 'I hope you're enjoying your retirement, ma'am.'

'I'm an enquiry agent now, so retired from nursing, but no' from life,' replied Mavis.

'Are you working on a case now? Here?' asked Clementine rather dismissively, as Henry and Stephanie handed drinks to Mavis and Althea. 'Could I have a G&T, Henry please?' she added, then, after what appeared to Henry to be no more than a glance from Nurse Thomas she added, 'Well, maybe just the T, with some lemon, please.'

'Absolutely,' was all he could manage as he made his way back across the room. *How had the Thomas woman managed to tame the terrible Clemmie in such a short time?*

'We are indeed working on a case,' replied Althea.

'What do you mean "we", Mother?' snapped Clementine.

'I'm an honorary WISE Woman. You'd know if only you bothered to keep in touch. I help out with their enquiries. At the agency.' Althea sat even more upright than her chair demanded. Henry thought she looked very small sitting in the large chair, but she did look proud.

Taking her drink from her brother and thanking him – *thanking him!* – Clementine said, 'I don't understand, Mother. What do you mean?'

'What Althea means,' said Mavis, 'is that she's able to bring a very special skill set to the table, and we at the WISE Enquiries Agency value her abilities greatly. The case we are working on at present is a very strange one. A young man from the village, usually reliable, has gone missing. His vehicle has been found, and some valuable items he was believed to have taken with him have turned up, here, I believe. Althea and I have come here this evening to discover if that part of the tale is true. Is it, Your Grace?'

Finally back in his favored spot in front of the massive stone fireplace Henry nodded. 'Yes indeed. Edward brought to our attention the fact that all three of the missing items had been left outside the New Buttery at some point late this afternoon. No one saw who left them, and no one can be certain about when exactly they were left, but they are back. Tudor Evans is due to collect them this evening. Probably while we dine.'

'And they're all in good order?' asked Mavis.

Henry looked to Stephanie for her agreement. He was glad when she said, 'Never having seen the items before we can't be one hundred percent sure, but they seemed fine to me. I'm sure Tudor will know best – he's the one who's handled them on countless occasions. We asked to be alerted if he thinks anything is amiss when he arrives and examines the contents.'

'I wouldn't mind a quick look at them myself, before he whisks them away,' said Althea. Henry noted that she leaned very close to Mavis when she added, 'We've become quite obsessed by them, haven't we? Don't you think it'd be nice to see them "up close and personal"?'

Henry felt his shoulders hunch as his mother spoke. He wasn't at all convinced she should be spending quite so much time with Mavis and the others. It certainly wasn't something he'd envisaged when he'd acceded to his mother's requests about offering the women office and living accommodation on the estate.

'Where have you stashed the loot?' asked Althea, confirming Henry's worst fears.

'Now, now, dear,' said Mavis quietly.

'We left it all in the morning room,' replied Henry. 'That's where we were when Edward brought it to us, and the great hall seems to be overrun with all sorts of people, bedecking every surface with some sort of diaphanous fabric, or wreaths of ivy. But you'd best be quick,' he added – unnecessarily as it transpired, because his mother and Mavis were both already on their feet.

As they made their way toward the door he could hear his mother saying, 'So, if the van and the artefacts have turned up, where on earth can Aubrey be? We have to find out about the missing girl up at the Morris farm . . .' Then they were gone.

'Could I have another tonic, brother dear? I seem to have finished this one,' whined Clementine.

Just about to snap, 'Get it yourself,' Henry realized he was at his sister's beck and call, so did as he was bid. He felt his shoulders slump as he plodded to collect Clemmie's glass. He couldn't imagine how things could possibly get worse, and all this before his wedding. *Might have another myself,* he thought, standing in front of the sideboard – where he turned his back so Stephanie couldn't see how much scotch was in his glass before he added water.

TWENTY-ONE

'You keeping up, Mavis?' called Althea as she made her way rapidly toward the doors to the morning room.

'Aye, you dinnae need to concern yoursel' on my account,' said Mavis absently.

'Och, that's very Scottish of you,' mugged Althea, stopping and turning to face her friend. 'What's up?'

Mavis stopped in her tracks. 'I don't like it, Althea. Yes, I want to see this stuff for myself, and, yes, I'm pleased – in a way – that it's all turned up. But that in itself is worrying.'

Pushing open the doors Althea entered the morning room, which was already illuminated by several standard lamps. 'Henry would save a fortune on electricity if he didn't have every room lit up like Blackpool,' Althea observed – somewhat acidly, thought Mavis as she followed the dowager's lead.

'There it all is,' said Mavis, passing Althea who plonked herself into a velvet-upholstered chair.

'You alright, dear?' asked Mavis. She was concerned Althea might be tired. That the dowager usually napped in the afternoon was a truth acknowledged by both women, but never mentioned by either.

'Glad to get away from the children,' said Althea heavily, which made Mavis grin. With grown children herself she knew how it felt to look at two adults and see two infants, or toddlers – or, worse still – two teens in their stead.

Without missing a beat Mavis replied, 'Ach, they'll be fine. Beneath all that sniping they love each other.'

'I don't doubt it,' said Althea quietly, 'but the sniping, as

you so correctly coined it, is extremely tiring. I had hoped
they'd grow out of it, but, of course, they never do. The whole
world sees them as fully grown human beings – but they are
unable to act that way when they are with each other.'

'Mine are the same,' said Mavis, seeking to console her
friend. 'Both good boys, good men even, but like wee ruffians
when they're together for more than two minutes.'

Mavis smiled as Althea motioned a salute and said, 'Once
again, so good to have someone about the place who understands the important things in life.'

'Aye, and the important things about this case,' said Mavis,
pulling open the wooden box sitting in the corner of the room
and peering in to see the silver bells it contained. She pulled
out a string of round silver balls attached to a leather strap
with a buckle at one end. The bells tinkled.

'Sounds like Christmas,' said Althea leaning forward in her
chair to get a better view of what Mavis was holding.

Mavis crossed the room and deposited the object in Althea's
lap. 'There's a whole bevvy of these in that box, and, I'll grant
you they look a bit old and battered, but if they're the age
we've been told, that's no' such a surprise. Let's have a look
at the staff. You stay there, I'll fetch it.'

Mavis had to lay the staff on the ground to be able to open
the outer casing of leather, then she revealed the artefact itself.
She turned it about in her hands, peering at the silverwork on
the wooden shaft, then at the gold cage that held an orb of
glass at its top. 'Beautiful workmanship,' she said quietly,
'even though you can see it's worn, the detail of the etching
in the precious metals is still there. And this glass ball? Must
have been quite a feat to make it – when did they say this
was made?'

'We think it was in the mid-1500s,' boomed Tudor Evans'
voice from the open doorway. Both Mavis and Althea started,
and Mavis almost dropped the staff on the floor.

'Good grief, you gave me quite a turn,' said Althea crossly.

Mavis saw Tudor flush with embarrassment. 'I'm sorry, Your
Grace,' he blustered, 'Edward showed me right to this door.
Said I should come in. I didn't know you hadn't seen me.'

Althea beckoned Tudor into the room. 'No worries. I dare

say we were too entranced by this wonderful thing. I've never seen anything like it. Though I dare say you're very familiar with the piece. Would you like to check everything is in good order?'

Tudor's expression told Mavis he'd be delighted to do just that. 'You're here a good deal earlier than we were expecting you,' she said, as she relinquished the staff to the man's eager hands.

She noticed he didn't look at her at all as he replied, 'As soon as I got word I came here as quick as I could. I really hope they're all alright. This is, thank heavens. And I can see that the bells in Your Grace's lap are also in good shape. But I'd just like to check everything else.' He picked up the case for the staff and shut it away with reverence and care, then reached for the suitcase and flung it open to examine the sticks it contained.

Mavis left Althea and stood behind Tudor as he pulled out stick after stick, and turned each one in his hands, banging pairs together. Again, his expression spoke volumes, and Mavis could tell he was relieved.

Standing up, and therefore towering over Mavis, she could almost feel the air vibrate as he said loudly, 'Everything's perfect. I am so pleased.' He beamed down at Mavis, then she saw his expression change. 'So what's going on with Aubrey then? This is all here and they've found his van. So where's he?'

'Now there's a question,' replied Mavis. 'It's an extremely concerning turn of events. Maybe we three could have a quiet chat, while we're away from the others. Won't you join us beside the fireplace?'

Although no fire was lit, the hearth still provided the focus of the room. Two small women and one very large man sat in an incongruous huddle and all gave the matter some thought.

'Do you know the Morrises out at the Morris farm?' asked Mavis of Tudor. He shook his head. 'Shame.'

'I do, somewhat,' said Althea hesitantly. Mavis judged she didn't want to say more in company.

Taking her chance to engage Tudor, Mavis added, 'And you've had no more thoughts about where Aubrey might have got to? You're sure he's never mentioned a young woman to whom he is especially attached?'

Again Tudor shook his head, but this time he added, 'I've been thinking about it a lot. And talking about it with Annie. But I haven't come up with any bright ideas. Sorry. I wish I could. I told her I'd phone her if I do think of anything . . . or would you prefer me to phone you?' he asked of Mavis.

She could tell by his eyes he was hoping she'd reply in the negative, so she did. 'No, you and Annie are building a rapport. Use her as your contact.' Although she wanted to use different words and a different tone, she judged it better to stick within professional parameters. 'But, if that's all . . .'

Tudor took his cue, rising from his seat. 'Would it be alright with you if I took the Morris equipment with me? I'll keep it safe, under lock and key all the time, at the pub.' He looked nervously from Mavis to Althea.

'It is neither mine nor the dowager's to give,' said Mavis simply, 'but it seems to make sense that you keep it for now, since you are the one who will be using it on Saturday. We'll have to see how things stand after that to know what to do with it then.'

Tudor nodded his agreement, packed everything up, scooped it all into his large arms and bade a good evening to the two women.

Alone again, Mavis said to Althea, 'Out with it then. The Morrises at the Morris farm. Who's this missing girl, d'you think?'

'Well, that's just it, I have been thinking, and I realize I can't be positive. I know there were two brothers and a sister. One brother inherited the farm, the other – Aubrey's grand-father – moved away. I believe the sister stayed and she married. As I recall she herself had a girl. Yes, that's right – the two sons had sons, the sister had a girl.' She looked across at Mavis and smiled her bright smile. 'Funny that. Anyway, it sounds like it's that girl, Aubrey's father's cousin Netta Roberts, Carol met at the Morris farm. If that's the case then we can infer, from what Carol told us, that it's *her* daughter that's missing, as well as Aubrey. Maybe she is Boudica.'

Mavis nodded. 'I think we can also infer Netta Roberts

married a man with a temper, who won't be pleased if his daughter has disappeared, and possibly eloped, with Aubrey – who would be . . . *what*? Her *great*-cousin? Her *grand*-cousin? Her cousin once, or maybe twice removed? I'll admit I've never been very clear on what they're called when they're not just first cousins. Is it second cousins?'

Mavis noted her friend's excited expression. 'Now that's where I can help. Marrying into a family like this, one has to be up on all that sort of stuff. It helps everyone to know how far back bloodlines go, just to avoid any nastiness when it comes to marriages – you know, recessive genes and all that. Mind you, most of the people in Britain with a title are related if you go back far enough, in the same way that almost everyone in the world with a European heritage is somehow related to Charlemagne. Now, if you say "removed", that means that you're talking about different generations. Aubrey and this unknown girl would be the same generation as each other – their grandparents being of the same generation too. So they'd theoretically be second cousins, because they had the same great-grandparents as each other, but . . .'

'So they'd be able to marry, no problem,' said Mavis. 'Henry VIII sorted that out, didn't he? Making sure cousins could marry.'

'But they aren't,' said Althea.

'They aren't what, dear?' asked Mavis, a little confused.

'They aren't consanguineous,' said Althea triumphantly. 'If that's who this girl is, who we think is missing.'

Mavis grinned. 'Now I think you're poking fun at me a wee bit, aren't you, dear? We've already established my only knowledge of Latin is that which I've picked up in my medical career, so, let me see if I can beat you at your crossword-solvers game. "Sanguine" comes from the Latin root for "blood", so I'm going with "consanguineous" meaning of the same blood. Would I be right?' Althea nodded graciously. Mavis continued, 'So you're saying that they wouldn't be related? But how could that be?'

'Aubrey's grandfather's sister wasn't a blood sister. She was evacuated from London during the war. To the Morris farm. Now I know this is all long before my time, but I seem to recall something about all her family being killed in the Blitz, so the Morrises adopted her, and she stayed. She didn't marry a Morris, so her daughter, and therefore her granddaughter, wouldn't have Morris blood either.'

Mavis sat for a moment and studied her hands in her lap. 'So why would the father be so angry if she was carrying on with Aubrey Morris? He seems like ideal son-in-law material; a steady man with a good business. And, if this is the same girl to whom he was writing as Boudica, it seems they had a great deal in common in terms of their knowledge of languages, if nothing else, before romance bloomed. It's very puzzling.'

'Dinner is served, Your Grace,' said Edward loudly from the doorway. 'Shall I escort Your Grace to the dining room?'

The heads of both women shot up. Shaking her head at the butler, the dowager said quietly, 'Mavis and I shall walk in together, thank you Edward.' Mavis noticed that Althea leaned heavily on her cane as she rose from her seat, then her friend said, 'I hope it's not a long dinner. I'm missing McFli.'

Taking the dowager's arm Mavis steered and tried to hide the concern she felt. 'I know Ian's gone across to the Dower House to make sure they are fully aware of what's happening with us this evening, but I agree that I hope it's not a lengthy meal. Speaking for myself, I could do with a relatively early night. How about we miss the dessert, however tempting it might be, and get away as quick as we can?'

Althea's relieved expression told Mavis she'd made an acceptable suggestion, so they moved off together.

Passing through the great hall toward the dining room, Mavis noticed a bright light shining through the glass panes of the front doors. 'What on earth is that?'

Althea looked toward the light. 'Looks like someone's trying to drive up the front steps. Edward? Edward!' she bellowed. Mavis was amazed at the strength of her tiny friend's voice.

Edward appeared, looking calm, as usual. 'Yes, Your Grace?'

'Something's happening out there. Take a look, would you?'

With a courteous 'Certainly, Your Grace,' Edward moved toward the door. Mavis couldn't help but think how the man seemed to skim the surface of the floor, rather than walking properly.

A moment later Edward rejoined the two women, holding a long, narrow box in his hands. 'This was on the front steps, Your Grace, and a motorcycle was leaving at a great rate of speed. It is addressed to His Grace. It was ringing a moment ago, but it has stopped now.'

'It was what, Edward?' Althea sounded puzzled.

'Ringing, Your Grace. As a telephone would ring.'

Althea looked at Mavis with a twinkle in her eye. 'This sounds like it might be fun. Let's take it to the table with us. You'll bring it, Edward, thank you.'

Mavis smiled as she saw how gleeful the package had made Althea, and the two women hovered beside Henry as he opened the box. Inside was a mound of tissue paper with a mobile phone nestling in it.

'Someone has sent me a telephone?' said Henry. 'How very odd. And the box seems a little on the large side for it, too.'

'There must be something in the tissue paper, Henry,' said Althea excitedly. 'Root about a bit.'

Henry threw his mother a withering glance, which Mavis saw the woman completely ignore. Pulling back the papers Henry said, 'Well that's decidedly odd.'

'What is it?' asked Stephanie, finally joining the others to peer into the box.

'It's an arm!' shouted Henry, pushing the box away and leaping out of his seat in horror.

'An arm?' said Stephanie, leaning to get a better look. 'It can't be an arm, there's no hand. Look – it's . . . oh no! It's a sleeve. One of the sleeves off my wedding dress!'

'It's what?' blustered Henry, then he dropped the lid of the box he'd held onto with a start as the telephone began to ring. He looked at the three women surrounding him, as well as his sister and her nurse. 'I'm not answering it. It can't be for me.'

Mavis noticed his eyes turn toward Edward who was hovering inside the door of the dining room. 'Ach, give it to me,' she said, picking up the phone. Pressing the button to accept the call Mavis said, 'Aye? Who is it, and what do you want?'

She noticed all eyes were glued to her as she listened. She put down the phone when the person at the other end hung up.

'What? What is it? Who was that? Why is the sleeve of my dress in this box – and where's the rest of my dress? It's supposed to be at the dressmaker's workshop in Bridgend,' wailed Stephanie. Mavis was quite alarmed by how unhinged the girl seemed to have become in just an instant.

'A young man with a thick Welsh accent informed me he has the rest of the dress, and will deliver it here, in time for the wedding, if you pay him five thousand pounds,' said Mavis without drama.

'Preposterous,' exclaimed Henry. 'Why would we do that? It's just a dress. It cannot be worth that much. Besides, how do we know he has it?'

Althea looked at Mavis with pleading eyes, and she knew she had to step up. 'I would suggest he delivered, or sent, the sleeve to prove he has the rest of the dress, and I can only imagine your bride-to-be would very much like to get married in the gown she's chosen and had fitted to her body for the occasion. Would that be right, Stephanie?'

Stephanie nodded dumbly.

'Very well, then,' said Mavis, 'I shall contact my team and we will begin an immediate investigation into what I have no doubt my esteemed colleague Annie, who enjoys giving our case files alliterative names, would refer to as "The Case of the Severed Sleeve". Stephanie, if you'd be so kind as to furnish me with the telephone number of your dressmaker, I'll make some enquiries. I shall return for a plate, if you would be so good as to keep something warm for me, Edward.'

TWENTY-TWO

Wednesday, February 26th

Speaking to Annie on the telephone, Carol used every euphemism she knew for 'fine' when she emphasized to Annie that she would be it. She was thrilled to hear that there was a 'new' investigation in hand, and agreed with Annie when she told her that Mavis had thought Carol's skills might come in handy.

Seeking escape in the downstairs loo from an annoyingly over-solicitous David, Carol had to admit she'd been lucky – in more ways than one. Of course she was happy she'd been sent home from the hospital with a completely clean bill of health for her and Bump, but she was also delighted she'd been able to move the case ahead just a little. David had banned her from speaking to Mavis for the entire day, but had relented insofar as she was to be allowed to visit the church on Thursday morning to help with the flower arranging for a few hours. She'd made it quite clear she'd sit down frequently and would avoid any and all areas that might be even a little damp underfoot. But, other than that, she knew she'd have to sit things out at home for the whole of Wednesday 'resting up'. And she wasn't looking forward to it. David had also made it abundantly clear during their drive from the hospital that he thought she shouldn't return to work at all before the birth of the baby.

'You alright in there?' David was knocking at the door.

'Yes,' she snapped, 'I'm fine. I've only been in here two minutes.'

'Five. You've been in there for five minutes.'

Carol flushed – unnecessarily – then flung open the door. 'I won't have you timing me in the toilet, David. It's ridiculous. It's demeaning. I'm a person, you know. Not a child, a grown-up person. I'll go do-lally if you watch over me every minute of the day.'

'I'm worried about you,' said her husband, sounding exactly that.

Carol marched into the kitchen and plonked herself on a chair beside the large, round scrubbed oak table. 'We need to talk,' she announced. 'Sit yourself down.' She pulled out another chair, into which David insinuated himself, looking cowed.

Carol sat quietly for a few moments, and David waited with an apprehensive look on his face. She could see his knee jerking up and down beneath the table. Gazing around the room Carol found she wasn't comforted by her collection of cat-themed knick-knacks, and decided she'd have a big clear-out of all the items not specifically featuring calico cats very soon. Nothing that bore no resemblance to Bunty would be allowed to stay.

Almost as though she knew she was being thought of, Bunty jumped onto Carol's lap and presented herself for petting, nuzzling Bump and pawing at Carol's leg. Carol stroked her beautiful fur, upon the dazzling whiteness of which was distributed the perfect balance of black and tan patches – the black patch over one eye giving Bunty a distinctly piratical look. Carol allowed Bunty's purring to rumble through her own body for a moment, and she felt instantly more calm. Just when she judged her husband couldn't take any more silence she said, 'I can't do it, David. It's not natural. I can't go on like this.'

David looked panic-stricken. 'What do you mean?'

As Carol continued to stroke Bunty she looked at her darling husband's tousled light-brown hair, tired amber eyes and pale complexion and said, 'We are about to be parents. Bump is as important to me as it is to you. Never forget that. But I cannot disappear as a person for possibly the next few weeks until Bump reveals itself, and you have to understand that. I'm pregnant, not ill. Millions of women all around the world are pregnant right now, and they are leading full, active lives. I am healthy. Bump is healthy. You cannot imprison me in this house just because I am pregnant. I had a little fall. We took all the necessary steps to make sure I am well, and I am. So, please, stop it, David. If you don't get a grip, this child could be born to a divorcing couple. There. I've had my say. Now it's your turn.'

David looked shocked. Carol hadn't seen him look that way since the day she'd first asked him out for dinner. On that occasion the shock had changed to delight, this time it turned to a wobbly chin and a threat of tears. *Sympathetic hormonal changes?*

'I know you're right, but I can't help myself,' whined David, running his hands through his hair. 'I tell myself off as I hear the words come out of my mouth, but out they come anyway. It's like I've become completely irrational. And you're right, it's getting worse. I've got to get a grip, but don't joke about divorce, love. That's not funny. If my being like this is that much of a problem, well, I've got to come to terms with it. I'll . . . grow up, as you put it.'

Carol sighed with relief. 'Thank you. That's all I needed to hear. You'll make the best father in the world, once you come to terms with the fact that you won't be able to wrap Bump in cotton wool for life. Now, with that sorted, I am warning you that Annie will be here soon with something for me to work on. I won't leave the house, but I will be doing something with my brain. I'll keep my feet up when I can – though you need to understand that's not very comfy for me at the moment, not unless I'm flat out.'

Half an hour later, having managed to shoo Annie away with many assurances that she would take it easy, and she was just fine, Carol was sitting with a mobile phone in one hand, a box with a torn sleeve in it on the table in front of her, and the knowledge that she could be of real help to Stephanie who, unsurprisingly, was very upset that her dressmaker had allowed her wedding dress to be stolen from her workroom.

She began her task by making some notes, set up two laptops, her mobile phone, and pulled a thumb-drive from a little cat-shaped box in which she kept precious things; in this instance, an enviable contact list she'd developed during her years in the City.

Now to work, she thought to herself. She examined the phone that had been delivered in the box, found the model, barcode and serial number, and consulted her list of contacts. Her first email went off to the head of IT for a telephone manufacturer in Singapore she'd met during one of the networking lunches she'd attended in the City. Knowing the man was a complete workaholic who owed her a big favor, she wasn't surprised to get a response from him within a couple of hours.

He then put her in touch with a logistics supremo in Hong Kong who said she was able to take the data gathered so far and would follow through with various shipping companies she knew and to get back to Carol as soon as possible with the final link in the chain.

Despite the fact she'd kept her promise to David and had, indeed, taken it easy and put her feet up as often as possible, Carol felt quite satisfied with her accomplishments for the day.

TWENTY-THREE

After dropping off the box containing the sleeve and the phone to Carol, Annie realized she needed a couple of packets of Fisherman's Friends to give to her dad when he arrived; they were his favorites, and she knew he'd appreciate the thought. She nipped across the green to the shop to see if they had any. When she entered the shop the little bell rang out, but there was no sign of Sharon. Odd, thought Annie. 'Sharon?' she called. 'Shar?' Nothing.

She peered behind the counters of both the shop and the post office parts of the store, then ventured to the doorway that led to the rest of the building. Sticking her head through the multicolored plastic ribbons that formed what couldn't really be called a privacy curtain, she shouted, 'Sharon?' again, and waited, listening intently.

'With you in a minute,' she heard from a distance.

'Alright, doll,' replied Annie.

'Sorry about that. It was my dad on the phone,' said Sharon rushing into the shop. 'There wasn't anyone in here when you came in, was there?' She looked about the place in a state of panic. 'I shouldn't have left but my mobile packed up and he wanted to talk to me about doing something for Saturday. Goodness knows what he's up to.'

'Do you mean he's doing something at the wedding?' Annie had no idea what Sharon meant.

Smiling, Sharon replied, 'Not as such. Marjorie Pritchard's been on at him to come up with some sort of device that will hold multiple layers of daffodils for either side of the chancel steps.'

'I thought Elizabeth Fernley, the duke's estate manager's wife, was overseeing the flowers,' said Annie.

Cathy Ace

'Probably,' said Sharon, fussing about behind the counter, 'but that won't stop Marjorie sticking her oar in, will it? Mind you, Elizabeth can give as good as she gets – can be quite chopsy at times. Nose put right out by the duke marrying, that one. Done most of the stuff his wife would have up until now, she has, and don't we all flamin' well know it.' She looked around as if to check that none of the nonexistent customers were listening, then leaned over the counter. 'Got it on good authority they've had a few ding-dongs up at the hall, Elizabeth and Stephanie.'

'Really?' said Annie, always eager to expand her understanding of the local goings-on.

Sharon nodded and gave a conspiratorial shrug. 'Nice woman, Stephanie. Got to know her a bit, 'cause she lived just opposite, in that cottage you're living in now. Till she moved up to the hall, of course. Bit of a change for her, especially since she's only normal, like us. Good for him, she'll be. Possibly good for all of us. Reckon she's got plans for the hall and the estate. You mark my words.'

Annie did, and suspected Sharon was right. She might be only a youngster, but she had the gossip gathering and disseminating skills of a woman three times her age. Annie wondered if she'd picked up the skills by osmosis from her own mother, who'd done what she was now doing for decades.

Realizing she had a chance to glean some possibly useful information, Annie opened by giving a bit, in order to get a bit. 'Did you hear that Carol took a bit of a fall up at the Morris farm yesterday.'

Sharon looked horrified. 'No! She's so close to her due date. Her and the baby alright?'

Annie nodded. 'They've both been given the all-clear by the hospital, but I wondered if you knew who it was that old man Morris's niece was married to? Carol said she caught a glimpse of a big, burly bloke when she was there.' She hoped this was a lie that might elicit useful information.

Sharon looked uncertain, but she spoke with conviction nonetheless. 'Couldn't have been him. Like a bit of string is Rhys Roberts.' She looked at the fluorescent tube above her head. 'They've got a girl, Ann – not Annie like you, very definitely Ann, she is. I know her a bit. But the father and the mother don't come to the village at all, to speak of. I knew Ann when I was little. A few years older than me, but we were at infants' school together. She went to big school in Builth but my Mam and Dad said they wanted me to go to Hay. Big stink about it, there was. Anyway, they won in the end so I just lost touch with her.'

'Big friends with Aubrey Morris at school, I hear,' dared Annie.

'What big ears you've got,' said Sharon with a wink. 'I'd better not rest on my laurels here, or you'll take over my reputation as the fount of all knowledge in the village. Where'd you hear that then?'

'As a professional enquiry agent, I can't say,' said Annie, returning Sharon's wicked wink.

'I never knew that competitive gossiping was a recognized sport, but if it's in the next Olympics, you and me are on! I think you're right, too. But they'd be cousins, wouldn't they? I don't know if that's proper. You know, if they were to become more than friends. I don't think I could ever fancy any of my cousins. Horrible lot they are.' Sharon pulled a face that showed to Annie just how horrible she thought they were. 'Hideous, most of them, too. Mam said I got all the looks in the family. But then she's me mam, so she would I suppose.'

Sharon began to tidy a few items on the counter, and Annie felt she only had one more chance to gather some useful information.

Girding her loins she went in for the kill. 'Another little gem I picked up is that the Rhys Roberts you mentioned earlier has a bit of a temper on him.'

Sharon looked across the counter at Annie with a strange glint in her eye. 'Gossip is one thing, and I'm all for it. It's how a place like this functions. I might be running this shop for the next forty years, so I won't go cutting off my nose to spite my face by saying anything nasty about no one. Even if it is true.' She nodded at Annie in a most significant manner.

'Got it, doll. You never said a word,' replied the enquiry agent, then added, 'I'll have two packets of Fisherman's Friends, please. That'll be it.'

TWENTY-FOUR

C hristine Wilson-Smythe woke up with a dreadful hang-
over. Luckily she was in her own bed in London, and
alone, so it didn't matter that the make-up she'd so
carefully applied the evening before made her look as though
she had two black eyes, bruised cheeks and a gash for a mouth.
Christine looked at her watch and was horrified to discover it
was almost eleven o'clock. She was due to collect her outfit
for the wedding at noon, had to drop by the designer's store
to deliver that invoice for Carol, and get back to Chellingworth
in time to have dinner with Henry and Stephanie.

Having been promised an 'unseasonably warm day in
London', Christine grabbed a beige two-piece trouser suit from
her wardrobe, a cream cashmere cardigan, which she buttoned
up to make it work as a sweater beneath her jacket and a
brown knitted wrap – just in case 'unseasonably warm' actually meant 'too chilly by half'.

Cursing the traffic inching across Battersea Bridge, Christine
pulled on her sunglasses and tuned in to BBC Radio 4. She
half-listened to a comedy, but her mind was wandering. Unable
to drive over the vehicles in front of her, Christine was glad
to have the distraction of a phone call from Mavis.

'Did you manage any of that Latin translation we sent you?'
were the first words out of Mavis's mouth.

'Aye, that I did,' mugged Christine.

'Ach, away with ya, you cheeky wee thing. No making fun
of my accent now. So, what did she say, this mysterious
Boudica? Hang on a mo, while I switch to speakerphone so
Althea can hear you too. Right, off you go.'

'It's been longer than I thought since I sat down and pored
over *De Bello Gallico* by Julius Caesar or *Historiae* by Tacitus.
I used to hate Latin translation classes. I'd stand there, with
The Gallic Wars or *The Histories* in my hand, shaking. They
were awfully boring and full of details about troop movements.

Still, I suppose it must have taken, because I quite enjoyed reading Latin again. It came flooding back to me – though I have to say there's some vocabulary that escaped me. Caesar and Tacitus must not have thought it worthwhile to write about fun things – but Boudica certainly did. From what I can gather the person to whom she was writing was very good with his hands.'

She heard Althea giggle in the background like a schoolgirl. 'Stop it,' said Mavis.

'I don't mean like that,' continued Christine. 'Apparently Caradoc could make anything; envisage, design and build or make things. He made her gifts, useful things that she took back to her farm with her. She spoke of each of them fondly. Since we know these letters were sent to Aubrey, that much makes sense. But – and here's the bad thing – she talks about him a lot, and their times together a great deal, and how she wishes they could spend more time together, but she doesn't talk about herself very much. All I got was that they are the same age as each other, she lives on a farm, they have visited the archeological site of Caerleon many times, and have very much enjoyed seeing it being excavated and explained more as the years have passed. She seems to like to throw in the odd Italian phrase along with the Latin. Not a surprise, I suppose, but I thought I'd mention it. As for the Welsh? I think she must be bilingual, and possibly first language Welsh. She almost scribbles in Welsh, but her handwriting is much more careful in Latin. The two early ones are not love letters in the normal sense; they don't proclaim love in the adult, or physical way, but she's clearly desperate to be with him more than she can be, poor thing. They speak of time spent together by two people who share common interests, common life-views, and have a common enemy. Again, no names, I'm afraid, just "him". No *amo, amas* or *amat*-ing, but sentimental stuff.'

'Amo means "I love",' said Althea somewhere in what Christine assumed was Chellingworth's Dower House.

'Aye, dear. Even my Latin runs that far,' replied Mavis. 'So, if that term's not in use, maybe we're talking about an unconsummated love. Any more news, Christine?'

'The most recent letter was written in Welsh more than

Latin, so I can't add much about that one – though the tone is different. She's now talking about their common enemy with real apprehension. One phrase she used was "stop at nothing to keep us apart", which I must say is worrying.'

Mavis was silent for a moment then said, 'I don't like the sound of that, but it's good to know. Anything more?'

'No, nothing I can add right now. I'm just about to try to park to collect my gown for the wedding, then I'll drop off that invoice, then I'm back onto the M4 to head for Chellingworth. I'm supposed to dine with Henry and Stephanie at the hall tonight.'

'Just a heads-up, dear, Clementine has installed herself, broken leg, wheelchair, nurse and all. Best be prepared for that.'

'How did she break her leg?' Christine couldn't imagine the heroin-chic Clementine doing anything that demanded physical exertion or danger.

'Apparently she drove her car over a bicycle and into a lamppost.'

'That's very careless of Clemmie. Was the cyclist hurt badly?'

'None to be found, dear.'

'How odd.'

'Aye, that it is.'

'Most things connected with my dear daughter are a little off kilter,' piped up Althea in the background. 'I dare say it's my fault.'

'Do as my parents do and blame the nanny,' replied Christine.

'I selected the nannies, so I'm even to blame for that,' said Althea. Christine thought she sounded a little tired, but didn't mention it.

'I'm about to park. Phone me if you need me, but now I have to concentrate.'

'Thanks for your help,' called Mavis, then Christine cut off the phone and wriggled the Range Rover into a space that was a very tight squeeze.

It took Christine just as long to park as it did to collect her ensemble for the wedding, and she was back in the traffic in about twenty minutes. Crawling along the King's Road she got stuck next to a lamppost for a while, and a makeshift sign caught her eye.

ARE YOU WITNIS TO ACSIDENT HERE THURSDAY 20TH? MAN VERY HURT ON BYSICLE. DRIVER GONE. WOMAN. BLACK CAR. BIG. WE NEED HELP!

The sign concluded with the word 'REWARD' in huge letters and a mobile phone number. As she finally began to inch forward, Christine couldn't help but wonder when exactly Clementine Twyst had hit a 'disappearing' cyclist. Realizing she wasn't getting anywhere fast, she phoned Mavis again, having snapped a photo of the sign.

'Something more to report?' was Mavis's businesslike reply to Christine's call.

'No, but I do have a question. It's about Clementine.'

'Aye.'

'Do you know exactly where and when she had her unfortunate encounter with a bicycle?'

Mavis chuckled. 'As befits Her Ladyship, she's been vague, but I believe it was last Thursday, somewhere along the King's Road. Do you have a reason for asking?'

Christine hesitated. 'I don't know yet. I need to check something out, but I'm in a bit of a rush. Tell you what, I'll phone Carol and get her to help. She'll be better at it than I would in any case. Thanks, Mavis. Bye.'

As the traffic finally eased a little, Christine realized she was approaching her destination, so decided to phone Carol after dropping off the invoice she'd promised she'd deliver. If anyone could find out if there was a connection between Clementine's smash and a poorly-spelled plea for help at the roadside, it would be Carol.

TWENTY-FIVE

Mavis hadn't made it as far as the office during the morning, though it didn't seem she'd needed to; she had her phone, her laptop and an endless supply of tea brought on little silver trays by Lindsey Newbury to see her through to lunch, plus the additional advantage that she was able to operate from a very comfy sofa in front of a warm fire with a good friend in the room and an endlessly entertaining dog to boot.

'We've had a very productive morning,' observed Althea as the women walked to the dining room for lunch. 'Don't fuss, McFli,' she added indulgently, as the little fellow yapped and circle-danced his way ahead of the women, then behind them.

'Aye, that we have,' agreed Mavis. 'Good leads from both Annie and Christine seem to confirm Ann Roberts is the girl Aubrey might have gone off with and an elopement is on the cards. Now we need to find out more about her father Rhys. It's clear the pair of them had a yen for Rome, so that might be where they were headed eventually. But how to begin that trip with no van? And our original research told us there were no flight plans made via Aubrey's computer.'

'Exactly,' replied Althea.

'I was thinking we might take a trip out to the Morris farm this afternoon, with Ian to drive us, so we could collect Carol's car. I'll drive it back to her house.'

'That's a very good cover story, Mavis. Do you think we should telephone ahead of time?'

'Och no. Let's allow it to be a wee surprise for them, having the dowager drop in,' said Mavis with a wink.

'Oh yes, let's,' said Althea, tucking into her leek and potato soup with relish.

'*Ydw*?' The tall, gangly frame of a man in his forties Mavis judged to be in need of a good bath stood in the doorway of the Morris farmhouse. Mavis had no idea what the man had said, but his expression meant she didn't need it translated to get the overall gist.

'I am Nurse Mavis MacDonald, retired, and this—' she said motioning to the diminutive figure next to her – 'is her Grace, the Dowager Duchess of Chellingworth, Lady Althea Twyst.'

As Mavis and the man in the doorway regarded Althea, she stared back at them both from beneath the brim of a waxed cotton hat that had seen better days, and from within the folds of a bilious yellow scarf which was stuffed into the front of her over-long waxed cotton jacket. Her daffodil-yellow wellies set off the outfit a treat.

'We don't want whatever it is you're selling, and we haven't got no money to give you neither,' growled the man. 'So whoever you are, you can just hop it.'

'We are not collecting for charity, young man,' said Althea in what Mavis knew to be her poshest tones, 'nor are we offering anything for sale. We are here to retrieve the motor vehicle that had to be abandoned when a pregnant woman was injured in your house, yesterday, and had to be rushed to the hospital. A matter which will be fully investigated, I am sure.'

At the word 'investigated' Mavis noticed the man stiffen. With a worried chuckle he said, 'Now, now. No need for an investigation. My missus told me some woman slipped in the hall here. That's all. Why? What's happened to her?' Mavis heard panic in the man's voice. 'What's she been saying? Wasn't even here at the time, me. I had nothing to do with it. Won't say another word, I won't.'

'Are you Mr Roberts?' said Mavis boldly.

The man's eyes narrowed. 'What's that to you?' His voice held a challenge.

Mavis was certain he was the man she was seeking. During her decades of nursing she'd met thousands of men who'd gone to do battle for their country, and she'd learned some of them were there for the simple reason that they liked to be in a fight – any fight, for any reason, with anyone. Their natural state of being was to always be ready to throw a punch when a well-formed sentence would do the trick just as well. She judged the Roberts man to be of that ilk.

'Sir, the health of the woman injured in this house is a matter to be discussed at a future date. For now, we are simply here to retrieve her car. Of course, we wouldn't have dreamed of removing it without telling a responsible person that we were doing so. Are you such a person? Do you have standing with the Morris family?'

It was clear to Mavis that her manner had caught the man off guard. He scratched his greasy hair with a grubby hand that held a half-smoked hand rolled cigarette and a book of matches. Turning in the doorway he shouted, 'Netta, there's someone here to take that woman's car. Can they have it?'

Mavis and Althea waited patiently. They, and the man at the door, knew they were under the watchful gaze of Ian Cottesloe who, once again, had followed his employer's instructions and was sitting in the dowager's car – with his head poking out of the window.

A tired-looking woman arrived at the door, which the man opened wider to allow her to see the two women.

'Good afternoon, I am Mavis MacDonald, and this is—'

'Your Grace!' said the woman, dropping the tea towel upon which she'd been drying her hands. 'What are you . . . Rhys, why didn't you say? Your Grace, did you want to come in?' Mavis could sense the woman's consternation and decided to make full use of it.

'Lady Althea and I have been unable to get any information out of this man. Who is he? And who are you?' Mavis used her gentle tone, with just a hint of the matron about it.

Pushing lank locks behind her ears, the woman all but curtsied. 'I'm Netta. Mrs Netta Roberts. This is Rhys, my husband. Mr Herbert Morris, who owns this farm, is my uncle. How is she, the poor woman that fell here yesterday? Is she alright? Is the baby alright? Ever so worried I've been about her. Her husband was so frightened when I spoke to him on the phone. Do you know how she is?'

Mavis judged real concern on the part of Netta Roberts, and allowed a warm smile to crease her face as she replied, 'Quite well, my dear. The hospital gave her and the baby a clean bill of health. But your husband could have been more helpful, had he but tried. We simply wanted to ensure we told a member of the family that we were taking Carol's car. You understand I am sure, my dear.' She touched the woman's arm as she spoke – a sign of reassurance and a bridge to build confidence, she always felt. Netta Roberts winced, which worried Mavis a great deal.

Glaring up at her husband, Netta said, 'Poor Rhys. Got a lot on his mind he has. Sorry about that. You take it. It's been there all night, safe as houses.'

Mavis reckoned it was time to play the professional card. 'Carol Hill, who was here yesterday, and I belong to the company of private enquiry agents retained to find Aubrey Morris. Do either of you have any information regarding his whereabouts?'

'No, we don't know nothin',' snapped Rhys Roberts. 'You've no business meddling in family matters. So why don't the two of you just take the blessed car and hop it.'

Pushing his wife aside roughly and starting to close the door, Mavis heard Netta cry, 'You can't speak to a duchess like that.'

'I'll speak to anyone I want any way I like,' then he added some remarks in Welsh Mavis guessed were a little more colorful and the door closed.

Trudging toward Carol's car Althea said, 'Didn't like the look of him. She seemed alright though.'

Mavis smiled at her fiend's perspicacity. 'You're a good judge of character, Althea. I agree with you.'

'And he's got something to hide, though she doesn't seem to know anything.'

'I agree, on both counts.'

'I wonder who could tell us about him,' said Althea as she waited for Mavis to open the passenger door.

'I think I might know,' said Mavis. 'Let's make sure this starts, then Ian can get off back to the Dower House. We both need to drop in on someone in the village.'

'Who's that?' said Althea, sliding on the car seat in her damp waxed cotton ensemble.

'How do you fancy a quick snifter, Althea? I saw Rhys Roberts was holding a book of matches from the Lamb and Flag pub. Now, given that I thought printed books of matches had gone the way of the Dodo, and the fact you haven't even been able to smoke in a pub for some considerable time, I might be setting us off on the wrong track. But we don't have another. So do you fancy finding out if Tudor Evans has a good sherry behind his bar before we go to dress for dinner with your son and his affianced?'

'It's very exotic being an enquiry agent, isn't it?' mused Althea as Ian led off down the rutted track that led to the main road, with Mavis taking things very carefully in Carol's car behind him.

'Exotic? I'd no' thought of it as being any such thing,' replied Mavis, bemused.

'I've been to an old house with a shrine to a dead mother and a living but mysterious girlfriend, to a farmhouse with a gruff man at the front door, and now I'm off to a pub in the middle of the afternoon. By my book, that's extremely exotic.'

Mavis smiled as she stared at the track ahead of her, not daring to turn to face her friend. 'Ach you toffs, all you really yearn for is to see how we normal folks live, and you're happy.'

'Not having been born a toff, but having become one, I'll grant you that,' sighed Althea. 'Tea brought on a silver tray can become very boring.'

Chuckling Mavis said, 'No' to me, my dear, no' to me.'

TWENTY-SIX

Annie's father received a loving welcome when he presented himself at her cottage. It took a while for Rodney Parker to dislodge his wife Eustelle from his midsection, but eventually she released him so she could make a pot of tea in the kitchen.

'Got something for you, Dad,' said Annie once they were alone, holding out the packets of Fisherman's Friends she'd bought. 'Don't know how you've got any taste buds left, the way you eat these things like Smarties, but I know you love them.'

Her father beamed, then said, 'And I got something for you too.'

He handed Annie a tin that had once held Cadbury's Roses – and Annie felt her tummy flip as she stood to open it.

'I didn't know you still had these,' she said, beaming. 'Do you remember we walked along one of the beaches in St Lucia, the morning before we all flew back home, and I picked up these shells along the shoreline? Look at them, Dad – they're like little jewels.'

Annie's father stood to peer into the tin. His thin fingers touched the mound of shells and little stones, and he swirled them about in their rusted metal container. Annie noticed his eyes had misted and she wondered what he was thinking.

'Penny for 'em?'

Removing his hand, Rodney Parker drew himself up to his full height, so he was almost as tall as his daughter. 'That was the last time I ever saw my home. Always said we'd go back, but we never made it. Those shells were there, and we brought them here. Not fair they should be locked up in an old tin. You should take them back to the sea. Give them a chance to be free.'

Annie was intrigued by her father's response to the shells. 'Do you feel like you've been stuck in an old tin box all these years, Dad? You know, in London, driving buses?'

Her father turned from her and spoke quietly. 'No. We came here for a better life, and we got that. Especially for you. But when you leave that light, that life – well, you cannot help but miss it. It's in your blood. Your mother, she tries to keep it all going with food, and decorating, you know. I'm surprised she hasn't got you to paint this place like ours back in Plaistow – bit of yellow here, a shelf unit or two of green there, bright blue on the trim. But, you see girl, it ain't until you get to be a bit older that you begin to wonder what "better" really means.'

Annie had never heard her father speak like this, and she felt uncertain about what to say next. 'That morning was special to me too, Dad, but for a different reason.'

'And what's that, my girl?' asked her father indulgently.

'It was the last time I walked on the beach with my dad.

But saying that, there's nothing to stop all three of us going back to St Lucia for a visit, you know. I've got a bit of money in the bank at last, and I'd love a chance to see everyone, and go everywhere, with me parents.'

Her father shook his head sadly. 'It's too late, girl. Too late.'

Annie wondered if there was something her father wasn't telling her. 'Are you alright, Dad? I mean, you're not ill or nothin', are you?'

'Don't I look alright?'

'Yeah, you look fine. Just like always. But . . . the way you're talking. You're worrying me.'

Her father reached out and put his arm around her. 'I'm sorry, girl. I don't mean to do that. No father would ever do that to his girl.'

Thinking about all the texts and emails she'd received from Mavis, Carol and Christine, Annie said, 'What *would* a father do for his girl, Dad?'

'How d'you mean?'

'Let's just say – and this for a case I'm working on – let's just say your daughter was sweethearts with a young man you thought was somehow unsuitable. We think they might be planning to elope, but, although the couple belong to the same family, they aren't blood relatives, so that's not the problem. If it's not about that, what would make you try to keep them apart?'

'Could be a lot a t'ings,' he replied simply. 'They love each other?'

'Well, that's the thing. There were letters between them over many years, and they were always a bit lovey-dovey, in an airy-fairy way. Not realistic at all. That's why I called them sweethearts. But a more recent letter suggests they might be about to run off together to get married. Any ideas about why a father would be dead set against a boy getting together with his daughter from the time they were kids?'

'Only two things gonna make a father do that, if he knows that keepin' them apart is gonna make his girl unhappy. One is his ego – he hates the family, and he won't have her joining it because of his reasons. The other could be his love for his girl – if he t'inks she'll be in danger somehow with the boy, or his family. Can only be them two t'ings. One comes from love of himself, one from love for her. Being a father is simple – you have to put your child first, not yourself. If it comes from love for her, even if he knows it's gonna cause her pain, he'll stick to his guns. Not knowin' this man, I'll give him the benefit of the doubt. The boy's dangerous for the girl.'

'But how can a *kid* be dangerous?' mused Annie aloud. 'If all that we're hearing is true, the father's tried to keep them apart since they were just little. It sounds a bit like Romeo and Juliet. You know, young love and all that.'

'Don't forget that play was about two teenagers who knew each other for three days, and six people ended up dead,' said her father with a twinkle. 'It's not a good way to t'ink about love and romance. I don't know what any other parent would do, but I know what I'd do; if a boy was dangerous for you, I'd keep you away from him, any way I could. Have you asked your mother what she t'inks?'

Grinning at her father, Annie said, 'Asked Eustelle? Nah – I wanted a father's perspective.'

'Never call her Mum, do you? Never did. Why is that?' said Rodney.

'Her name's Eustelle.'

'I know, girl, but she's your mother. Don't you t'ink she might like you to use that name for her? You're the only person in the world with the right to do so.'

Annie was surprised. Her father had never said anything like that before. It was as though her world had shifted off its axis just a little. Not usually lost for words, she found the experience unsettling.

'Tea's up,' called her mother from the back of the house. She walked into the sitting room carrying a tray. 'Now, tell me what you t'ink of this hat, child.'

Eustelle Parker might have been wearing a plain yellow apron over a simple red dress, but the edifice on top of her head was a riot of color. Three feet wide, eighteen inches from back to front, not only was the flying-saucer shaped hat a monster, but the fact it seemed to have twice as many colors woven into its straw construction as a rainbow stopped Annie in her tracks.

'Gordon Bennett, I'd forgotten it looked like that! It's so
. . . colorful.'

'Sure t'ing,' said Eustelle with a grin, waving a tea towel
and strutting in circles around the tiny room. 'Goes wit'
everyt'ing, this does. That's why it's lasted thirty years. Lookin'
good, right?'

Eustelle clearly expected a supportive, if not enthusiastic,
reaction, and she got both from her husband.

Grabbing her arms in a formal dance pose, Rodney swung
his wife about, making little growling noises. 'You know what
that hat does to me,' he said making faces that alarmed Annie.
'Remember the last time you wore it? Winston's grandson got
married, and we danced all night.' He grasped his wife who
let out a little squeal.

'Come on you two, there are children present,' said Annie
squirming.

'You shouldn't be listenin',' replied her happy mother with
a wink.

Annie left her parents to act like kids as she slipped upstairs
to get her phone. Reaching Mavis, the women had a good
discussion about the possibility there might be something in
the background of Aubrey Morris's part of the family that
would have Ann Roberts's father dead set against even a
budding romance. Something that might drive Rhys Roberts
to do any number of things to keep a young couple apart.
Finally Annie asked, 'So, what have you been up to?'

'We've just left the Lamb and Flag,' replied Mavis, 'though
we didn't get much out of your Tudor Evans.'

Annie chuckled throatily. 'He's not *my* Tudor Evans, Mave.
How is he, by the way?'

Annie thought she could hear Mavis smiling when she
replied, 'No much different than when you saw him yesterday.
He confirmed Ann Roberts's father used to be a sometime
drinker at his pub, but that he's seen little of him since the
smoking ban. He assured me that's not unusual, especially for
the smokers. I judged him to be choosing his words carefully
when he spoke of the man, though it's clear to me he didn't
care for him much. He mentioned his well-known temper, and
the fact he'd had to ban him from the Lamb and Flag, on three

separate occasions, for a month each time. He knows little else about the Roberts part of the family up at the Morris farm.'

'So he seemed alright then, did he?' pressed Annie, as innocently as possible.

'Tudor seemed concerned that your dad would arrive in plenty of time for the wedding, and to see him perform,' added Mavis.

Annie knew she was grinning when she answered. 'Really?' She hoped she'd managed to sound nonchalant. Annie felt both fourteen and fifty-four years old at the same time, and, for some reason she couldn't fathom, she was just fine with that.

TWENTY-SEVEN

As Edward stood back for Althea and Mavis to enter Chellingworth Hall, Althea announced, 'Young Ian will return with our luggage presently. Mrs MacDonald has asked that you do not unpack for her.'

'No, thank you, Edward,' said Mavis, smiling as brightly as she could. It seemed most peculiar to her that there was a class of person for whom folks poking through their most private possessions was quite acceptable, yet who baulked at the suggestion those same people should be permitted to share a meal at the table with them. But, Mavis reasoned, she hadn't had over fifty years to get used to it, as had Althea.

'We'll not be late at dinner, Edward,' warned Althea, and Cook Wilson and Miss Jennifer will be coming with Young Ian when he returns. We'll all be here at the hall from tonight until the day after the wedding. I know it's an upheaval for all of us, and you too, but I think Miss Stephanie is correct when she says it makes sense to have all hands available here, on the spot.'

Edward's reply of, 'Certainly, Your Grace,' did nothing to inform Mavis of his opinion on the matter, though she noticed he was a little more fleet of foot than usual when he left them at the open door to the drawing room, which was still acting as a reception room before dinner.

Henry, Stephanie, Clementine, Nurse Thomas and Christine were already enjoying drinks, and some brittle conversation.

Stephanie looked disappointed as Althea and Mavis entered. 'Lost a tenner and found sixpence?' asked Mavis of Stephanie as she accepted a sherry from the duke.

The bride-to-be rallied. 'Sorry, I was hoping you'd be Mum and Dad. They're late coming down for dinner.' She looked at her wristwatch. 'I don't know where they can have got to. I said six thirty for seven, and it's ten to. Oh, there they are.' A relieved smile suffused Stephanie Timbers' face with a genuine warmth, and Mavis turned to see the parents of the bride. This was their first opportunity to meet Althea, their home in Spain meaning Henry and Stephanie had flown out for him to seek their permission to marry their daughter.

Whatever Mavis had expected, John and Sheila Timbers were not it. Following Carol's disclosures about the man, which Mavis had suggested were best kept to herself, she'd half thought he'd look like a bit of a thug. Instead, he was short, dapper in a dark suit, deeply tanned, with silver, well-barbered hair and gray-green eyes that glittered in the firelight. The mother was equally well-tanned – *surely it wasn't that sunny in Spain in the winter?* – and obviously a devotee of both the gym and a clothing designer who favored angles, zips and very bright colors.

Mavis noticed Clementine had perked up as she called from her chair, 'Is that a Teikikomo?'

Sheila Timbers smiled an affirmative, but was not to be swayed from her main objective, Henry Twyst's cheek, which she kissed firmly, leaving a smear of pink lip gloss on Henry's wintry-pale skin. Mavis noted his look of alarm, and also the way he steered Stephanie's parents directly toward his mother.

'My mother, the Dowager Althea,' said Henry – quite formally thought Mavis.

'Your Grace,' said Sheila, bobbing. Mavis tried to hide what she felt was an unfair smirk. Having got to know Althea as a person, she found it most peculiar that anyone would think of curtseying to her.

'Your Grace,' said John Timbers, nodding his head.

Mavis's heart warmed even more to her friend when Althea stood up and hugged each of them saying, 'I'm not Her Majesty, you are allowed to touch me, you know. Come along now, let Henry get you a drink. We'll all be family before too long, and we should make an effort to get to know each other. In company such as this I am to be Althea, plain and simple. You may save the correct form for when we aren't just a family group – or as good as,' she said grinning at Mavis and Christine.

The rest of the introductions that followed took quite some time. Both Sheila and John Timbers seemed to be surprised to hear an enquiries agency was being operated on the estate, that two of its members were in the room and Althea was also involved. 'Been running background checks on any of us, have you?' quipped John Timbers – maybe a little too jovially, thought Mavis.

'Why? What would we discover, other than that you're a man who built a fair fortune as a lumber merchant, then sold up to enjoy his retirement in a villa on Spain's Costa del Sol?' said Mavis cheerily. She knew a few things she could have added, but chose not to.

She was sure she noticed a flush beneath his tan as John Timbers chuckled heartily and said, 'Not much else to know, really.'

'Just back from the Caribbean, Sheila?' asked Christine. Mavis suspected she wanted to show off her powers of deduction a little.

Looking a little taken aback the petite blonde answered, 'Yes, actually. Though how did you—'

'How did I know? The tan. Your jewelry. The designer label clothes. As Clementine noticed, that's a Teikikomo dress. He has a store in that new upmarket area in St Thomas, I understand.'

'Have you met him? He's delightful. Doesn't say much, of course,' piped up Clementine from her wheelchair. Mavis realized maybe Lady Clementine's broken leg hadn't been explained to Stephanie's parents – she assumed Stephanie would have done so herself, but the worried look on her mother's face made Mavis wonder about that. Sheila Timbers kept staring at Clementine's appendage as though it were some sort of cannon taking aim at her; she kept trying to move herself out of the line of fire, but Clementine – who seemed to have gained some level of competence at maneuvering her chair – kept shifting so that her foot was once again pointing directly at Mrs Timbers.

'We don't really mix with designers and such,' said Sheila quietly, eyeing Clementine's foot.

Unsure about taking a seat, Sheila Timbers hovered beside her husband, becoming gradually paler beneath her tan. Mavis felt sorry for the couple, especially when she worked out that Stephanie's fiancé was probably only a few years younger than her father – dwelling on the unpredictability of love sent Mavis's mind back to the case of the missing Aubrey Morris. She sidled toward Althea and hissed, 'Where's the New Buttery?'

'Pardon?' replied Althea.

'The New Buttery, where they found the Anwen Morris artefacts. Where is it?'

Mavis noticed Althea was smiling as she whispered back, 'You've seen it. It's that neoclassical monstrosity out behind the stables. They built it in the 1700s to replace the old buttery, which I suppose they used to simply call the buttery.' She paused and looked around before she added, 'Given the size of it, they must have liked their butter around here. It's huge.'

Mavis tried to visualize the building Althea had referred to. It wasn't at all what she'd have imagined to be a buttery – old or new. She and Althea often walked the grounds around the hall, and she was now more than passingly familiar with most of the parts of the hall itself, and the many buildings that adjoined or surrounded it. From the folly in the water garden to the original Elizabethan stables, she was in awe of it all. The building Althea had mentioned was about half the size of a football field, had a collection of classical female figures wearing diaphanous garments made of intricately carved stone acting as though they were supporting the portico and roof, and blank, windowless walls. Mavis wondered how they'd had enough light in there to churn butter all those centuries ago, and why on earth they'd made the building so large.

'Did you have a lot of dairy cattle back then?' asked Mavis quietly, nodding and smiling as though having a much more socially engaging conversation than she was.

Althea followed her lead and laughed a little too loudly, drawing a surprised glance from Henry, who was occupying his favorite spot in front of the fireplace. 'I'm not quite that old, dear, but I know what you mean. And no. I understand the Twysts provided buttery facilities for any and all of the dairy farmers in the area. A sort of community service, I suppose.'

'The Morris farm was all sheep, wasn't it, back then, as it is now?' asked Mavis.

Althea paused and gave the matter some thought. 'I do believe there was a friendly rivalry between the Twysts and the Morrises about something to do with the church and sheep, but that would have been back before the New Buttery was even built. Does it matter?'

'Isn't it lambing season?' said Mavis, rather more loudly than she had meant to.

'Yes, it is for some farms,' replied Stephanie. Mavis suspected it was because the poor girl was trying to find a topic of conversation that wouldn't flag. 'The farmers hereabouts try to plan it so that their ewes – all being well, of course – give birth over about a three-week period, and they also try to stagger those times. Some might go for an early start date, like March 1st, or some might hold back until April. That way it means they're more likely to be able to call upon experienced local help with the lambing, get easier access to vets as needed, and, of course, there are the students who get work experience through the National Sheep Association. From next week for the next couple of months it'll all be about the lambs around here.'

Mavis was surprised by Stephanie's very comprehensive answer.

'Thank you so much,' she replied quietly.

'It sounds so odd, thinking about creatures all giving birth to some sort of a timetable,' said Sheila Timbers brightly. 'It's not how I've ever thought about country life.'

'But your family business relied upon the natural cycle, didn't it?' said Henry airily from beside the hearth. 'The growth of trees, their harvesting and processing into lumber. You cannot have been completely unaware of the natural rhythms of country life, surely?'

Mavis could tell John and Sheila Timbers were far from familiar with Henry's dismissive tone, and she felt sorry for Stephanie who – now used to her fiancé's ways – rushed to her parents' defense.

'Not really, Henry, dear,' she said cheerily. 'Trees take such a long time to grow – even the fast-growing softwoods – that those who plant them are rarely those who benefit from their harvesting. And the connection between grower and harvester isn't as clear either. Daddy used to buy swaths of timber, not saplings, didn't you, Daddy?'

'Indeed,' was all that John Timbers could manage.

Mavis sensed yet another avenue of conversation had been run to ground, so decided to act in a rather cavalier manner. 'Lady Clementine was telling us about her accident. She's very fortunate to have come out of it so well, weren't you, Lady Clementine?'

Mavis judged that giving Clemmie a chance to act the wounded diva would provide an entertaining distraction that would last just long enough to get them all into dinner. She hoped it would be a light, and not overly long, meal, because she had to unpack her bags, settle in to her room, and get a good night's sleep. She was determined to go out and take a good look around the New Buttery early the next morning, before she headed off to St David's Church to be an extra pair of hands for the flower arranging there. She didn't want to rush to any conclusions, but she hoped as soon as she refreshed her memory of the lay of the land around the building in question, she might have one more inkling about how the ancient Morris implements had come to be delivered, unseen, to Chellingworth Hall.

TWENTY-EIGHT

Thursday, February 27th

C arol had slept very poorly, and suspected the midnight snack of ice cream might have had something to do with her discomfort. Bunty was curled on the chair next to the Aga when Carol shuffled into the kitchen. 'Not even going to acknowledge I exist, are you?' she said to the sleeping cat. Bunty didn't stir. Not even a whisker.

'I'd do the same if I were you,' said Carol aloud. 'Nice and cozy in here, it is. Rest of the place could do with a bit more heat, and a few more draft excluders. I'll pull out that old pattern I had for making decorative stuffies to put at the bottom of our doors. What do you think, Bunty, my girl? Fancy some stuffies to play with?'

At the word 'play', Bunty deigned to open an eye and peered at Carol. But that was it.

When David Hill joined his wife for breakfast she'd already finished. 'Right, I'm off to the office, which, for the sake of comfort, will be the table in the dining room today,' she announced. 'Nothing too strenuous, I promise. As you know, I'm going to help with the flowers at the church later on, but I've got some stuff I need to do here first.'

Her husband kissed the top of her head and fussed about with something in the fridge as he replied, 'I'm glad you'll just be doing some quiet desk work. It's what you need after a fall like that. I'm sure the others can manage without your help on this case.'

Carol decided it best not to mention she was working on two new cases on behalf of the WISE women, so she simply grabbed her glass of milk, and set herself up at her makeshift desk.

Right-ho, she thought as she powered up two laptops, checked her phone signal and set about seeing if the plans she'd put in place the day before were beginning to pay off. She was eager to see what had happened overnight, and was delighted to see a good deal of useful information in her inbox.

Sitting at a dining table in deepest Powys, Carol thanked the logistics genius in Hong Kong for supplying her with data she'd been able to unearth about the mobile phone sent to the duke. Carol's purpose had been to track the manufacturer, shipper and ultimate retailer of the mobile phone that had been dumped into the box, and then to speak to the retailers who had sold the phone, in an effort to discover who had bought the item. With the answers her contacts had furnished her with, she was able to contact a curious shopkeeper in Cowbridge, who confirmed the identities of two young men who'd bought the phone a couple of days earlier. He happened to know both their names because they were local lads, and he was delighted to pass the names on to Carol because he was sick and tired of them lolly-gagging about outside his shop.

Carol phoned Stephanie's still distraught dressmaker, Megan Davies, and discovered she knew the two young men in question – referring to them as local Jack the Lads who had a running dispute with one of her brothers. She assured Carol she'd pass the information on to her local police, who'd already been to her workshop to investigate the break-in. Carol made Megan promise to phone her back when she had any news, which the grateful woman did.

Carol knew she couldn't just twiddle her thumbs while she waited for an update about The Case of the Severed Sleeve, so decided to follow through with her other, unpaid, work. A lengthy conversation the previous afternoon with an old colleague of hers, who now worked for the Met Police in their data management center, had helped her formulate what she thought was a rather cunning plan. Her friend had told her the sign Christine had seen on the King's Road was not unusual; many people who needed witnesses to an accident would display such notices close to the scene, hoping people who traveled a regular route might have spotted something useful.

What had really interested Carol was that her friend also mentioned that, although no pattern was yet discernible, such signs were appearing with increasing regularity near places where no injuries had been reported to the police other than those sustained by a motorist who'd – somehow or other – managed to crush a bicycle. Bound by professional ethics, Carol's old chum hadn't been able to say much more, but Carol had got the gist; there was some sort of con going on, and it looked as though Clementine Twyst was just about to be dragged into an unpleasant situation.

Off the record, Carol and her mate had discussed an 'hypothetical situation' which involved a moneymaking scam perpetrated by an organized group comprising 'victims' and 'witnesses', with hapless, and often injured, motorists being convinced they could make an expensive lawsuit go away by paying off a cyclist they'd 'hit' who was suffering from whiplash. Carol's idea had been to use social media to try to build a profile of 'evidence' from the public at large, so she was delighted to find that #crushedcyclistcon was trending on Twitter by the morning.

As she scrolled through the online feed her initial Tweets to her considerable list of networked contacts had spawned, she saw snippets of despair and anger from all parts of London, and even beyond. Hiding behind their anonymous 'handles', people seemed happy to share information about times, places, amounts paid, threats received and injuries sustained in what appeared to be a spate of 'accidents' that bore a striking similarity to that which had caused Clementine to break her leg so badly.

Carol typed in a few more Tweets with judicious wording, and watched as the responses rolled in. It was quite clear Lady Twyst was not alone in believing she'd hit a bicycle but no cyclist, she just hadn't been contacted about the amount she'd have to cough up to shut up her 'victim' yet. Carol was delighted – not for the poor people who'd already been conned, of course – because she could now go back to her Met Police contact with enough evidence to allow them to start piecing something together that might at least stop the scam from spreading. Maybe, if the police had known about the con when they'd interviewed Clementine, they could have warned her about possible demands for money. Carol knew such a warning would be a great comfort to those who'd suffered the trauma of an accident, so she phoned her friend and directed her to the trending information on Twitter. A conversation about the usefulness of social media ensued, and Carol finally hung up feeling she'd achieved a great deal by tackling what she thought of as The Case of the Crushed Cyclist Con, even though the WISE Enquiries Agency wasn't being paid a bean by anyone to even look into it, let alone solve it before it impacted someone they knew.

Carol finally realized she needed to get herself sorted out if she was going to be on time to meet Mavis at the church to help with the flowers, but she knew she wouldn't be able to settle her mind until she'd spoken to Stephanie's dressmaker again. She wondered about the wisdom of phoning a woman who'd promised to give her any updates, but did it anyway.

'Hello again, Megan – sorry to bother you, but I wondered if—' she began, only to be interrupted with a joyous: 'They've got it!' at the other end of the line.

'They've found Stephanie's wedding dress?' asked Carol, wanting to be clear.

'Yes,' squealed Megan. 'They've been ever so good, our local bobbies. Went right over to the house of one of the boys, who wasn't home, so then they went to the other one's house and found both dresses there. Only the one sleeve is damaged, they said, and they won't hold it for evidence or nothin'. I can go and get it now. I was going to phone you before I jumped in the car, honest I was. Isn't it wonderful? Aren't they lovely?'

Carol was delighted, of course, but curious too. 'So the boys stole two wedding dresses, did they?'

'Yes. Stephanie's and another one.'

'And who's the other dress for?' Carol thought she might have an inkling.

Megan sounded wistful. 'An old schoolfriend of mine, from up your way. Ann Roberts. Due to collect it on Monday, she is. So now she won't even need to know it was ever missing. Bit of luck, really, 'cause I've still got some hemming to do on it, but maybe that can wait until after I've sorted out Stephanie's sleeve. You've got it there, safe, haven't you?' Panic tinged the poor woman's voice. 'And you promise it's not badly ripped or nothing, right? I'll never be able to match the fabric, see.'

'No worries, Megan. The sleeve is here, in its box, and it looks to have been ripped off at the stitching, so the fabric is fine. I'll get it over to Chellingworth Hall. I'm guessing you'll be visiting there for a final fitting?'

'Absolutely. I'm going to phone Stephanie as soon as I've got the dress in my car, so I know it's safe.'

'Right-ho, I'll leave that up to you then,' said Carol, 'but, tell me, did you have any other wedding dresses there at the time of the break-in?'

'Yes, about half a dozen.'

'But only Stephanie's and Ann's were taken?'

'Yes.'

'And were the dresses labelled – did they have the bride's names on them?'

'Oh yes, and their contact details, fitting information and photos of them wearing them. Got to keep it all together, see.'

'I see. Thanks for that. I just want you to know I'll be getting in touch with your local police. I want to let them know about a connection with a possible missing persons case we're working on up here. Nothing for you to worry about, but who would you say has been the most helpful person you've been dealing with there?'

Carol thought she could hear Megan smile as she replied, 'PC Duffy, she's been great. If you need anything, you should talk to her. I'd better go now, alright?'

'Yes, you go, and thanks,' said Carol, and hung up feeling very satisfied. She immediately checked the number for the police in Bridgend and finally reached PC Duffy. She explained who she was and suggested she might have some useful information pertaining to the break-in at Megan's workshop.

PC Duffy turned out to be a good listener, but not very forthcoming with regards to the case. She grudgingly agreed to phone Carol if anything came of a possible link between Ann Roberts's stolen wedding dress and Rhys Roberts, father of the planning-to-elope bride.

'Modern technology mixed with good old-fashioned enquiring triumphs again,' said Carol to herself as, feeling supremely satisfied with her efforts, she went to shower and dress. Ready to head out to help with the flower arranging, she made herself a Marmite and lime marmalade sandwich which she stuffed into her handbag and tramped across the green just in time to meet Mavis at the gate to the church grounds. As they walked along the path through the graveyard catching up, Mavis was suitably impressed with Carol's achievements of the day and was intrigued by her idea that maybe there was some connection between the two lads in Bridgend and Rhys Roberts. Neither woman could think of anyone else who might want Ann Roberts's wedding dress stolen, but both were convinced it was a planned theft, because there couldn't be a good reason for only stealing the two dresses that had been selected.

Finally taking in their surroundings, Carol said, 'I don't suppose they bury anyone here anymore. All cremations now, I should think.'

'Planning that far ahead, are you?' quipped Mavis.

Carol knew her colleague was half-joking, but she wasn't. 'Sort of. I like it here. It feels right. I fit. I never fitted in in London. Not really. I do here. And I think Bump will too.'

Their pace slowed. It was a dry day, if bleak, so they both snuggled into their collars as Mavis said, 'I'm glad of that. You deserve it. And I feel the same. I don't know how long it will last, but I enjoy Althea's company, and what's not to love about living at the Dower House?'

Carol smiled. 'Yes, our house is lovely too. And now that we've cleared all our decorating plans with the estate office, we can make it more our own. They're being very good to us, aren't they? Us, and Annie and Christine too, of course.'

'Aye, that they are. Seems to me Althea and the late duke set a good example to Henry, and they were following in some good traditions too. I went out to the building where they found the Anwen Morris pieces this morning – it's in a place where almost anyone could have laid those pieces down and no one would have seen them. However, I think it would have been difficult to *get* there without being seen. I had a word with a few people in the kitchen, which looks out in that general direction, and a couple agreed they'd seen an old Land

Rover out there for a wee while. Now I know that doesn't narrow things down a great deal around here, but one of the things Tudor Evans told Althea and me yesterday afternoon was that Ann Roberts's father used to drive such a vehicle. Tudor commented he'd had to leave it outside the pub on a few occasions when hc'd had one, or five, too many. So that's another indicator he might be mixed up in all this.'

'Good point, though I can't imagine why Tudor didn't tell you about knowing the Roberts man earlier in the day. You did say you'd asked him, didn't you?' said Carol.

'I dinnae think he was tryin' to hold anything back. I believe I asked him about knowing the Morrises, and Tudor tends to take things quite literally.'

Carol nodded her agreement. 'I'm starting to feel there might be enough circumstantial evidence for us to go to the police again and present them with our findings. What do you think? Do you think they might take Aubrey Morris's disappearance more seriously if we could point them toward a possible elopement, the Morris farm and the violent Mr Roberts?'

'I think we need a team chat about it. Unless something comes up that prevents us from doing it, I'd like all four of us to have a face-to-face meeting early this afternoon. At the office if we can manage it, you could Skype in from your home. I'd like us to be able to speak to the police before the end of the day. What do you think?'

The two women had wandered down a side path rather than heading into the church, to allow them to carry on talking. Having now reached the end of their chat, Carol once again cast her eyes across the verdant grass, the grey, brown and glinting white marble headstones of the graveyard, and she pointed to two graves side by side. 'Two Morrises. I wonder which ones they are.'

Crossing the wet grass she bent down to read the inscriptions. 'This one goes back to 1793. Look at this – three children, all less than a year old, a mother, father and a grown daughter. How sad.'

'It comes to us all,' observed Mavis.

'This one's much more modern,' said Carol, her voice

muffled by her scarf. 'I think this must be Aubrey Morris's grandparents. The dates look to be about right.' Her head popped up and she looked around. 'There's another stone that's even fresher, and that's a Morris too.' She strode out and stooped to read. 'Yes, this is Aubrey's mum and dad. See? "Beloved wife and mother". Gosh, none of them made old bones, did they?'

'Those were the times,' said Mavis sadly.

Carol stood upright. 'Not really. Yes, I get it that the ones back in the 1700s might not live into old age, but neither did Aubrey's parents or grandparents. Look at these other people, at much the same time.' Carol's ability with numbers always astonished Mavis. Making rapid calculations, Carol said, 'The average age of a man buried here is about seventy-odd, and the women a little older. But the last two generations of the Morris family? In their forties or fifties. Very sad. Maybe they just aren't a strong family.'

'It can happen,' said Mavis. Carol noticed she was looking particularly thoughtful when she added, 'Annie said something interesting last night on the phone. She said her dad would do anything to keep her from coming to harm. Now Ann Roberts and Aubrey Morris aren't related, but what if her father thought her life might be endangered simply by consorting with, or eventually marrying, Aubrey?'

'You mean as if Aubrey has some sort of disease he could pass to her, that's led to early deaths in his part of the Morris family?'

Mavis shook her head. 'Aye, that's what I mean, but it makes no sense.' Carol saw Mavis's expression change as she spotted someone scurrying along the path to the church.

'There's our boss for the day, Marjorie Pritchard. We'd best be on our way, or I've a feeling we'll be chided for tardiness.'

Carol grinned. 'She's almost a professional chider, you know?'

'Come away then, let's be off. Let's leave the dead and join the living.'

'Good plan. So, what's in store for us, do you know?'

'No idea. This was the only thing I could offer to help with, so I hope I can do a good job. I dare say I can follow instructions, if they're given.' Mavis winked.

'This is Marjorie we're talking about, there'll be instruction a-plenty, trust me,' replied Carol with a grin.

Upon entering the oak doors to the ancient church it was immediately apparent to Carol that some sort of kerfuffle was taking place at the chancel steps where Sharon from the shop and her father were having a loud discussion with Marjorie. The serried ranks of the Jacobean wooden pews had been polished, the narrow nave was full of women rushing about holding vases of daffodils in bud, and the hangings on the altar and pulpit (the kind gift of the third Duke of Chellingworth in thanks for the safe delivery of his first son) and even the stone font near the door (the kind gift of the third duke on the safe arrival of his second son) had all been changed to white, in readiness for the wedding.

'Once we manage to escape from here I'll phone everyone to arrange getting together at the office for a meeting this afternoon. How about that?'

Carol nodded, then they entered the fray, both determined not to be forced to take a side in the battle being fought over the positioning of the daffodils.

TWENTY-NINE

It was half past two when three of the four women of the WISE Enquiries Agency found themselves sitting in a circle around the coffee table in their office, with Carol on Skype via a laptop.

'Althea sends her apologies,' announced Mavis bringing the meeting to order. 'She agreed to join Stephanie and Sheila Timbers for the final re-fitting of Stephanie's wedding gown, which was being driven up from Bridgend by the dressmaker. It's all thanks to Carol's amazing skills and contacts that the dress has been found and returned. I understand this fitting, and the reattachment of the sleeve, is a process that might take some time, so I suggested we had this meeting without Althea. As our client in this matter she has agreed to abide by our decision, whatever it might be.'

'I think it's time we get back to the cops,' said Annie slurping coffee.

'We should discuss our findings first, then reach a team agreement,' said Mavis very properly.

'Mavis is correct,' replied Christine. 'We need to see where we stand, especially if we're going to ask the police to become involved in the case of a missing person.'

'Given that we only really began to work on the case just before lunchtime on Monday, I think we've done quite well,' added Carol, 'but Mavis and Christine are right, in order to get the police to recognize that Aubrey Morris and quite possibly Ann Roberts are truly "missing", we have to get our ducks in a row. Do you want to take it from the top, Mavis?'

Everyone knew the answer would be yes, so the three women waited as Mavis began by standing and walking about – which they all knew meant she was thinking.

'Are you up to creating a workmanlike document as I speak?' she asked Carol, who nodded at the laptop screen's camera, her hands hovering over an invisible keyboard.

'Ready when you are – and I can cut and paste in the more detailed parts of reports we've been sending each other to make it look even more impressive, plus the photos we have of the missing man, the van etc. You kick off with the major points, I'll build an outline then fill it in later. How about that?' Carol beamed at her colleagues, who all smiled back – glad to see she was back to her usual self, and none the worse for her episode at the Morris farmhouse.

'Very well,' began Mavis. 'Aubrey Morris failed to keep an appointment with Tudor Evans on Sunday evening, and we were brought into the case late on Monday morning. We have established the following facts from more than one source in each case: Aubrey Morris is a likeable, well-respected handyman, with a reputation as a quiet, studious, reliable person. Something of a loner, he has taken on the family business and run it well, even growing its reach. Both his parents are dead. He is related to the Morris family at the Morris farm. He lives

modestly at the family home, which was given to his grandfather by the Morris family. He seems to have had a very
particular friendship over the years with Ann Roberts, the
granddaughter of the Morris at the farm. Aubrey and Ann are
not related by blood, but we believe there is a definite insist-
ence by Ann's father that the two of them not be involved,
even as friends. We believe Aubrey and Ann planned to leave
the village of Anwen-by-Wye after Henry's wedding. We have
evidence of the following: his removal of thousands of pounds
from his post office account; his purchase of a travel insurance
policy for Europe; his cancellation of various jobs around the
village; her making plans to collect her wedding dress for their
planned elopement. However, we also believe he would not
have let down the Anwen Morris for their very important role
in Saturday's ceremonies. We have worked under the assumption that Aubrey left Anwen-by-Wye some time on Sunday,
probably late in the afternoon, in his van, taking with him the
Anwen Morris historical artefacts which properly belong to
his family, though are used and viewed as "village property".
The fact I believe he did not pack for a trip, as I saw at his
home, means his departure must have been unexpected.'

Mavis paused, then added, 'Do we believe these assump-
tions are correct? We have no evidence to confirm Aubrey
took his van and the Morris dancing equipment, and both have
since turned up – though in two places and on two separate
occasions.'

Annie half-raised her hand. 'If he didn't take his van, then
how'd he leave at all? No buses that time of night, and no
one's said they gave him a lift.'

'Good point,' chimed in Christine, 'though Mavis is correct.
We don't *know* he drove off in his van. He could have been
conked on the head at his house, bundled into it and spirited
away.'

Carol looked into the camera, though her expert fingers kept
moving. 'No sign of a break-in or struggle at the house, no
sign of blood or any real disturbance in the van. He must have
driven off himself.'

'I'm inclined to agree,' said Mavis with some finality. 'But
why a week *early*? We have evidence of a strong bond between

him as Caradoc and Ann Roberts as Boudica covering many years and mentions in a letter about her becoming his wife, and there's the wedding gown. Their shared love of all things Roman suggests maybe a trip to Italy, but we have no evidence to confirm that to be the case. Indeed, we only know of the possible disappearance of Ann Roberts because of an overheard comment made by her mother. The local police have at least told me no one else has been reported as missing from this area. We are working under the assumption that Aubrey and Ann are both missing, and that there is a connection. Again, do we agree this to be the case?'

Christine, Annie and Carol all nodded.

Mavis took a deep breath and began another lap of the interior of the barn. 'We have established that Ann Roberts's father, Rhys, is a man with a tendency to unpleasantness and even violence, and her mother appears to be cowed by him. Her reaction when I touched her arm when we met gave me cause for concern, that's for sure. A woman only winces when she's touched if she's hurting. Of course, ladies, as professionals we must remember that not everyone who is rude, unpleasant, given to intoxication or even violence lives down to our expectations of them, but, having met him myself, I would like to say there's no' much I'd put past Rhys Roberts. He might very well see fit to impose his will upon anyone who chose to challenge it. His build might be slight, but I believe he would be able to call upon a wiry strength, developed over decades as a man used to handling sheep.'

'I trust your instincts, Mave,' said Annie, raising her coffee mug toward the petite woman, who replied to her colleague's comment with a withering glance. 'Sorry, Mav*is*,' added Annie, sulking.

Mavis pressed on. 'We've established Rhys Roberts's dislike of Aubrey Morris and his daughter being even friends has a long history. It cannot be based upon a concern about their being related, because they are not. Aubrey Morris could not, to be fair, be cast as a dashing young man, but he has a well-earned reputation for steadiness, which I cannot believe would be frowned upon by any father when considering a potential mate for his offspring. So we are stuck, ladies. Why might

Rhys Roberts have caused the disappearance of both Aubrey and his daughter? And, if he did, then was it he who dumped the van at the side of the road – and if so, why? And why did he deliver the Anwen Morris implements to Chellingworth Hall, if he did? We only have one sighting of a vehicle somewhat like his to go on for this aspect of the case.'

'There must be something we don't know about Aubrey,' said Christine thoughtfully.

Annie nodded. 'If a father is dead set against his little girl not being with a boy, it's 'cause that boy can harm her somehow – other than, you know, by generally breaking her heart and making her life a misery, which they all do anyway. Unless the dad's got a screw loose and just wants to shut his daughter away from all blokes for her entire life, that is.'

'He might be that sort,' said Carol. 'I haven't met him, but his wife Netta? The one who came to help me when I fell? She sounded really frightened when she said she was worried about what he might do. I don't think a person would sound like that unless there was some past behavior to go on.'

'I agree,' said Mavis. 'But there's so little here to take to the police. We have a *suspicion* that Ann Roberts and Aubrey Morris are together. If only the two lads who stole the wedding dresses would talk, they might be able to connect that incident with Rhys Roberts. There's no word from your contact in Bridgend yet, is there, Carol?'

Carol shook her head. 'PC Duffy said she'd phone if they made a link, but I'm not sure we should wait on that, though it would help.'

'So we *think* her father might have something to do with our *belief* they are both missing. The police have been quite clear, when speaking to Althea, that there is nothing they can do about an adult who simply chooses to be somewhere other than where he's expected to be. If only they would listen, they'd have the authority to at least search the Morris farm for Aubrey. They might not be in the Morris farmhouse, but I imagine they have a good many outbuildings, and any number of places that people, or, heaven forbid, bodies might be secreted.'

'Come on now, Mave – Mav*is* – if we really had anything

to suggest foul play we'd have been off to the cops days ago,' said Annie.

'Yes,' agreed Christine, 'that's a leap. I mean, we can't even think why he'd have kidnapped them, or whatever, let alone why he might kill Aubrey, or his daughter. But, you know what concerns me most?'

'That it's been so cold at night?' replied Carol.

Christine nodded. 'I don't know what the temperatures were like here over the past few days, but it's been freezing in London. I can't imagine an outbuilding in the depths of the Welsh countryside would have been a particularly pleasant place to be holed up.'

A little voice said, 'If we can't talk the police into searching the Morris farm buildings, could we do it ourselves?'

Althea had entered the barn in silence and no one had noticed her hovering at the door.

Welcoming her friend and encouraging her to take a seat, Mavis answered, 'No, we cannot, Althea. We have no right to do that. Private property is just that. Indeed, the only reason I felt we were able to enter Aubrey's home was because you yourself had a key, and owned the land upon which the house stood.'

'We own quite a lot of the Morris farm too,' said Althea quietly.

Mavis looked shocked. 'What do you mean? You haven't mentioned this before.'

'I only just found out,' admitted Althea, pulling off her sturdy jacket. 'After we'd stopped fussing about with Stephanie's gown – which is lovely by the way – I popped in to see Bob Fernley, our Estate Manager. I thought I'd check about access routes to the New Buttery, to see if I could work out how someone could get there without being seen, and the topic of property lines arose. It seems the Chellingworth Estate bought up a few hundred of the Morris acres around the time old man Morris died. They needed the cash. I suspect it was so they could buy the house where Aubrey and his parents lived. We don't own the land where the houses are – you know, the part we saw when we were there, Mavis – but we do own a good deal of their pasture. Would that make a difference?'

Mavis gave the matter some thought. 'Carol – you're the bookworm here. What's your pseudo-legal opinion?'

Carol unhunched and stopped typing. 'I'll need to check it out, but I believe if the Chellingworth Estate owns the land, then it – by which I suppose I mean you, Althea – would have the right of entry to that land, and everything on it. Of course, the Twysts and the Morrises might have signed a contract forbidding such an act, but, otherwise, I think you could go where you wanted on your land, and do as you pleased. Of course, what you own might be just green fields and hillsides, without so much as a shack upon it. But let me check some satellite shots of the area while you all talk, and I'll let you know. So, to be clear – the Chellingworth Estate *owns* the land, and – what? The Morris family rents it from you to use for grazing?'

'Here,' said Althea, handing Mavis a couple of pieces of paper she'd screwed up in her pocket. She flattened them out as she passed them across. 'Bob Fernley said this contract would explain it all properly and he drew a sort of outline on an Ordinance Survey map to show me our boundaries.'

'Thanks.' Mavis took the note and read it, then flattened the map and looked at it thoughtfully. She photographed them both and emailed them to Carol. 'Carol – would you check the photos I just sent you, please?'

Carol nodded, and turned her attention to her keyboard.

'Althea, following discussion, we don't feel confident we have enough to go back to the police to get them to act,' summarized Mavis. 'We've only been on the case for three days, and we're happy to continue, but we think we've hit a bit of a dead end.'

'That's not good news,' said Althea, looking crestfallen. 'I feel more and more that we need to find Aubrey. And that poor girl, too.'

'What if we went and confronted the father?' suggested Annie. 'All of us go, mob-handed, and put it to him we know he's done something. If we could get the mother on our side, and the grandfather as well, that might swing it. You know – strength in numbers.'

The women considered the idea. 'Not much of a mob are

we?' said Christine, voicing the opinion of all. 'I mean, look at us. This enquiring business was never formulated on our physicality – it's all about us using our brains, our knowledge and our contacts to ferret out information. All he'd have to do would be slam the door in our faces and we'd be finished.'

'I could ask Tudor to come with us. And there's Ian, right, Althea? He'd come, wouldn't he? And I could bring me dad – though maybe Eustelle would be more frightening,' offered Annie.

'I'm not convinced a couple of cars full of a rag-tag group would be a good way to go about it. It would look as though we were threatening physical violence,' replied Christine.

'Well . . .' said Annie huffily.

'You can go where you like here,' said Carol triumphantly, bringing up a map on the laptop screen instead of her face. Her voice continued, 'The agreement between the Twysts and the Morris family gives clear map coordinates for the land owned by the Twysts, and that remaining in the Morris family. I have outlined the area the Twysts own in green, that owned by the Morrises in red. As you can see, the parcel owned by you, Althea, abuts your other land, whereas theirs is quite close to the main farmhouses, and runs to the road. It's almost a complete half-and-half situation. If I open up the satellite imagery too you can see where the Morris and Roberts houses are – here and here – as well as the major collection of barns and outbuildings – here.' Carol remotely moved a little pointer as Mavis pushed her spectacles onto her nose.

'Got it,' said Mavis eventually. 'Look – there's a narrow track that leads down to Chellingworth Hall through the Morris/ Twyst area. And see where it ends? Not far from the New Buttery. Rhys Roberts could have driven along that track to deliver the Anwen Morris packages. He'd not have been seen approaching the hall along the main driveway, which might be why only a couple of people recalled seeing a Land Rover that day.'

'Well spotted,' said Annie. 'I bet that's what he did.'

'Now here,' continued Carol, stretching the image on the screen so that it became enlarged and using the pointer again, 'is the spot where Aubrey Morris's van was found. See how

close it is, across country, to the Roberts house? Given it was
parked out of sight, he might have left it there to go to Ann
Roberts's house on foot. And look, there are a couple of other
buildings. Because it's just an overhead shot I can't tell you
what they are, but, given how close they are to a couple of
the stone walls we can see forming a lattice on the hillside,
I'd say they might be feed stores or shearing barns, I don't
know. I must admit it's difficult to get a good sense of scale,
but they don't look very big, and one of them appears to have
only half a roof. Maybe they are completely abandoned.
Maybe—'

'Maybe that's where Rhys Roberts is hiding Aubrey and
Ann,' interrupted Althea. 'Can we go there without the police?
Are they on Twyst land?'

'They are,' replied Carol, making the image smaller again
so the women could tell that they appeared in the green zone.
'But as for getting there? It would be quite a hike. As you can
see, they aren't near any visible tracks – which makes me think
it's even more likely they aren't in constant, current use. If
they were, and they were for storage, you'd expect to see
tracks for vehicles. You could certainly use the track that leads
from Chellingworth Hall for some distance, but then you'd
have to cut across country for about a mile or more before
you got there. I don't think I'd be much use, in fact—'

'Down to me and Chrissie, in't it?' said Annie with a sigh.
'Only two up to it, I'd say – with all due respect Mavis, Althea.'

'I have absolutely no doubt that Althea and I would be more
than capable of undertaking such a hike, Annie,' said Mavis
tartly. 'On a weekly basis we cover several miles of energetic
walks, whereas I'm not sure I've seen you do much more than
amble from the village to this office.'

Annie pulled a face that spoke volumes.

'Come on now ladies,' said Carol. 'I know I can't volunteer
because, of course, David would go ballistic and I've got to
admit to myself I wouldn't be up to it. But, in any case, what
are any of us going to do when we get there? If there's nothing
there but abandoned buildings, then, OK, you'd just walk back
to Chellingworth Hall again. But what if there's a situation that
demands an immediate response? If Aubrey, Ann, or both of

them are there, needing medical attention, or just assistance to get back to civilization, what then? Would you carry them out? It's just not practical. What if there's no mobile phone signal there – and it's likely there isn't – how would you summon help? See? We can't, any of us, just go yomping off around the countryside looking for lost souls. It's silly, and probably dangerous.'

'What if Rhys Roberts has got a gun?' said Annie, still looking and sounding sulky. 'He could have. Farmers do, don't they?'

'They'd be allowed to own guns for certain purposes, and with the correct paperwork,' replied Mavis. 'But this isn't the Wild West, Annie, nor Downtown LA in the 1940s. People don't go about the place with rifles on their hips or revolvers in their waistbands. This is Wales.'

'We've got a lot of guns up at the hall,' said Althea brightly. 'We could take some of them with us.'

Mavis leaped to her feet. 'Now hold your horses, no one's going anywhere, with or without firearms. Carol's made a fair point. Those buildings are a good distance from anywhere. We'd need vehicles that could get us there.'

'There are no tracks shown on the map,' said Christine simply, 'but my Range Rover's pretty good at most terrains, I could take that.'

'Walls,' said Carol. 'There are no gates in the walls. I don't think even your Range Rover can jump over those dry-stone walls.'

Silence. Annie leaped to her feet as though she'd been electrocuted. 'Hang on a minute, girls, I think I've got the answer. You're right, Mave – we'd better hold our horses. Let me give someone a quick ring. Don't talk about it without me – vamp for a bit.' She took her handbag with her to the far end of the barn and the women could see her searching for her phone.

Sighing and stretching Christine asked wickedly, 'Will McFli be at the church?'

Mavis glared and said, 'Ach.'

Althea returned Christine's impish grin, 'I did discuss the possibility with Henry, but only because I knew it would send him into a fit. No, McFli will remain with me at the hall until the ceremony, then he'll be taken to the Dower House. He's a delightful creature, but there will be hundreds of pairs of feet at the reception, and he could get trampled. Certainly he'd become too excited. It's best he stays in a place where he's safe and comfortable, even if he is alone.'

'Horses,' announced Annie rejoining the group. 'Great inspiration, Mave. I spoke to Tudor and he can get us a couple of horses to ride out to the barns or whatever they are, and he'll come too.'

'Very clever,' praised Mavis as Annie stood tall with pride. 'Though I cannot imagine you're much of a horsewoman yourself, Annie. Knowing how you feel about cars, how can you possibly be prepared to sit on a horse?'

Crestfallen Annie replied, 'I'm not one for horses myself – to be honest, I find them frightening, but if we need to get there, that's the best way. I'm sure I'll manage. Tudor said I'd probably be very good at managing a horse because they know who's in charge right away.'

No one said a word. Their expressions did the talking.

Clearing her throat Althea said, 'Having ridden for half a century, believe me when I tell you a Welsh hillside is not where you want to be when you find out whether you're a natural horsewoman or not. It's far too dangerous – both for you and the horse. Mr Evans might have every faith in your innate ability on the back of a beast, but beasts they are, and while he might be correct in stating they know instinctively if a rider is in charge, they are equally aware if a rider is nervous. Annie, my dear, I think you've had a good idea, but it's not one I can condone. Maybe we could ask Tudor to undertake the search on our behalf.'

'I'm a very good horsewoman,' said Christine. 'Maybe I could ride up there with Tudor?'

'Tudor Evans was a sound hunt rider, when we hunted,' said Althea thoughtfully. 'Good seat, excellent handling, and I'd trust him to do our bidding. And you, Christine – Irish horses? Bareback?' Christine nodded and grinned. 'Good, then you'll know how to handle pretty much any sort of mount. Since I stopped riding our stables are empty, I'm afraid. All given over to the making of honey, beeswax candles and soap for the little shop at the hall. If Tudor can get you some good steeds, you two would make quick work of the ride there and back. You could take some emergency medical supplies with you, and of course you'd have your mobile phones. Even if they didn't work at the structures in question they might at other spots. What do you think, Mavis?'

Mavis stood, taking control of the situation. Checking her watch she said, 'It'll be dark in half an hour. You can't go now. Too dangerous, however good the two of you might be on horseback. Annie – do you think Tudor might be able to arrange things for first light tomorrow? If there's someone out there I hate to think of them having to endure another night in such frigid temperatures, but I cannae see we have any alternative. Could you check with him, Annie?'

Annie nodded. 'He said he had to pop out for an hour or so – to see a man about a dog he said, so I don't know what he's *really* doing. I'll drop by the Lamb and Flag on my way back to the cottage.' Mavis and Althea exchanged a knowing glance.

'Very good,' agreed Mavis. 'So, if this is our plan, what else can we be doing this evening to progress the investigation?'

'I can write all this up, properly, with photos and such, so our case is as prepared as possible to be put in front of the police tomorrow, depending on what Christine and Tudor find,' said Carol.

'I'll see Tudor,' added Annie, 'but I'll have to make sure I spend some time with Eustelle and Dad too. Maybe I'll treat them to a bite to eat at the pub.'

'Good idea,' said Carol. 'Your dad would probably like that, and it'll give Eustelle a chance to have another natter with Tudor. She's quite taken to him, I understand.'

Annie sucked her teeth by way of a reply.

'I'll dig out something to ride in – though I'm not sure what I've got here that will do,' said Christine. 'There again, I never was one for proper riding boots or anything.'

'You'll wear protective headgear at least,' said Althea. 'That's something I am able to provide. Come to the hall with me – we have any number of hats there. Something's bound to fit.'

Mavis chipped in next: 'With Althea and myself at the hall again tonight, I could offer to—'

'You'll be on dinner guest entertaining duty with me, dear,' said Althea. 'The hall is overrun with people. Your parents don't arrive until tomorrow, Christine, am I correct?' Christine nodded. 'Good,' said Althea, 'I'm not sure how the Timbers would cope with two more titles at the table. Poor things, they are so completely at sea. Sheila looked terrified at dinner last night – wouldn't touch the cutlery until I did. It's all so silly. They are good people with a lovely daughter, and I'm no snob.'

'I don't think it's you they're worried about,' said Mavis quietly. 'Henry can be a bit, *you know*, sometimes.'

Althea nodded. 'Stuffed shirt. My fault.'

Mavis patted her friend's hand. 'Not your fault, remember? It was the nanny, right?' the two women shared a smile.

With the meeting at an end, the women took their leave of each other; Althea, Mavis and Christine headed for dinner at Chellingworth Hall, Carol signed off and Annie trudged to her cottage where it was her plan to talk her parents into joining her at the Lamb and Flag for a tasty treat from Tudor's menu.

All of them tried to push to one side the thought that, somewhere in the chill of the night, a young man and woman might possibly be hoping for release from an unpleasant captivity.

THIRTY

Friday, February 28th

Annie set off the next morning when it was still almost dark, and did as she had promised – she phoned Carol so they could catch up as she walked to the hall. 'Hiya doll, feelin' alright?' she opened.

'Fine thanks. It was a big help to sit and organize everything last night and get it into one file. I like the sense of control I get from arranging facts in order. That's not weird, is it?'

'Nah,' said Annie, thinking it was. Annie yawned. 'Sorry,' she said in a sleepy voice, 'it's not *that* early I know, but I couldn't sleep. Something's got up Eustelle's nose and she's thrown some sort of wobbly with Tudor. Wouldn't tell me what. Went off on one at the pub last evening when we all went there for dinner. And for no reason at all.'

'What was she doing when she "went off"?' asked Carol.

'Nothing. Well, getting cutlery from the side of the bar while Tudor went to get our food, that's all, so as good as nothing. One minute she was all over him, pleased as punch to see him and me dad having a good old natter, then she went weird. Like she couldn't get us out of there fast enough.'

Carol spoke quietly, 'Sorry, Annie. Maybe she'll be alright by this afternoon.'

'Yeah. Hope Stephanie's doing alright too,' said Annie with a sigh. 'I wonder what it's like to be a bride. I s'pose she must love him. I dunno, Henry's nice and all that, and he's being very kind to all of us, but he's got the personality of a stick. The sort they shove up your backside at Eton, you know, to keep you upright through thick and thin. He's so different from Althea. Good old laugh, she is. I can see why she and Mave get on so well. She's the sort of old bird anyone would like to have as their gran. Jolly, you know. *Cor*, there's Tudor – a real sight for sore eyes.' Annie waved. 'Gotta go, Car. Phone you later, alright. Sorry you're missing it all, doll, but keep your feet up, let us know if you hear from Bridgend and look after Bump.'

Just as Annie walked up to the front steps of the hall, Christine arrived looking svelte in a full-length waxed cotton riding coat. Annie wondered how she managed it. She even looked good with the lump of a riding hat on her head. Annie reckoned if she tried it on she'd look like something out of a Thelwell illustration. She sighed. Alexander arrived moments later, perfectly turned out in a country suit that made him look very dashing.

'Hello, Alexander,' said Annie shaking his hand warmly. 'I

knew you were arriving today but you've managed to get here very early.'

'He surprised me when I got back to my apartment at the barn after dinner last night,' said Christine quickly, blushing a little.

Annie let out a raucous laugh. 'I can imagine what he surprised you with,' she mugged.

'Annie!' chided Christine, nonchalantly walking toward the steed Tudor was leading toward her.

'I'll wait here with you, Annie,' said Alexander easily. 'Christine assures me she doesn't need my help with this part of the investigation. Apparently I earned my keep in Brighton.'

'And how'd you do that, exactly?' said Annie with a wicked grin.

'By helping her find the perfect wedding gift for Henry and Stephanie, of course,' replied Alexander, his eyes sparkling with mystery.

Mavis and Althea arrived next, and they were all joined by Henry and Stephanie, who'd decided they didn't want to miss out on the proceedings. With everyone present and correct, Mavis handed over the maps she'd printed out from Carol's emails and Christine assured her she was excellent at using a compass, which she showed Mavis three times to prove she was properly equipped. Saddlebags holding basic medical supplies had been prepared and the horses were inspected one last time. Just as the riders were about to set off, Bob Fernley came rushing out of the estate office waving his arms.

'Don't frighten the horses,' said Althea abruptly as she held up her small hand in a most arresting manner.

'Sorry, Your Grace, I just wanted to bring these out.' He held something toward Tudor, who, to Annie's eyes at least, looked every inch the country squire on his large steed.

'What's that then?' said Tudor in his booming voice.

'They are distress flares,' said the estate manager. Looking over at the dowager he added, 'I suggest you only use them far enough away from the animals so as not to cause them concern – they're silent, in that they don't bang, but they will make a loud whooshing sound. I suggest you use one if you need us to organize an immediate police presence, and two if you also need medical assistance. If you do, I happen to know we have at least one local paramedic who rides well.'

Tudor looked impressed. 'You're very well prepared.'

'Her Grace told me last night what was planned for this morning. I've done all I can think of,' replied Bob Fernley, 'given the circumstances.'

'Let's not hang about then. Are you ready?' asked Tudor of Christine. She nodded, and the two set off at a canter.

Annie felt she wanted to pull a hanky out of her pocket and start waving it at Tudor's receding figure, then she told herself she was being stupid and said, 'I could kill for a cuppa. I suppose we've got time. Any chance I could make one in your office, Bob?'

Bob Fernley hesitated for a second, looked at the duke, then the dowager and said, 'But of course. Would you all like to come over?'

'Thank you, Bob,' said Althea, 'but I think it's much better if we all go to the long portrait gallery on the second floor and wait there. I'm sure someone at the hall will be able to rustle up a tea tray. It's an excellent vantage point. We'll be able to watch their progress and keep an eye open for flares. Come along.'

'Good thinking, Mother,' said Henry as the strange group began its progress toward the hall. 'The long portrait gallery has not yet been overrun by the hordes, though I suspect it's only a matter of time.'

'I'll be having some photographs taken there tomorrow morning, before the ceremony,' said Stephanie. 'I thought it would be a good setting for a bridal portrait – watched over by dozens of former Twysts. But you don't need to worry about that, Henry dear. It'll all be taken care of without you having to become involved – though you might think it's a good idea for us to have some shots taken there when we are married. The newlyweds standing among the ancestors might be a nice touch.'

Annie noticed Henry almost winced at the idea, but that Stephanie seemed oblivious to his pain.

'Have Stephanie's parents arrived yet?' asked Alexander

as Annie and he made their way up the stone steps. 'Or Christine's?'

It's Christine's parents you're really interested in, was what Annie was thinking as she replied, 'John and Sheila Timbers arrived the day before yesterday, but the Wilson-Smythes won't be here until – oh, now, by the looks of it. Isn't that them?'

They turned and glimpsed the viscount and his wife alighting from a sleek Audi. 'Yes, that's them,' Alexander said, but Annie could tell he was distracted. 'Did you say "John and Sheila Timbers"?' he added. Annie picked up on the tension in his voice as he spoke. 'Don't suppose you happen to know where they're from, do you?'

'Well, as luck would have it, Car told me she'd done a bit of nosing around about him.' She glanced over her shoulder to make sure no one was listening. 'He ran a business out near the Catford dog track in South London back in the 1980s, then grew it from there. As Car tells it, he had quite a number of lumber yards between the Thames and the M25, but largely south and west. He sold up years ago, and they live in Spain now. Have you met 'em?' she wondered what Alexander would say.

Alexander's eyes narrowed. 'Would you excuse me? I think I'll go and tell Fiona and Aiden what their daughter's up to, and try to make sure they don't panic. How about I invite them to join everyone in the long gallery?'

'Alright, doll, can't see why not. The more the merrier,' said Annie as she continued on her way, noting silently that Alexander had managed to wriggle out of answering her question about his knowing John Timbers.

By the time everyone had assembled and tea had been brought, the atmosphere in the long gallery was quite festive.

Annie overheard Edward whispering as he deposited the last tray on an occasional table, 'Your parents were asking about going down to the village, Miss Stephanie, I told them I would tell you. They are in their room.'

'Thanks, Edward. I did promise I'd take them on a tour – I just don't seem to have had the time.'

'We'll be fine dealing with all this,' Annie whispered to

Stephanie jovially. 'It won't take you more than an hour – why don't you go and have a bit of time with your mum and dad, alone? I know that sort of thing means a lot.'

Stephanie flashed a grateful smile and checked her watch. 'I could be back by lunch – plenty of time to eat and get ready for this afternoon's arrivals. The harps won't be here until after lunch so I suppose . . .'

'Go on,' urged Annie with a wink.

Stephanie bent to her fiancé's ear, whispered something then left without further ado.

Annie sipped her tea, wolfed down a few of the tasty, crumbly oatmeal biscuits brought to accompany it, and watched as Mavis strode the length of the gallery, constantly looking out of the windows which gave onto the surrounding country-side and the hill up which Christine and Tudor had ridden. Annie didn't reckon Mavis would want to run any risk of missing a flare.

Looking at her watch Mavis announced, 'They should have reached their goal about fifteen minutes ago. I'm sure they'd have alerted us by now if they needed any help.'

Annie was on edge, anxiously perched on the same window seat as Alexander, straining her eyes for any sign of Tudor.

'There they are,' called Alexander, rising. 'They're galloping, but they're alone. I'm going down to meet them. Anyone coming?'

The entire group replaced cups and saucers on trays and moved *en masse* toward the staircase leading off the paneled room which ran the entire length of the main body of Chellingworth Hall – designed to allow seventeenth-century ladies to exercise during poor weather.

By the time Christine and Tudor's horses clattered across the cobbled courtyard beside the hall, the entire group was assembled. Annie felt so proud when she looked at Tudor, it made her worry about her sanity. Then she told herself it wasn't odd, because he looked very handsome as he dismounted and allowed Bob Fernley to take his horse to a water trough, along with Christine's steed.

'So? What did you find?' Annie was breathless as she finally reached Tudor to speak to him, but it was Christine who answered.

'Hello there, Mummy, Daddy,' began Christine, waving at her parents, who'd been left straggling at the back of the assembled huddle. 'We found the buildings but there was no one there. However, there were signs at least one person had been kept in each of the two buildings. Look, I took photographs.' She pulled her phone from her pocket and handed it to Mavis, who passed the phone around for all to see. As the phone moved from person to person, Christine addressed the group.

'Someone had piled up straw to make beds – one in each of the two buildings. There were empty bottles of water, protein bar wrappers, even plastic sandwich containers, strewn about both buildings. Someone has "lived" in each building for some time. Days, I'd say. Also in each building there was evidence ropes had been used to restrain a person. And in one there was blood. Not much, but certainly enough to give concern. We must inform the police. They *must* listen now, surely?'

Mavis handed the telephone back to Christine and took control, 'So, we're working on the theory that Rhys Roberts has kidnapped and confined his daughter Ann, and Aubrey Morris, in these buildings, but that he has now moved them. Do you agree WISE women?' Annie, Christine and Althea all nodded.

'I've got to say, for what it's worth, I've never liked the man, and I wouldn't put this past him,' said Tudor quietly. 'But it's shocking. I mean, you never think it'll happen on your own doorstep, do you? And that he'd do this to his own daughter, too? Unbelievable – even though I suppose I can believe it of him, if anyone.'

'We've got to get in touch with the police immediately,' said Annie. 'Look, Car was at the Morris farmhouse, and she didn't think that Aubrey and Ann were there then. I bet if Rhys has moved them, he's probably taken them to his own house, or – and this is more scary – he might have carted them off somewhere else altogether. And as for where that might be, I don't know. As Tudor said, this is a man who's crossed a line, and he might have lost all perspective.'

'Maybe they've got a point about the curse after all,' said

Tudor quietly, then he shook his head and added, 'Nah! It's all nonsense.'

'What's that?' asked Althea.

'The curse,' replied Tudor, speaking very slowly and clearly.

'There's nothing wrong with my hearing, I just didn't catch what you said – or rather I did, but I have no idea what you mean,' snapped Althea.

Annie noticed Tudor blush, and suspected if he'd had a forelock he'd have tugged it. She felt embarrassed for him. Rallying he said, 'There's supposed to be a curse on the Anwen Morris artefacts. All nonsense, of course, but I understand it's something to do with whoever owns it dying before their time. Load of old rubbish.'

Annie couldn't help but speak up. 'Do you mean people believe the *owner* of the Anwen Morris artefacts is cursed – or just the artefacts themselves?'

Tudor replied, 'I'm pretty sure it's the owner, because I've never had any of my men refuse to use the implements when we dance.'

All eyes turned toward Annie, and she didn't disappoint. 'Well, that's it then! I bet you that's it – Rhys Roberts didn't want his daughter getting hitched to someone in the family that owned the implements. I bet they were given to Aubrey's grandfather to get them out of the part of the family that stayed at the Morris farm in the first place. Whatever you might think of curses – and I have to say I agree with Tudor that they are all a load of twaddle – with what we've found out during our enquiries, it's clear that the main Morris family didn't do well when it owned them. The great-grandfather's death was unexpectedly early, if you recall. Since then everyone in Aubrey's part of the Morris family has died at a relatively young age, as Mavis and Carol said they discovered in the graveyard yesterday. Maybe that bolstered Rhys Roberts's belief that his daughter's life would be in danger if she built a friendship with, and then went on to marry, Aubrey. I know we've all been trying to work out what would make a father go to such extremes to keep two people apart – and for that to have begun when Ann and Aubrey were so young. Believe me, as someone whose dad is very much a man who'd do *anything* to protect his daughter, I can tell you fathers might go to extreme lengths to keep their little girl safe – and then some. Any parent would, wouldn't they?' As her gaze swept the group she noticed how Christine's parents looked at Alexander when they nodded their agreement.

'That's true,' said Althea, 'the love of a parent for a child is a powerful thing, even if it is misdirected by some weird belief.'

Mavis took control again. 'Well, whatever the motive might be, and however wrong-headed it is, we need to get hold of the police. *Now*. Finding blood cannot be a good sign. Carol has furnished us with a comprehensive electronic file on the case to date and, if Christine will send those photos showing the blood on the floor of the shack to me right now, I can put it all together and send it to whomever I manage to speak to on the telephone at the Builth Wells police station.'

'Go to the top,' said Althea. 'Use my name – use Henry's. Use anyone's to get hold of someone who will take this seriously, and take action.'

The result was that half an hour later Mavis was able to report to the entire group, which had reassembled itself in the long gallery once again, that police cars were being dispatched to search the Morris farm, and all its buildings. 'It seems my phone call arrived just after they received information from their colleagues in Bridgend that the two lads they're holding there confessed they'd been sent to steal Ann Roberts's wedding dress by her father. When they spotted Stephanie's gown hanging close to Ann's, they saw an opportunity to make some money for themselves, so they pinched that too, and came up with their hare-brained scheme to ransom the dress. They knew Rhys Roberts because he's hired them as casual laborers during the lambing season before now. They also told the police he told them he found out about Ann and Aubrey's plans to elope, and has prevented them from doing so. They did not have any information about how he has been doing that, so the information and evidence we have gathered arrived at just the perfect moment to allow our local police to do their job. They've promised to keep me informed, though, to be honest, I don't think we should expect them to take the time to do so.'

'So what do we do now?' asked Althea looking at Mavis.

'As private enquiry agents we've done all we can,' replied the Scot with resignation. 'When we reach a point in a case where it's obvious it's a police case, and they're willing to take it from us, that's what we do – we hand it over to them. There's only so far we're allowed to go, you know.'

'It's very frustrating,' said Althea petulantly. Annie knew what she meant because she'd had the same feeling on many occasions herself.

'Mave's right. Best let the cops deal with it now,' said Annie with resignation.

'I can hear sirens,' said Althea, peering out of the window. 'Why would we hear sirens so far away from the Morris place?'

Annie noticed Mavis had pulled out her phone and was listening intently. Putting away her phone Mavis announce, 'Rhys Roberts has bolted. Apparently, when the police arrived at the main farmhouse he ran to his Land Rover and sped off. They reckon he's coming this way.'

'He can't be,' said Christine. 'Tudor and I jumped a lot of walls to get to those buildings. He'd never be able to make it here.'

'Don't forget the track that leads here from the Morris farm,' said Mavis. 'It doesn't go anywhere near those outbuildings you visited, it takes quite a different route. But we know where he'll come out – near the New Buttery – and I told the police that. They're coming here to try to pick him up at this end, and, apparently – oh, yes, I hear it now – they've sent up a helicopter to keep an eye on him.'

Everyone crowded to the windows, then Henry shouted, 'I'm going outside. I cannot wait inside here any longer. This is terrible.' Annie noticed he looked quite excited.

As soon as Henry made for the door it seemed everyone decided to do likewise, and they all trooped down the main staircase, across the great hall and out onto the steps. Two police cars were racing up the driveway spitting stones in all directions, their sirens and lights blaring and blazing. Overhead a helicopter buzzed over the hall and everyone instinctively ducked, then stood again to watch as it swooped toward the hillside. Behind the police vehicles was Stephanie's car, her father's head sticking out of the back window, his arm pointing skywards.

The police cars rounded the hall and stopped where Bob Fernley stood, agog. He spoke to one of the drivers, pointed, and the cars continued toward the rear of the hall. Just as they disappeared from sight a battered old Land Rover shot out of the same area, skidded on the pea gravel as it came around the side of the hall, then side-swiped Stephanie's car, sending it skidding onto the lawn, before taking off along the driveway.

'Stephanie!' shouted Henry as he ran toward his fiancé's now-stationary car. Before he could get there the two police cars that had just disappeared, reappeared and screamed their way back around the hall, setting off in pursuit of Rhys Roberts's vehicle, only narrowly missing the duke as they did so.

There was a general surge toward Stephanie's car, and Annie was relieved to see all three of its occupants get out, seemingly none the worse for wear. The police helicopter swooped overhead again, though fewer people ducked at its second pass.

Holding his fiancé to his chest Annie saw Henry swaying, rocking her like a baby, kissing her head, her hands – anything he could. Her parents exchanged a hug and turned their attention to their daughter.

'Let me through,' called Mavis, 'I am a nurse.'

'Me too,' shouted a deep voice from the steps, where Nurse Betty Thomas had deposited Lady Clementine in her wheelchair and was now running toward the car that had been hit by the Land Rover.

Annie didn't rush anywhere, she did what the panicked duke had asked and dialed 999, then she hung on with the operator until she knew an ambulance was on the way. From her vantage point on the steps she watched the pandemonium unfold before her. It was quite a sight but, luckily, it seemed that no one was hurt.

Annie thought the chaos of the day was behind them all, but the events that followed proved her wrong. There was the arrival of an ambulance, then the checking of the Timbers family members by the paramedics, finally the removal of the badly dented car by Bob Fernley using one of the estate's Land Rovers was undertaken, so the eventual flocking of the group to a very delayed luncheon only took place after a couple of hours. She was just about to join everybody to enjoy some much needed sandwiches and cold meats in the drawing room when she noticed Edward was looking flustered – for him – and dithering about in the great hall.

She went across to the door of the hall where he was hovering distractedly. 'What's the matter, doll?' she asked.

'The lorries have just arrived with the harps and one of the drivers said there's been a nasty accident. The man the police were chasing after went off the road a few miles along, and it's serious they say. Critical. After all that's happened I don't know if I should tell His Grace.' Annie felt sorry for Edward who looked as though he was about to snap under the accumulated stresses he'd been facing.

'I'll do it, you go and have a cup of tea.'

'Tea? No time for tea! I must make sure they know what they're doing with those harps,' he replied looking worried. 'They look a lot bigger that I'd thought they'd be. I hope we've left enough room for them at the bottom of the staircase.' He hurried down the steps waving to the burly men who were unloading the harps and shouted that they should stop doing what they were doing and come inside to check where they were to bring the huge instruments. Through the open doors Annie caught sight of a procession of four hatchback vehicles making a stately progress along the driveway toward the hall. As they slowly navigated the space between the now-rutted lawn and the large lorry she could see Marjorie Pritchard was driving the lead car, and it was full of plates, containers and bags. The Young Wives' Welsh cakes had arrived.

THIRTY-ONE

Saturday, March 1st

T he day of the wedding dawned bright and clear. Gone were the clouds and sleety rain of the previous days, even the birds in the still-bare trees seemed to think it was time to break into song.

Despite all the recent disastrous events, the plans for the day had gone ahead as originally envisaged. By noon, when Stephanie Annabel Timbers agreed to love, honor and obey Henry Devereaux Twyst at the fifteenth-century chancel steps of St David's Church in the picturesque Welsh village of Anwen-by-Wye, the sun was just high enough to pour through the ancient stained-glass windows, throwing a rainbow onto a packed nave full of happy faces and some dubious fashion choices.

'Love Divine' and 'The Lord is My Shepherd' had been sung with real *hwyl* and some spontaneously beautiful harmonies, a reading from Corinthians about adulthood and the importance of love was delivered by Tudor Evans – who struck an intriguing chord in his Morris Green Man garb – and the entire congregation had been delighted by a blessedly brief sermon from the Reverend Ebenezer Roberts about the different types of love that exist between human beings, culminating in praise for the sacrament of marriage.

Then the real fun began. According to tradition, the newlyweds and the procession of attendees were led along a thankfully dry pathway toward Chellingworth Hall by the energetic dancing of the (sadly, not quite complete) Anwen Morris, replete with their precious tools of the trade. Althea's arm was taken for the walk by Edward who, as per Twyst tradition, had acted as Henry's best man, while Clementine and her extended limb were dispatched in a car with Nurse Thomas.

The crowd gathered at the entrance to the hall and waited

expectantly as Henry and Stephanie Twyst stepped gracefully over the extra-long broomstick that had been fashioned for the purpose and was wedged across the doorway. A cheer went up, the broomstick was removed, and hundreds of people flooded into the great hall to partake of tasty morsels provided by caterers who even Cook Davies had to admit had done a good job. The Young Wives' Welsh cakes were swarmed over – under the delighted and watchful eye of Marjorie Pritchard – and the six harpists and the musicians from Cardiff University did a splendid job of making themselves heard above the hubbub, especially when only the harpists played the traditional Welsh tune of 'The Ash Grove' which silenced everyone with its sheer beauty and simplicity.

The Hills wandered hand in hand as Carol showed her husband around the rooms that were open; it was David's first visit to Chellingworth Hall and he enjoyed it very much, though he kept asking Carol if she needed to sit down any time they were near an unoccupied seat. She finally gave in, to make him feel better, but insisted upon selecting a chair in the upper gallery near the balustrade so she didn't miss anything happening in the main body of the great hall below.

Christine Wilson-Smythe's parents chatted with as many of the locals as possible, while all the time trying to keep an eye on their daughter. She, meanwhile, had managed to find a quiet corner where she tried to find out from Alexander why he'd made such an effort to completely avoid Stephanie's father. It had annoyed her, but she wasn't sure why it should have done. All she could say for sure was Alexander had been acting in a most peculiar manner since he'd been sharing air with the Timbers couple, and she wanted to get to the bottom of it all. She managed to winkle out of him: 'It's something and nothing. He's a retired timber merchant I once did business with. It didn't turn out to be a satisfactory experience. I just hope the apple has fallen as far from the tree as possible.'

'You did,' was Christine's heartfelt response.

'This is true,' acknowledged Alexander with a grin.

'Was it bad?' asked Christine pointedly. 'Whatever you

and Stephanie's dad went through, I mean. Was it when you were . . .' – she glanced around, making sure no one could overhear them – 'Issy?' she hissed, using the name by which Alexander had been known during his more nefarious years.

Alexander shook his head. 'Not the Issy years, I'm pleased to say. At least he wouldn't have anything from those times to hold over me, I don't believe. But it wasn't long after, and I was still learning the ropes of property development. I made some poor choices. He was one of them.'

'Will he remember you because of it?' she pressed.

'Don't know if he's put two and two together, yet, but, with his now being the father of a duchess, and me here with you on my arm, maybe I have to reconsider the meaning of Mutually Assured Destruction, and, if it comes to it, make sure he understands it the same way.'

She didn't like the expression on Alexander's face as he spoke, but, not wanting to spoil the day, Christine decided to pursue the matter at a later date. What history might Alexander Bright and the father of a freshly-minted duchess have in common . . . and how bad could it be?

Althea Twyst held court in the morning room, as befitting a dowager duchess. She and Mavis had settled on two seats in a corner, and those who wanted to find the matriarch of the possibly-soon-to-be-increasing Twyst family were directed to the correct general area. She looked to be thoroughly enjoying the whole affair, though at one point Mavis suggested she might slow down on the sherry intake.

'You have a point,' agreed Althea grudgingly. 'I am finding that with each glass my level of anxiety about what I should do about Clemmie is increasing.'

Both women regarded Lady Clementine Twyst whose wheelchair was backed into the unused fireplace of the room, her entire body and outstretched leg swathed in yards of lemon voile, offsetting her vivid pink hair which was gelled into swirls and peaks that looked quite alarming. Nurse Thomas was dressed in her best navy uniform and standing guard beside her charge.

'Aye, kids.' Mavis sounded resigned as she spoke. 'We only

want what's best for them, but they never see it that way, do they?'

Annie Parker and her parents were impossible to miss – not only were they among the tallest people in the room, but the size of Eustelle's hat meant they also had to be given a pretty wide berth. As soon as Annie spotted Tudor, who'd changed from his Morris dancing outfit into a dark suit, she called him over, much to her mother's disgruntlement. Knowing she had to get to the bottom of whatever it was that was going on between them, Annie confronted her mother.

'Eustelle, this is ridiculous. You've taken against Tudor for no apparent reason, and I want to know why.'

Tudor and Annie looked at Eustelle apprehensively, while Rodney whispered to his wife, 'You got to say. Go on.'

Eustelle drew herself up to her full height – plus hat – and said, 'There's no point you denying it, Tudor Evans, so don't you bother. I heard you talking to that boy who works for you in your kitchen last night when we were all there and you called my daughter a black you-know-what. And I won't stand for that. You are *not* a nice man.'

Tudor and Annie looked at each other with amazement. 'I said she's a black what?' said Tudor simply.

'The "b" word.' Eustelle looked about then whispered, '*Bitch*. A black bitch. And her legs is too long. That's what you said.'

Rodney held his wife's hand tightly, and nodded at his daughter. 'That's what she heard,' he said sadly.

Eustelle shot a hateful glance at Tudor and Annie's mouth dropped open – lost for words, for once.

To their surprise Tudor broke his silence by laughing, at first a quiet chuckle, then a full gale of laughter, which caused heads to turn.

'I don't know what you t'ink is so funny,' said Eustelle, 'you be quiet now. You insulted my child, and I won't have it. Annie, this man is not the sort of person you should mix with. I t'ought he was a good man, but he ain't.'

Annie still hadn't spoken, but Tudor eventually answered the pleading in her eyes. He held up the screen of his phone for her to see. 'Look. I was talking about a dog. I'm getting a puppy. A Labrador. The bloke I've been dealing with got me over to his place the other day – that's where I had to go off to for a few hours. I told you Annie – I *said* I had to go to see a man about a dog. Anyway, there are only these two puppies left. See?' He held the screen toward Eustelle. 'A yellow and a black. Both are bitches, but the black one looks a bit leggy to me, and she might not turn out to be a good proportion. Besides, she's always tripping over her own paws. Her balance seems right off. Might be something wrong with her ears. The yellow is perfect. But he reckons he doesn't want to split them up. Says they've "bonded". But I was telling him on the phone – which must have been what you heard, Eustelle – that I'm not interested in the black one, I just want the yellow one.' He laughed again, then stopped when he saw the expressions on the faces of all three of the Parkers.

'I'm sorry you got your wires crossed, Eustelle, but that's all it was,' he added in a more subdued tone. 'If you'd listened a bit better you'd have heard me tell him I also thought that calling them "Sooty" and "Sweep" was a stupid idea because dogs should have proper names like – oh, I don't know—'

'Like Rosie and Gertie,' said Annie, smiling at Tudor. 'Rosie for the one that looks just like the Andrex puppy 'cause she's perfect, and if you had her she'd be Tudor's Rose—' she winked – 'and Gertie for the gangly one. They used to call me Gangly Gertie at school.'

'There you go, see, *they* are proper names, though I'm sorry people were so spiteful to you when you were little—' Tudor smiled gratefully at Annie – 'but, see, I can't cope with two puppies, and the pub's certainly not big enough for two energetic, full-grown Labradors. I know it's a shame to split them up, but I just can't take both.'

'I'll have Gertie,' said Annie.

Her mother, father and Tudor all stared at her.

Annie suddenly looked coy. 'Well, if I'm going to settle in the countryside I should probably have a dog, you know, for security. And I dare say it wouldn't do me any harm to have to take her for walks. There are some lovely places around here.'

'We could walk Rosie and Gertie together,' said Tudor quickly.

'Maybe we could,' said Annie, 'so long as Mum doesn't object.'

Eustelle Parker looked stunned. 'Who are you? And what have you done wit' me daughter?' she asked Annie. 'What's with you, callin' me "Mum"? Sayin' you'll get a dog *and* take it for walks? You sick, child? Never called me Mum before.'

Annie winked happily at her father who said, 'Getting yourself a puppy sounds like a great idea, my girl, it'll help you settle here, I t'ink.' He returned his daughter's wink then added, 'Now I'd better find your mother a drink, and I don't mean tomato juice.'

Stephanie and Henry Twyst finally managed to find a moment to catch up with Christine and Alexander, interrupting their strained conversation.

'Thanks for the gift, it's lovely,' said Stephanie, kissing Christine on the cheek. 'Where on earth did you find it?'

'I'll be honest,' replied Christine, 'Annie sort of inspired me, though she had something rather more modern in mind. I spoke to Alexander who asked around, and, through his various contacts, we tracked it down. One of the dealers who owns a shop in Brighton had it in his personal collection. I knew it would be perfect for you both, if only I could find it.'

'Thank you, Alexander,' said Henry, 'my hat's off to you. No, *our* hats are off to you.' He circled his wife's waist – which looked tiny in her perfectly-sleeved, simple yet elegant gown of cream duchesse silk which some had said reminded them more of Princess Anne's wedding dress than Lady Di's or Kate Middleton's – and squeezed her lovingly.

'You're very welcome, Your Graces,' said Alexander with a grin.

'I've heard about them, of course,' said Henry, 'but I've never actually seen one before. I understood they were terribly difficult to find outside a museum. Wonderful provenance. Jolly clever. Very thoughtful. Now, whenever we have visitors, we can show it off and joke that they might have to use it. Mother is always saying I don't have a sense of humor – this'll shut her up. A genuine Elizabethan chamber pot, exactly the sort of thing they'd have used when this place was built. Wonderful.'

The foursome raised their glasses to each other and Henry grinned as he said, 'Bottoms up, my dear wife!' Henry drained his glass, then noticed Edward was clearing his throat in the manner he reserved for attracting the duke's attention. Handing his empty glass to his butler Henry said to his bride, 'Back in a tick,' and left.

Moments later Edward rang the dinner gong atop the main staircase. The crowd became quiet. 'My Lords, Ladies and Gentlemen, your hosts, their Graces the Duke and Duchess of Chellingworth.'

Fueled by generous quantities of alcohol, the guests' applause was hearty rather than polite, and Henry enjoyed having to ask everyone to stop after a moment or two.

'My wife and I thank you all for helping us mark this very important day when we begin a new life together.' Henry spoke hesitantly – he'd felt much more confident when he'd made his speech to himself in the bathroom mirror that morning. He cleared his throat in an attempt to give himself time to reflect upon what he wanted to say next. Not good at thinking on his feet, he spoke more quietly and slowly as he added, 'We all know what's been going on around here this past few days, and if you didn't know about it until yesterday, the local constabulary made sure you noticed then. I think the helicopter was the final giveaway.' Henry blushed when people laughed aloud. 'So, without further ado, I have someone who wants to speak to you.'

Henry and Stephanie Twyst stood aside as Aubrey Morris walked out of the crowd at the foot of the stairs where he'd been standing largely unnoticed, and climbed up to join the happy couple.

His arm was in a sling, he limped, had two black eyes and an obviously broken nose. He was also blushing to the roots of his thick, sandy hair. A buzz ran through the crowd as his slight frame finally appeared high enough up the staircase for everyone to see him, then spontaneous applause rang out.

Licking his dry lips he smiled nervously as he said, 'Thank you, Your Graces. I . . . I'm not sure how to begin, but I know I want to thank everyone who was involved with getting me and Ann away from her father. Ann's not too bad, just a bit dehydrated, they said. She's stayed at the hospital to be with her mother, who's in a bed there with three broken ribs, a broken arm and a hairline fracture of the skull.'

'Give 'em our love, poor dabs,' shouted a female voice in the crowd.

Aubrey nodded. 'Yes, I'll do that. I'm going straight back there after I leave here.'

'Did Rhys do that to Netta?' asked a bass voice from the back of the hall.

Again Aubrey nodded. 'Yes. By then Ann and me were up at his house. He'd taken us back there. I saw him hit Netta flying when she tried to stop him getting away from the police. Knocked her flat, he did. Like I said, Ann'll be fine, and they think her mam will be too, in time. Him though – Rhys – who knows? The accident he had when he was driving along the main road left him in a bad way. He . . . um . . . he might not make it.'

'Who cares?' shouted someone.

Aubrey Morris looked around to see who'd spoken, but gave up and said, 'That's the funny thing, see. Ann does. Whatever he's done, he's her father, and we think he did what he did to us with her health and well-being in mind. To him, he was protecting his child.'

'What happened?' shouted another voice. 'Tell us what happened.' A general nodding of heads and a rumbling of support followed.

Aubrey looked at Henry, seeking approval, which he got, then he straightened his sling and began, 'Ann and I were planning a week's holiday in Rome – next week, after the wedding here, and after our wedding on Tuesday.' Aubrey blushed as gasps hissed around the great hall. 'We've been planning it for a while, see. I'll be honest, it was the duke who inspired us to make the move. If someone like the duke can take a big step like this and follow his heart, then so can we – that's what we said. We thought if we went and got married

Rhys wouldn't be able to keep us apart any more. He'd have to lump it. So we got it all sorted out for Swansea Register Office, next Tuesday, then we were off for our honeymoon to Rome, where we'd always dreamed of visiting. Anyway, Rhys got wind of our plans last Sunday afternoon. He saw Ann coming into their house with a suitcase to pack, and frightened her into telling him what was going on. Went ballistic, he did, then locked her in her bedroom. Ann managed to hang onto her mobile, so she phoned me and we decided it was best if we both made ourselves scarce right away. I jumped into my van, and I went to get her. I parked it where I always do when I visit her, out of sight, just near a lay-by at the bottom of the hill where her house is. It's where there's a stump of an old tree where we've been forced to hide letters to each other. Rhys began to check her email and her phone, and he started to steal her letters too, see. Anyway, I waited a bit, then she phoned me when she thought he'd gone out, but he hadn't, so when I got there it all went a bit wrong. He's pretty strong, is Rhys Roberts, and I've never been what anyone would call physical.'

'You do a lovely job with loose slates on the roof though, Aubrey,' called a woman's voice, breaking the tension in the great hall.

Aubrey smiled, blushed again, and continued, 'When he'd knocked me down for about the third time, I must have passed out, because I woke up in a barn or something, cold and hurting all over. I was all on my own, and I didn't really know what had happened. I was tied up with some old rope to a couple of iron rings attached to the wall, and I couldn't move much. As time passed I heard Ann shouting from somewhere nearby. I gathered she thought we were probably in a couple of old sheep sheds out on the hillside, and that's where we were both stuck. For hours. Just when it got dark Rhys brought us supplies and blankets, but not much else. I told him I'd be missed, and did my best to persuade him to at least let Ann go, but he just hit me. I told him about the Anwen Morris regalia I had in my van ready for the meeting I was due to have here that Sunday night, which really set him off. He hit me more then, and kicked me too, and he told me in no uncertain terms he didn't want Ann anywhere near me because of the curse that's on the Anwen regalia. I tried to explain it was all rubbish, and begged him to let Ann and me go, but he wasn't having any of it. He took my keys and said he'd get rid of the Morris dancing stuff once and for all. I thought he meant he'd chuck it in the river, or something, but I heard him muttering the best thing to do was to give it to someone else and let them have the problem of everyone in their family dying young. He sounded really bitter when he said it, but I don't know what happened to it all. I'm sorry if it's gone forever.'

'I've got it all safe and sound, Aubrey, never you mind. I'll keep it till you want it all back,' said Tudor in his deepest bass.

Aubrey brightened a little. 'That's good news, that is, Tudor. Thanks.'

Someone in the group of rapt guests shouted, 'It's a terrible curse that, you know, Aubrey. Look what's happened to you. Maybe you *should* dump the lot of it.'

'There is *no* curse,' replied Aubrey forcibly. 'My family's not been blessed with the best of health, it's true, but you can't put that down to the fact we own a set of *things*. But Rhys thought it was all real, see, and he was terrified Ann would die before her time if she and I ever became more than friends. We'd both known that Ann's dad had been trying to stop us being together since we were little, but we never knew it was because of *that*. So Ann and I sat there in those sheds for days. The nights were awful cold, and he'd only given us a couple of blankets each. She cried such a lot, and I couldn't help her at all. It was terrible. Worst time of our lives. I have no idea what Rhys's plan was, because he never told me that. Maybe he didn't have one, I don't know. It seemed to me he'd acted out of anger and fear, then didn't know what to do with us once he'd carted us off. But I can tell you it was frightening and I hated it, and I was very worried about Ann. I didn't know what he was doing to her, see. Then, for no reason I could fathom, he came back the night before last and dragged us both into his Land Rover, still tied up, and dumped us in a shed at the back of his house. Ann's poor mother was beside herself when she found us there yesterday morning. Went at it hammer and tongs they did then, Netta and Rhys. Then, once he heard the sirens, Rhys was off in the Land Rover. I'm sorry he had the crash. It would have been better if he hadn't. But there it is. Anyway – when this lot's healed—' he raised his sling a little and motioned to his face – 'I'll be back at work, *after* Ann and me get married. Which we will do as soon as her mam's able to be with us. Thank you to everyone who helped find us and get us freed. I don't know the people concerned but I understand we have a group of women here who never gave up on Ann and me, and were the people who finally managed to get the police involved. They've been very good, have the police. Sorry they didn't take things more seriously, I think. One of them was very insistent I should see it all from their point of view, that they thought I'd just gone off on my own. I do understand, in a way, but you think they'd have done something when they found my van abandoned. They said they thought I'd just left it there.'

'Never do that with your van, would you, Aubrey?' called a female voice.

Aubrey managed a weak smile, 'You're right about that. After Ann, I think I love my van more than anything. It's part of my name round here. Part of me, my family. Morris the Van is a good way to be known. Anyway, I hope the women who kept investigating all come and find me in a minute so I can thank them in person. Now I'll hand the proceedings back to His Grace, thank you all very much.'

As Edward helped Aubrey descend the staircase, Henry motioned that Stephanie should speak. She allowed the applause for Aubrey's speech, and the heartfelt greetings from his friends and neighbors to die down, then said, 'Thank you for that, Aubrey. His Grace and I also want to thank the women of the WISE Enquiries Agency for their tenacity and investigative diligence. On a personal note, I'd like to thank them very much for ensuring I can stand here in this gown. Ladies, please do take Aubrey up on his request to meet you all. You all deserve his, and our thanks.' This time the applause was more festive, various shouts of 'Welcome to Anwen-by-Wye' and 'Glad you're here on the Chellingworth Estate' resounded, and Althea, Carol, Annie, Mavis and Christine allowed themselves to be congratulated by those positioned closest to them.

'Looks like the locals have accepted us,' whispered Mavis to Althea as they began to make their way back to their seats from the spot they'd occupied in the great hall for Aubrey's speech.

'Quite right too,' replied the dowager.

Once the hubbub had subsided, Stephanie continued, 'Now, with your indulgence, I think I should return to a very important aspect of a wedding day. I have removed the living myrtle from my bridal bouquet, which Henry and I will plant in the garden to ensure a fertile marriage, a tradition we are both happy to observe—' she smiled coyly at her groom who shuffled from foot to foot somewhat uncomfortably – 'so now I invite every unmarried woman in the great hall to come forward – come along now, don't be shy ladies, girls – so I can perform a very important task. On the count of three, I shall throw this bouquet into the air, and we all know tradition tells us the person who catches it will be the next to marry. Come along now – yes, Annie, Christine this means you too – everyone come forward – ready now? And . . . one . . . two . . . three . . .'

Stephanie Twyst, Duchess of Chellingworth, had a good arm on her, and the floral arrangement arced high above the waving arms at the foot of the stairs. For once in her life, Annie Parker was delighted to be a good head taller than anyone else in the place and, as she looked at the bouquet in her upstretched hands, she saw the smile on her friend Carol's face gazing down from the gallery.

'Good catch!' shouted Carol, then she winked at Tudor Evans, who blushed.

'Now isn't that something,' said Mavis, rising to her feet to applaud. 'What a lovely way to wrap up a case. I'm surprised Annie didn't fall and break her neck trying to catch it, which would be just like her.'

'Annie's a good girl, and Carol's been the clumsy one these past few days,' said Althea smiling, then she started to hum and whistle 'Always look on the bright side of life' as she took a full glass of sherry from the little table beside her.

'Not appropriate, Althea dear,' chided Mavis gently.

'The extra sherry, or the ditty?' asked Althea wickedly.

Mavis coughed politely as Althea wrinkled her nose at her friend and colleague. 'Oh go on with you, Mavis MacDonald, have one yourself and live a little. Or why not ask Edward to bring you a "wee dram" which I know you prefer. My only son is married, let's celebrate. Now all I have left to deal with is that one, over there.' She jerked her thumb in the direction of Clementine, whose wheelchair was still backed into the fireplace. 'Children – such a worry for a parent.'

'Aye, and it's a worry that never goes away, whatever their age,' agreed Mavis with a nod.

'True,' said Althea, waggling her cane in the air to attract the attention of Edward, who was hovering in the general vicinity, 'and what we'll do for them – well, it's anyone's guess. Though I must say I feel my duty towards Henry is largely undertaken at last. Now it's up to him and Stephanie to produce an heir because I cannot do that for them. Think they're up to it, Mavis?' She winked at her friend, who tutted loudly then accepted the glass of single malt with which Edward had magically appeared.

'To the Duke and Duchess of Chellingworth,' said Mavis, raising her glass toward Althea's.

'And to the future patter of tiny feet,' replied Althea, swigging back her sherry in one gulp. 'And I don't mean McFli's paws,' she added.